DON LESSEM

DINOSAUR WORLDS

NEW DINOSAURS • NEW DISCOVERIES

BOYDS MILLS PRESS

Published by Caroline House
Boyds Mills Press, Inc.
A Highlights Company
815 Church Street
Honesdale, Pennsylvania 18431
Printed in Spain

Publisher Cataloging-in-Publication Data
Lessem, Don.
  Dinosaur Worlds: new dinosaurs, new
discoveries / by Don Lessem.—1st ed.
[192]p. : col. ill. ; cm.
Includes index, bibliography, and maps.
Summary: Reconstructions of sixteen
prehistoric habitats and examinations of fossil
evidence that place dinosaurs in their
ecological roles and tell the story of the
dinosaurs' rise and fall.

ISBN 1-56397-597-1

1. Dinosaurs—Juvenile literature.
2. Paleontology—Juvenile literature.
[1. Dinosaurs. 2. Paleontology.] I. Title
567.9 / 1—dc20   1996   CIP
Library of Congress Catalog Card Number:
95–83194

First edition, 1996

Book designed and produced by
  Bender Richardson White, Uxbridge, England.
Managing Editor: Lionel Bender
Art Director, Designer: Ben White
Text Editors: Lionel Bender, Andy Boyles,
  John Stidworthy
Picture Research: Don Lessem and
  Madeleine Samuel
Media Conversion: Peter MacDonald and
  Diacritic
Production: Kim Richardson

The text of this book is set in Clearface and
Trade Gothic

10 9 8 7 6 5 4 3 2 1

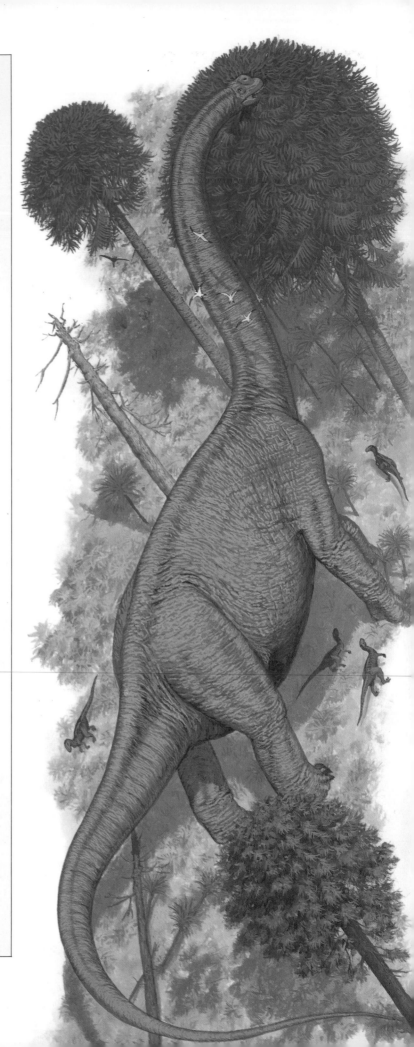

CONTENTS

AUTHOR

"Dino" Don Lessem, one of the world's foremost authors and presenters of dinosaur information for children and adults, has traveled the world, from Mongolia to Alaska, on dinosaur digs. Recently he went to Argentina to research *Dinosaur Worlds*.

Founder of the international, nonprofit Dinosaur Society, Mr. Lessem created its children's newspaper, *Dino Times*, and is currently Dinosaur Editor at *Highlights for Children* magazine. He has written fifteen dinosaur books. Twelve of them are for children, including these National Science Teachers' recommended books: *Jack Horner: Living With Dinosaurs* and *The Complete T. rex* (with Dr. John R. Horner.) Recent books include *Dinosaurs Rediscovered* and *The Dinosaur Society Dinosaur Encyclopedia* (with Donald F. Glut). He has written and hosted NOVA documentaries and was an adviser on the film *Jurassic Park*. His other books are about endangered species, human prehistory, and humor.

Don Lessem lives in Newton, Massachusetts, with his wife and two daughters.

Don Lessem (left) and Steven Spielberg, director of *Jurassic Park* and its 1997 sequel, *The Lost World*.

SENIOR SCIENTIFIC ADVISOR Dr. Peter Dodson is professor of anatomy and geology at the University of Pennsylvania School of Veterinary Medicine. Dr. Dodson has studied dinosaurs in Canada, the United States, India, Madagascar, and China. He named the smallest ceratopsid (horned dinosaur), *Avaceratops*. He has written studies of dinosaur death and burial, and on dinosaur diversity. He is coeditor of *The Dinosauria* reference text. His popular books for adults and children include *The Horned Dinosaurs—A Natural History, An Alphabet of Dinosaurs,* and *Giant Dinosaurs*. Dr. Dodson is a vice-president of The Dinosaur Society. He is also a research associate at the Academy of Natural Sciences of Philadelphia and adjunct professor at the Wagner Free Institute of Science in Philadelphia.

ADDITIONAL ADVISORS
ANIMALS

Dr. Hans Sues is curator of paleontology of the Royal Ontario Museum in Toronto, Canada. He is an expert on land animals of the Mesozoic Era. He has participated in digs in Nova Scotia, Virginia, Morocco, Niger, and many other sites. He is responsible for naming several species of dinosaurs. He is also an editor of the *Journal of Vertebrate Paleontology*.

PLANTS

Dr. Leo Hickey is a senior professor of paleobotany at Yale University's Peabody Museum of Natural History. Dr. Hickey's research includes plant fossils of the Mesozoic era, particularly the Hell Creek region of Montana.
Dr. Robert Spicer is a professor of paleobotany at the Open University, England. He is an authority on plants of the Mesozoic and has collected plant fossils in many localities, including Arctic Alaska.

INSECTS

Dr. Conrad Labandiera is curator of paleobiology at the Smithsonian Institution's National Museum of Natural History, specializing in fossil insects.

The author would also like to acknowledge help given by:
Dr. Kenneth Carpenter of Denver Museum of Natural History;
Dr. Anusuya Chinsamy-Turan of the South African Museum, Capetown, South Africa;
Professor Rodolfo Coria of Museo Carmen Funes, Plaza Huincul, Argentina;
Mr. Ben Creisler, Seattle, Washington;
Dr. Philip Currie of Royal Tyrrell Museum of Paleontology, Alberta, Canada;
Dr. William Hammer of Augustana College;
Dr. Kirk Johnson of Denver Museum of Natural History;
Dr. James Kirkland of Dinamation International, Colorado;
Dr. Paul Olsen of Columbia University Lamont Laboratories;
Dr. Thomas Rich of The National Museum of Victoria, Melbourne, Australia;
Dr. Paul Sereno of the University of Chicago;
Dr. Edith Taylor of Ohio State University;
Dr. David Weishampel of Johns Hopkins University;
Dr. Peter Wellnhofer of Bayerische Staatssammlungen, Munich, Germany;
Dr. Rupert Wild of the Staatliches Museum für Natur, Stuttgart, Germany.

Dr. Peter Dodson and *Tyrannosaurus rex.*

ABOUT THIS BOOK

Dinosaurs first appeared on Earth about 230 million years ago in what scientists call the Triassic Period. They thrived throughout the following Jurassic Period and died out at the end of the Cretaceous Period, 65 million years ago. During this time, the environment—the geography, climate, and plant and animal life changed continuously.

Dinosaur Worlds takes a close-up view of the dinosaurs, other animals, and their world throughout the Mesozoic Era—the Age of the Dinosaurs. The Age of Dinosaurs was a time of dramatic change in the land and seas, and in the creatures that inhabited them. Dinosaurs were the most varied and successful animals in the history of life on land. Some of them achieved sizes never equaled before or since. Some were as tall as office buildings, as heavy as twenty elephants, and as long as three school buses.

A wide variety of other giant creatures lived among dinosaurs, including flying reptiles, the pterosaurs. Some of these grew as big as small airplanes. Giants of the sea included marine reptiles such as plesiosaurs. Giant crocodiles were the longest meat-eaters of all, with one species growing even longer than any meat-eating dinosaur.

Many smaller creatures also lived in the time of the dinosaurs. Near the start of this era the first mammals, our ancestors, appeared. Insects lived throughout the era, but some familiar ones, such as butterflies and bees, did not appear until late in the dinosaurs' reign.

At the beginning of the Age of Dinosaurs there were no flowers, and the landscape had vegetation with a very different look from today's. By the time of the last dinosaurs there were many flowering plants, and the vegetation was quite similar to the present. Throughout the time of the dinosaurs, landscapes varied from deserts to forests to swamps. Dinosaurs lived in every area, from the Arctic to the South Pole.

This book describes and illustrates what the dinosaurs looked like. It also discusses how they lived, how they died, how they were preserved, and how they were discovered. It highlights "dinosaur ecology"—the relationships among dinosaurs, plants, and other animals alive at the time.

Enjoy your journey of discovery to the lost worlds of the dinosaurs!

"Dino" Don Lessem

LIFE AND TIME

We think of dinosaurs as ancient creatures, but they evolved recently in terms of Earth's long history. The planet Earth is estimated to be 4,600 million years old. The first multicellular animals, as large as a human thumb, appeared in the sea only about 600 million years ago. Land animals first evolved about 400 million years ago. Dinosaurs lived from 228 million years ago to 65 million years ago. Humans appeared approximately 1 million years ago.

Paleontologists divide the history of life on Earth into four eras, which are further divided into periods. There was no complex life during the first, longest period, the Precambrian. It lasted until 600 million years ago. In the Paleozoic Era, from 570 million to 245 million years ago, most major groups of animals first appeared—shellfish, spiders, fish, reptiles, insects, and amphibians.

The Mesozoic Era, from 245 million to 65 million years ago, was the Age of Dinosaurs. Mammals emerged at nearly the same time as dinosaurs, but in this era they stayed small. Reptiles ruled the skies and the oceans. Birds appeared midway through the Mesozoic. Flowering plants became dominant only at the end of this era. As the Mesozoic ended, dinosaurs and many other creatures, including flying and marine reptiles, became extinct.

In the Cenozoic, from 65 million years ago until today, mammals have become the dominant land animals. Birds, insects, and bats fly through the skies. Fish and marine mammals rule the seas. Flowering plants are now widespread.

This chart shows the main periods of Earth's history, including when various forms of life evolved.

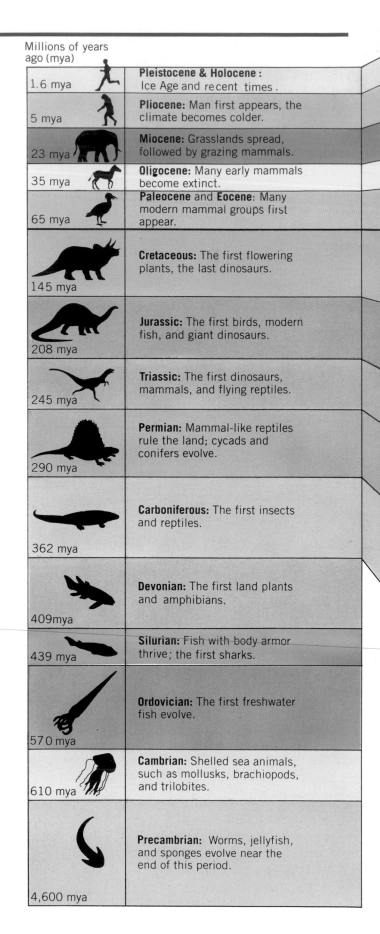

Millions of years ago (mya)

1.6 mya	**Pleistocene & Holocene:** Ice Age and recent times.
5 mya	**Pliocene:** Man first appears, the climate becomes colder.
23 mya	**Miocene:** Grasslands spread, followed by grazing mammals.
35 mya	**Oligocene:** Many early mammals become extinct.
65 mya	**Paleocene** and **Eocene:** Many modern mammal groups first appear.
145 mya	**Cretaceous:** The first flowering plants, the last dinosaurs.
208 mya	**Jurassic:** The first birds, modern fish, and giant dinosaurs.
245 mya	**Triassic:** The first dinosaurs, mammals, and flying reptiles.
290 mya	**Permian:** Mammal-like reptiles rule the land; cycads and conifers evolve.
362 mya	**Carboniferous:** The first insects and reptiles.
409 mya	**Devonian:** The first land plants and amphibians.
439 mya	**Silurian:** Fish with body armor thrive; the first sharks.
570 mya	**Ordovician:** The first freshwater fish evolve.
610 mya	**Cambrian:** Shelled sea animals, such as mollusks, brachiopods, and trilobites.
4,600 mya	**Precambrian:** Worms, jellyfish, and sponges evolve near the end of this period.

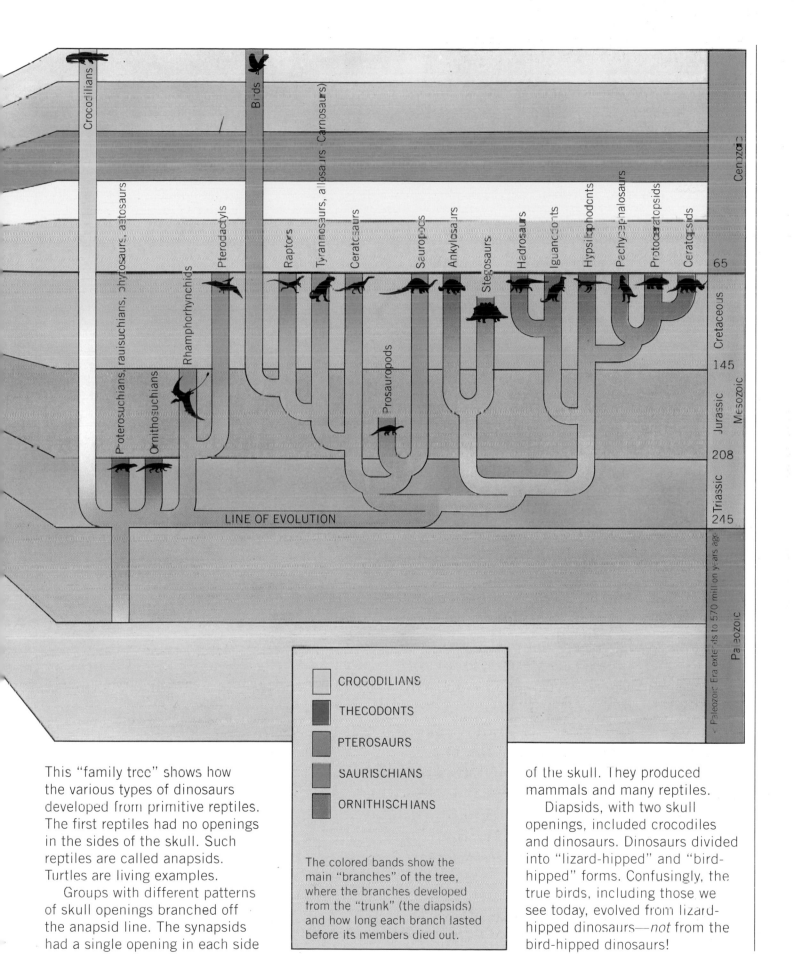

					Cenozoic	
Crocodilians	Birds	Tyrannosaurs, allosaurs (Carnosaurs)				
		Raptors	Ceratosaurs	Sauropods	Ankylosaurs	Stegosaurs	Hadrosaurs	Iguanodonts	Hypsilophodonts	Pachycephalosaurs	Protoceratopsids	Ceratopsids	
					65	

Proterosuchians, rauisuchians, phytosaurs, aetosaurs

Pterodactyls

Rhamphorhynchids

Ornithosuchians

Prosauropods

	Cretaceous	
	145	
	Jurassic	Mesozoic
	208	
	Triassic	
	245	

LINE OF EVOLUTION

| | Paleozoic | |

‹ Paleozoic Era extends to 570 million years ago

Legend:

- CROCODILIANS
- THECODONTS
- PTEROSAURS
- SAURISCHIANS
- ORNITHISCHIANS

The colored bands show the main "branches" of the tree, where the branches developed from the "trunk" (the diapsids) and how long each branch lasted before its members died out.

This "family tree" shows how the various types of dinosaurs developed from primitive reptiles. The first reptiles had no openings in the sides of the skull. Such reptiles are called anapsids. Turtles are living examples.

Groups with different patterns of skull openings branched off the anapsid line. The synapsids had a single opening in each side of the skull. They produced mammals and many reptiles.

Diapsids, with two skull openings, included crocodiles and dinosaurs. Dinosaurs divided into "lizard-hipped" and "bird-hipped" forms. Confusingly, the true birds, including those we see today, evolved from lizard-hipped dinosaurs—*not* from the bird-hipped dinosaurs!

DINOSAUR ANATOMY — *T. REX*

Scientists and artists have the enormous task of trying to reconstruct prehistoric life. Here, *Tyrannosaurus rex* (*T. rex* for short) serves as an example of how different kinds of evidence are used to bring an extinct creature "back to life." *T. rex* was king of all predators in North America.

Cutaway drawing of a *T. rex*
This shows the major parts of the dinosaur. Soft tissues, such as muscles, lungs, and guts, rarely become fossilized because they decompose quickly.

FOSSILS
Bones fossilize most often when sediment covers the bone. Then minerals enter the bone, turning it to rock. Bones, eggs, dung, footprints, and skin impressions can all become fossils.

TAIL
T. rex held its long muscular tail well off the ground. The tail was strengthened by rodlike, bony tendons.

SPINE
This is also known as the backbone and is made up of bones called vertebrae. An animal with a backbone is known as a vertebrate.

SKIN
From fossilized skin impressions, scientists think *T.rex* had leathery skin with a pebbly texture. We can only guess its skin color.

PYRAMID OF NUMBERS

The diagram shows the numbers of several typical land animals and plants that would have been present in the same habitat as one *Tyrannosaurus rex*. It is based on estimates by paleontologists. Giant predators such as *T. rex* are at the top of a "pyramid" of thousands of organisms. Just below are smaller predatory dinosaurs and large plant-eating species such as *Triceratops*. The smallest creatures are at the bottom of the pyramid.

To find enough food for its massive body, each *T. rex* probably had to roam over a large area.

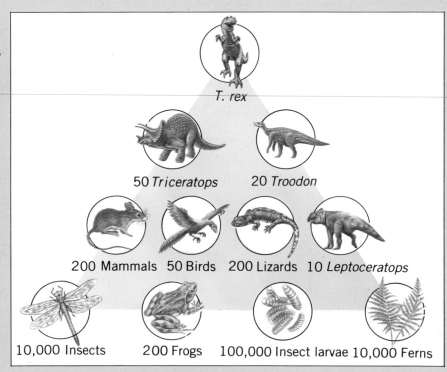

T. rex

50 *Triceratops*   20 *Troodon*

200 Mammals   50 Birds   200 Lizards   10 *Leptoceratops*

10,000 Insects   200 Frogs   100,000 Insect larvae   10,000 Ferns

Fossils do not hold the answers to every question about an animal's diet, posture, behavior, or internal organs. Only in the past decade have new discoveries allowed scientists to create a reasonably complete picture of the fearsome killer, *T. rex*. Scientists can also reconstruct its life by comparing *T. rex* with living animals. In addition, some basic ideas about ecology—such as how many animals and plants might have lived in one habitat—hold true for many different kinds of environments.

Tyrannosaurus rex, or "tyrant lizard king," was the last and largest of the tyrannosaurs. The only other big predator known to have shared its habitat was *Nanotyrannus*, a 15-foot-long, one-ton "pygmy" tyrannosaur.

SKELETON
T. rex's skeleton was a rigid framework that supported its body, protected its internal parts, and provided attachment points for muscles used in movement.

RIB CAGE
This protected the heart and lungs and helped the lungs expand and contract during breathing.

NECK
T. rex's neck was short and curved. Strong muscles supported its head as it attacked and bit its prey.

SKULL
The skull of *T. rex* was large and powerful. Inside, the brain was long and large for a dinosaur.

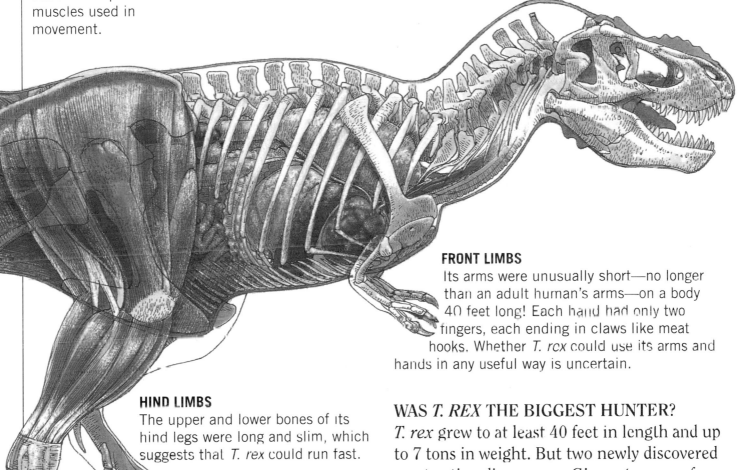

FRONT LIMBS
Its arms were unusually short—no longer than an adult human's arms—on a body 40 feet long! Each hand had only two fingers, each ending in claws like meat hooks. Whether *T. rex* could use its arms and hands in any useful way is uncertain.

HIND LIMBS
The upper and lower bones of its hind legs were long and slim, which suggests that *T. rex* could run fast.

FEET
Each foot measured nearly 3 feet across. The three large front toes had long claws. On the inside rear of each foot was a tiny toe.

WAS *T. REX* THE BIGGEST HUNTER?
T. rex grew to at least 40 feet in length and up to 7 tons in weight. But two newly discovered meat-eating dinosaurs—*Giganotosaurus* from Argentina and a *Carcharodontosaurus* from Morocco—were bigger than *T. rex*. Individual allosaurs may have grown bigger than *T. rex*, and other meat-eaters, such as *Spinosaurus*, may have grown to the same size. But *T. rex* was the most powerful predatory dinosaur.

DINOSAUR ECOLOGY

For more than 160 million years, dinosaurs lived across most of the Earth. During this time there were many changes, but dinosaurs thrived in all kinds of climates. In dry environments and swamps, in cool forests, and along hot lakeshores, dinosaurs survived. They fed, drank, grew, breathed, excreted, migrated, and mated. They hid from enemies, searched for food, rested, and slept, just as animals do today. In all of this they were affected by their surroundings, which included the host of plants and animals that lived alongside them.

Dinosaurs were part of a larger community of animals and plants. Most dinosaurs were plant-eaters. They ate from the ferns, cycads, and evergreen trees that covered the land during most of the Age of Dinosaurs. Some plant-eaters were equipped with many grinding teeth to digest tough plants. Others had scissorlike jaws for snipping plants. Each species was adapted for a unique way of life.

Ecology is the scientific study of animals and plants in relation to all other living things around them and to their surroundings. It includes feeding, mating, migrating, communication, competition for living space, and many other interactions.

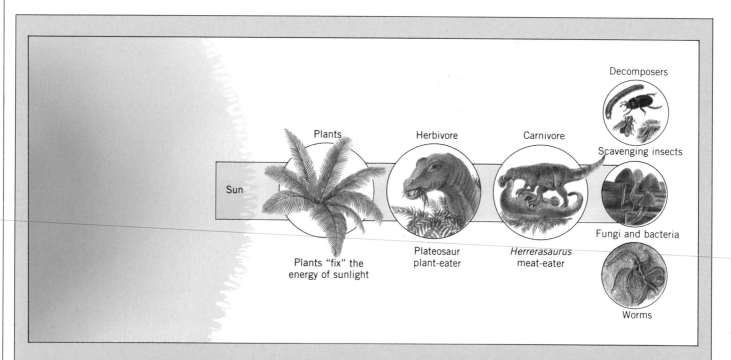

Sun

Plants

Plants "fix" the energy of sunlight

Herbivore

Plateosaur plant-eater

Carnivore

Herrerasaurus meat-eater

Decomposers

Scavenging insects

Fungi and bacteria

Worms

ENERGY AND FOOD CHAIN

Living things need energy to live and grow and to drive all their chemical processes. They get this energy by breaking down complex food materials. Sunlight contains energy. Plants use this energy to make their food from water and carbon dioxide gas. The food acts as stored energy. When animals eat plants, they capture some of this energy. Meat-eaters (carnivores) get their energy by feeding on plant-eaters (herbivores). Decomposers and scavengers get their energy by feeding on animal waste or on the remains of dead animals and plants. Some dinosaurs got their energy from plants, some by eating other animals.

FOOD WEB

In most wild habitats, the food chain is not simple. Instead, a number of plants and animals depend upon one another for survival in a food web. Two or three kinds of meat-eaters might live off several of the same types of plant-eaters, which may feed on many different kinds of plants. In these complex systems, the survival of each dinosaur species depended on interactions with a number of different kinds of plants and animals.

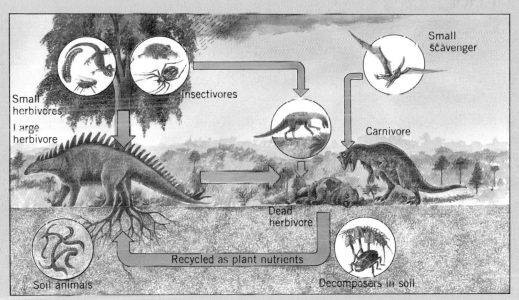

The largest dinosaurs had tiny heads and teeth. They relied on their huge stomachs and rocks that they swallowed to help them digest enormous amounts of plant food.

Meat-eating dinosaurs ranged in size from creatures smaller than a man to animals longer than a school bus. Some ate tiny mammals, lizards, eggs, and perhaps insects and fish. The largest meat-eaters ate other dinosaurs. The dinosaur carnivores were probably both hunters and scavengers. Eating the dead and dying members of the herds of plant-eating dinosaurs may have allowed them to feed without much hunting.

Within a forest ecosystem there are several distinct habitats, ranging from the forest floor to the tops of trees. In each area, there are many communities, or collections, of living things.

COLD-BLOODED LIFESTYLE

Many species of dinosaur were very likely cold-blooded. The individual dinosaurs might have used some strategies of modern reptiles to control their body temperatures. They might have basked in the sun (1, 2) to increase their body heat, then sheltered beneath rocks or vegetation (3) to retain warmth as the air cooled at night. Also, they constantly changed the angle of their bodies to the sun to adjust warming (4, 5). Meat-eating dinosaurs were the ancestors of birds, which are warm-blooded. So some dinosaurs may have been more warm- than cold-blooded.

DISCOVERING DINOSAURS

We know dinosaurs and the plants and animals of their time only from fossils. Paleontologists have been digging up dinosaurs for nearly two centuries. In all that time, they have discovered about 330 different kinds of dinosaurs and scarcely 2,000 good skeletons. Half of all dinosaurs are known only from a single specimen. Even so, our knowledge grows every year, and scientists today understand much more about dinosaurs and the world they lived in than ever before.

1

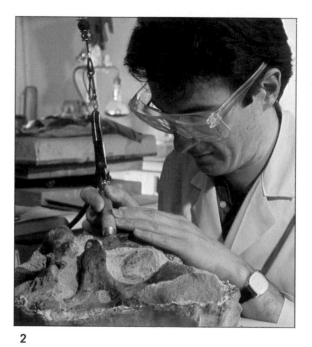

2

3

Preparing fossil finds This sequence of photographs shows the excavation, preparation, and display of *Baryonyx* fossils. Sometimes bones on the surface are just the tip of what is still in the ground. A little digging by a scientist may reveal that well-preserved fossils lie below. Then a professional crew excavates the site. The location of each fossil is mapped. This helps determine how the animal died and was buried. Then the fossil is taken away for further study. Scientists from the Natural History Museum in England put bones of *Baryonyx* in plaster jackets **(1)** to take them back to the laboratory.

Fossils are created only when the remains of creatures are protected from air, wind, and rain for thousands of years. Usually, the animals must have lived in an environment where sand or mud covered them soon after they died. The rock containing fossils must be at the surface of the earth so they can be discovered. In badlands and deserts, where the rock is not covered by trees and buildings, winds may expose long-hidden rock layers.

Digging up fossils is both hard work and a scientific process. Paleontologists look for clues to the ancient environment and the behavior of the animals in it. They still dig out bones with picks, then wrap them in plaster, as scientists did a century ago. Today they also look for fossil footprints, eggshell fragments, the bones of youngsters, and fossil plants and pollen. They analyze the fossil-bearing rock for clues to ancient climates and landscapes.

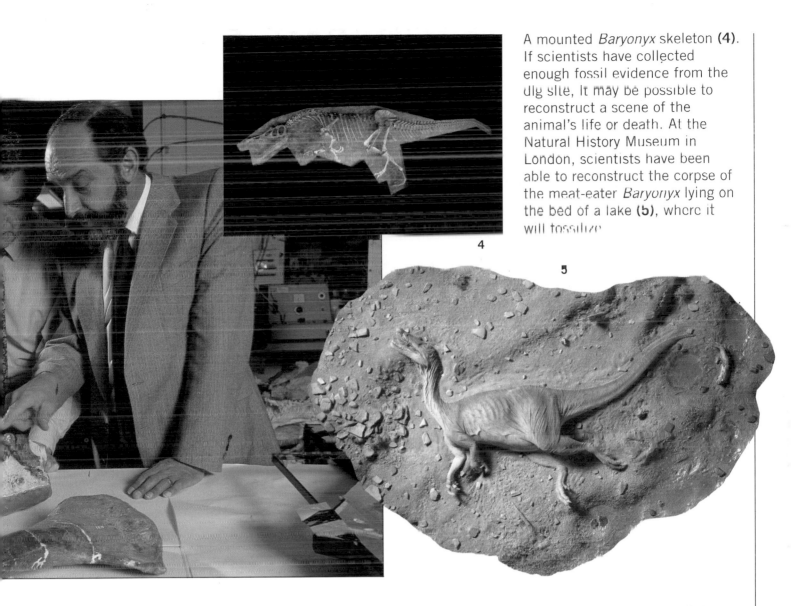

A mounted *Baryonyx* skeleton **(4)**. If scientists have collected enough fossil evidence from the dig site, it may be possible to reconstruct a scene of the animal's life or death. At the Natural History Museum in London, scientists have been able to reconstruct the corpse of the meat-eater *Baryonyx* lying on the bed of a lake **(5)**, where it will fossilize.

4

5

In the laboratory, a "preparator" starts to clean rock from the fossils **(2)**. A wide range of tools may be used in preparing dinosaur bones, from saws and sandblasters to an engraving tool, as here. Once a dinosaur skeleton has been cleaned, casts may be taken to make replicas, or copies, of the bones.

These are mounted on a frame so that the skeleton can be put on display in the museum. Missing bones may have their shape "guessed" by scientists. Here, Dr. Angela Milner, Mr. Ron Croucher, and Dr. Alan Charig of the Natural History Museum study the *Baryonyx* bones to reconstruct the skeleton **(3)**.

Fewer than fifty scientists worldwide search for dinosaurs each year. Yet, on average, a new kind of dinosaur is discovered every seven weeks. Most scientific work on fossils goes on in the laboratory. The researchers may examine the fossil under a microscope to see the pattern of wear on teeth, or the cells inside a bone. The size of a bone can show whether the animal was mature or young. Marks on the bone may show where its muscles were.

Sometimes the remains are complete and unusual enough that a museum or university will mount a skeleton of its discovery. Years ago, the actual bones would have been used. Now scientists usually make casts of the bones, perhaps in fiberglass, and keep the valuable original bones for study. The casts are painted and linked together with metal. Building a dinosaur skeleton requires months of work and many thousands of dollars.

THE LATE TRIASSIC PERIOD

The first dinosaurs evolved from other reptiles in the Late Triassic Period, nearly 230 million years ago. They were one of many new groups of land creatures, just as other new life-forms were conquering the air and the sea. All of the Earth's slowly shifting land was joined into one supercontinent along the equator, and the climate everywhere was warm and growing drier. Conifer trees, palmlike cycads, and ferns grew wherever there was enough water. Grass, flowering plants, and the broad-leaved trees we know today had not yet evolved.

The tiny skull of the early meat-eating dinosaur *Eoraptor* is held between the thumb and forefinger of paleontologist Dr. Paul Sereno—in an X-ray photograph. The large hole at the center was filled by an eyeball, and the hole at the tip of the snout was the location of a nostril. At the rear of the skull was the braincase.

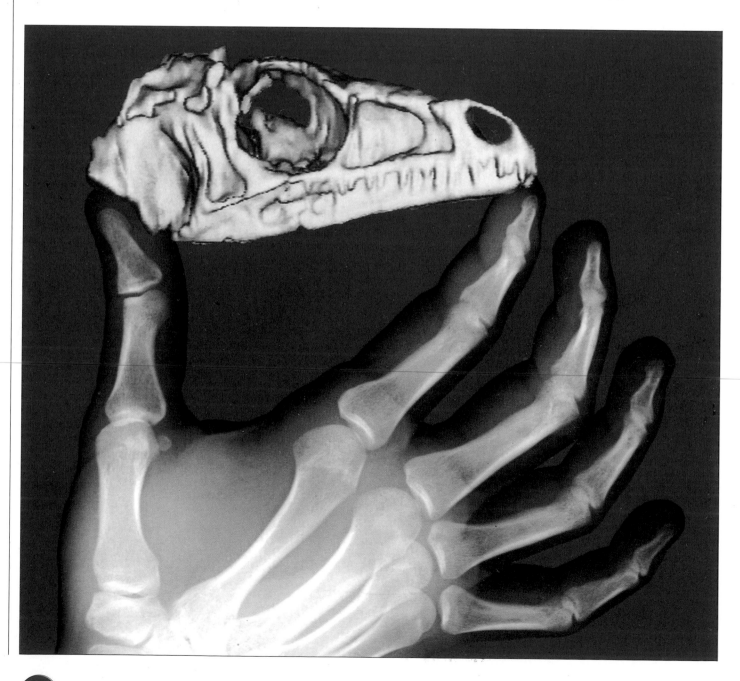

In the Late Triassic, mammals had not yet appeared, and their mouselike reptile ancestors were dwarfed by giant reptiles. These big animals included fat-bodied, plant-eating land reptiles. Among them, the piglike rhynchosaurs and the cow-sized dicynodonts were the most widespread.

Toward the end of the Triassic Period and the beginning of the Jurassic Period, big plant-eaters, the prosauropod dinosaurs, emerged. The meat-eaters on land included both the solidly built, straight-legged phytosaurs and the first meat-eating dinosaurs. Unlike most other reptiles, Late Triassic and Early Jurassic carnivorous dinosaurs were swift. They ran on two legs positioned directly beneath their bodies.

CONTINENTS—THEN AND NOW

Around 230 million years ago, there was just one landmass, which is now called Pangaea. This supercontinent straddled the equator. By the end of the Triassic Period, Pangaea had begun to split apart. Within the following Jurassic Period, two distinct giant landmasses, Gondwana in the south and Laurasia in the north, would form.

FOSSIL FINDS AROUND THE WORLD

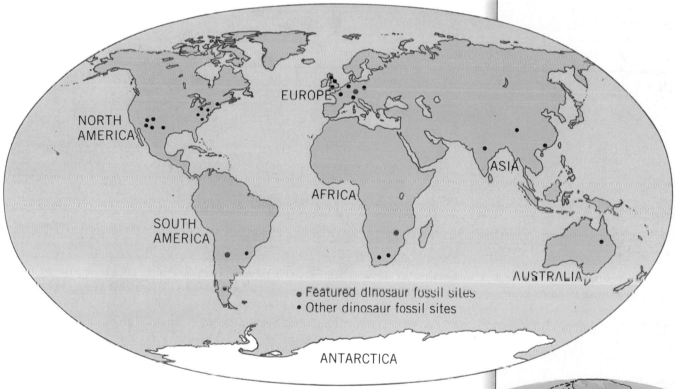

- Featured dinosaur fossil sites
- Other dinosaur fossil sites

This map shows the present-day continents and the major dinosaur fossil sites from the Late Triassic and Early Jurassic Periods. The four sites featured in this book are shown in red.

The Valley of the Moon in northwestern Argentina was home to the first dinosaurs we know well. **Western Europe** was one of the first areas to be inhabited by plant-eating dinosaurs, the prosauropods. Fossils found in **Nova Scotia** in Canada reveal the time when large reptiles died out while plant- and meat-eating dinosaurs survived. Fossils from Zimbabwe in **southern Africa** have given scientists some of the best evidence of how dinosaurs grew.

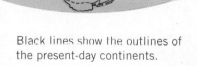

Black lines show the outlines of the present-day continents.

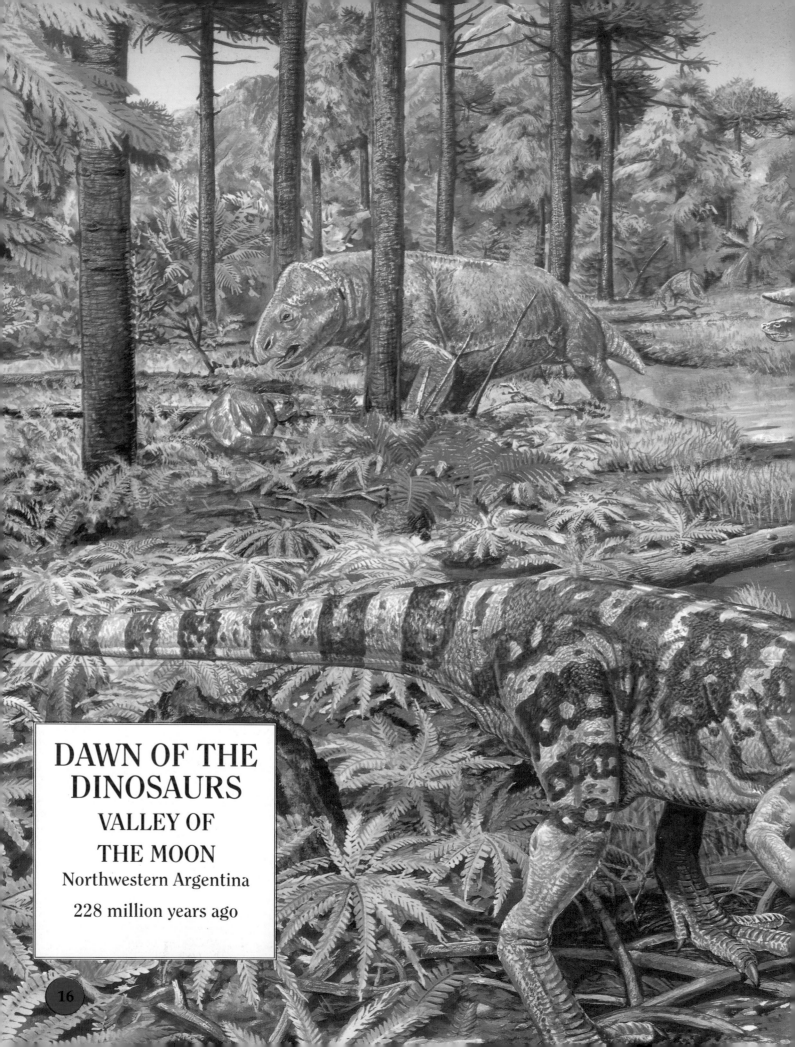

DAWN OF THE DINOSAURS
VALLEY OF THE MOON
Northwestern Argentina

228 million years ago

Beside a riverbank, huge plant-eaters browse on ferns, and a pig-sized herbivore has been killed by a new form of killer, a meat-eating dinosaur. This dinosaur, in turn, is preyed upon by a big reptilian hunter and by a smaller dinosaur.

NORTHWESTERN ARGENTINA

The first dinosaurs appeared about 230 million years ago, when the world's land was one giant continent. In what is now a desert in northwestern Argentina, the warm, lush riverbanks were home to many creatures. Here, scientists have discovered many spectacular skeletons of early dinosaurs and other, even larger, reptiles.

Soaring over the riverbanks were the first flying reptiles, the pterosaurs. In the water and on the land, crocodile-like creatures prowled. Some were as small as house cats. Others were as large as pickup trucks. Several of these animals had flat teeth, specialized for chewing plants. Others had sharper teeth for killing other animals.

The largest animals in this world were not dinosaurs but rauisuchians—meat-eating reptiles like *Saurosuchus*. Other large animals around at this time were the slow-moving plant-eaters, the dicynodonts. They had strong muscles in the back of their skulls. Their jaws could slide back and forth to slice plants. The most common animals of all in Late Triassic Argentina were the rhynchosaurs. These were plant-eaters as big as pigs, with beaks like those of parrots.

A spider builds a web among the branches to trap its insect prey. Other small creatures, such as therapsids and lizards, also ate insects.

Valley of the Moon—Today The riverbanks where dinosaurs first roamed dried up millions of years ago. Today's desert badlands, with their dry valleys and sunbaked landscape, look like the surface of the Moon, giving the valley its popular name.

A small meat-eating dinosaur called an *Eoraptor* peeks around the base of a conifer tree. With its keen eyesight, speed, and grasping hands, *Eoraptor* is an efficient hunter of small creatures and larger, slower plant-eaters. This *Eoraptor* has seen a tiny mouselike therapsid that is feeding among fungi and ferns. Even in a slight breeze, the leaves of these delicate plants rustle. The therapsid hears the hunter and might escape.

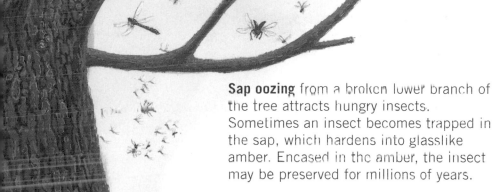

Sap oozing from a broken lower branch of the tree attracts hungry insects. Sometimes an insect becomes trapped in the sap, which hardens into glasslike amber. Encased in the amber, the insect may be preserved for millions of years.

FACT FILE

Plant-eaters and meat-eaters, big and small, fed along the water's edge in the ancient Valley of the Moon. The following plants and animals are shown in the panorama.

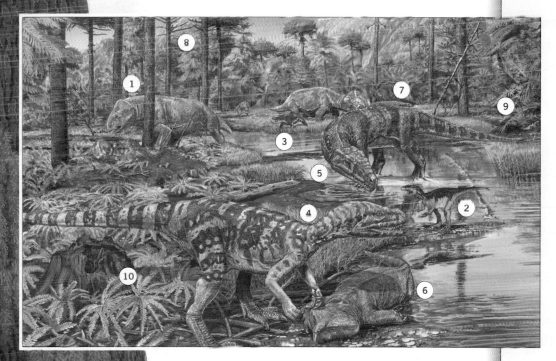

ANIMALS
1. *Dicynodont* (die-SY-no-dahnt)
2. *Eoraptor* (EE-o-RAP-tur)
3. *Exaeretodon* (EX-eye-REE-toe-dahn)
4. *Herrerasaurus* (huh-RARE-uh-SAW-rus)
5. *Saurosuchus* (SAW-ro-SOO-kus)
6. *Scaphonyx* (skah-FAHN-icks)
7. *Sphenosuchid* (SFEE-no-SOO-kid)

PLANTS
8. *Araucarian conifer* (AR-ah-CARE-ee-un)
9. Cycads (SY-kads)
10. *Dicroidium fern* (DIE-crow-ID-ee-um)

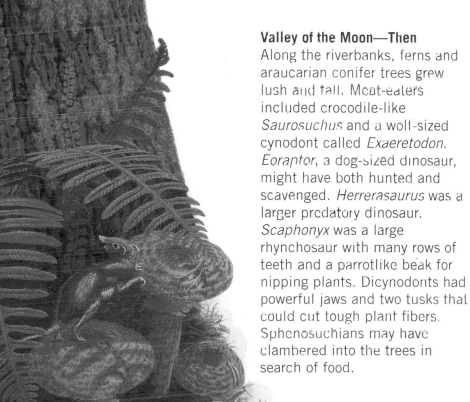

Valley of the Moon—Then
Along the riverbanks, ferns and araucarian conifer trees grew lush and tall. Meat-eaters included crocodile-like *Saurosuchus* and a wolf-sized cynodont called *Exaeretodon*. *Eoraptor*, a dog-sized dinosaur, might have both hunted and scavenged. *Herrerasaurus* was a larger predatory dinosaur. *Scaphonyx* was a large rhynchosaur with many rows of teeth and a parrotlike beak for nipping plants. Dicynodonts had powerful jaws and two tusks that could cut tough plant fibers. Sphenosuchians may have clambered into the trees in search of food.

Globe shows the continents now

Argentina, Then and Now Today, Argentina is about 1,500 miles south of the equator. It is cooler and drier now than it was in the Late Triassic, when it sat on the equator.

THE DINOSAURS EMERGE

The Valley of the Moon was home to some of the first dinosaurs we know about. They stood upright and were fast-moving killers. The overall design of meat-eating dinosaurs, as two-legged runners with powerful jaws as weapons, helped them to be successful until the end of the dinosaurs' reign.

Eoraptor and *Herrerasaurus* were among the earliest dinosaurs known. *Eoraptor* is a recently discovered dinosaur, and fossils of both have been excavated from rocks of similar age in the Valley of the Moon. Like modern reptiles, these creatures probably had scaly skin and laid eggs. They were small compared to some later meat-eating dinosaurs. But among the animals of their time, they showed several new features special to dinosaurs. For example, they walked on their toes, with their legs positioned directly beneath them and their tails held off the ground.

HERRERASAURUS

Meaning of name: "Herrera's lizard," named after Victorino Herrera, its discoverer
Order: Saurischia
Size, Weight: 10–19 feet long, 800–1,000 pounds
Locations: Northwestern Argentina, possibly southwestern United States
Diet: Meat

With its large jaws, *Herrerasaurus* might have swallowed small animals whole, as a present-day snake does. But more often it probably used its strong jaws and sharp teeth to gnaw and bite its prey.

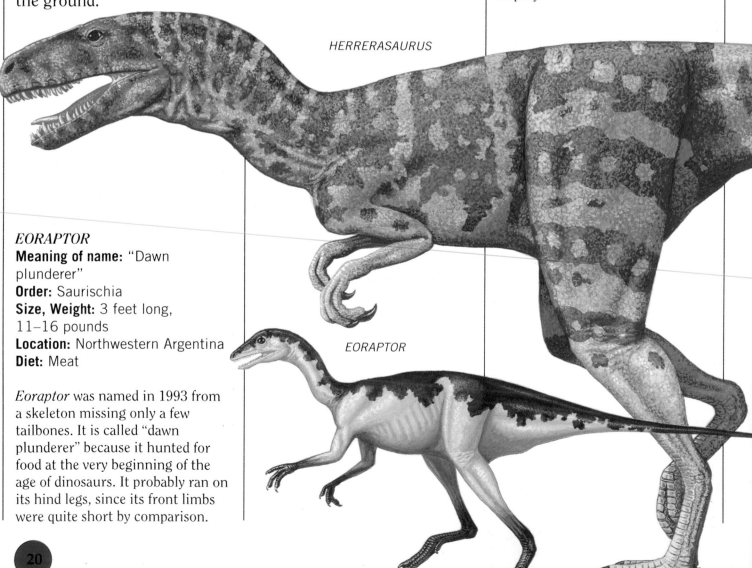

HERRERASAURUS

EORAPTOR

EORAPTOR

Meaning of name: "Dawn plunderer"
Order: Saurischia
Size, Weight: 3 feet long, 11–16 pounds
Location: Northwestern Argentina
Diet: Meat

Eoraptor was named in 1993 from a skeleton missing only a few tailbones. It is called "dawn plunderer" because it hunted for food at the very beginning of the age of dinosaurs. It probably ran on its hind legs, since its front limbs were quite short by comparison.

INSECTS

In the boggy conditions around streams and ponds, many kinds of insects flew through the air. They included grasshopper-like creatures with wings a foot long. Lizards and amphibians preyed on the insects.

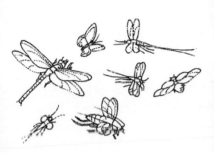

Dinosaur with upright posture

Standing up

Why did the dinosaurs survive and flourish when most other big animals of the Late Triassic died 208 million years ago? The first dinosaurs were probably no more intelligent than other large animals of their time. But dinosaurs were faster because they ran on two legs beneath their bodies. So perhaps they were better hunters than others in the Late Triassic.

The therapsids were ancestors of the first mammals, which appeared soon after this time. Early mammals remained small animals, no bigger than house cats, while dinosaurs were alive.

Megazostrodon—an early type of mammal

PLANTS

A dense forest of evergreen trees called araucarians covered the valley of the first dinosaurs. In the shade of these odd umbrella-shaped trees, hardy ferns and other nonflowering plants grew. The treetops spread out like fans more than 100 feet above the ground.

SAUROSUCHUS
Meaning of name: "Lizard crocodile"
Order: Rauisuchia
Size, Weight: 20 feet long, 2,200 pounds
Location: Northwestern Argentina
Diet: Meat

Saurosuchus was the largest rauisuchian. It may have resembled a crocodile, but it lived on land. *Saurosuchus* walked with its legs positioned farther under the body than do modern lizards, but it did not walk or run as efficiently as dinosaurs did.

SAUROSUCHUS

FOOTHILL FORESTS

No place in the world today is exactly like northwestern Argentina 228 million years ago. And there exist no life forms resembling the creatures that lived then in the region. But the forests at the base of the Rocky Mountains in western Wyoming in the United States have some important features in common with the environment of the ancient Valley of the Moon.

As in Triassic Argentina, these forests are made up mainly of tall conifers, with few plants in the deep shade of the trees. Large and small predators such as wolves, badgers, and weasels live here and feed on a variety of large plant-eaters, including deer, elk, and moose. Because modern and prehistoric carnivores faced the same basic problem of hunting and killing large animals for food, it is possible that they had similar ways of solving these problems. For example, predatory dinosaurs might have hunted in packs, as wolves do. Does that mean that they also had sophisticated ways of communicating with one another? Is it possible that they might have lived together in groups?

Though no bigger than a small dog, *Eoraptor* may have been much more vicious. Perhaps it hunted in packs, using its speed to ambush prey like this young dicynodont.

In most places, including ancient Argentina and modern Wyoming, large meat-eaters prey on plant-eaters and small meat-eaters. Some hunting dinosaurs in the Valley of the Moon may have stalked prey on their own, as the bobcat does today in Wyoming. And like the bobcat, they may have hunted within separate areas of the forest and attacked animals many times their size.

In the snow, a bobcat kitten stands over its prey—a snowshoe hare. *Eoraptor* possibly hunted and killed like the bobcat, catching its victims with its claws, then using its sharp teeth to tear at the meat. In western North America, bobcats, coyotes, cougars, and wolves are all hunters of plant-eaters. And like the carnivorous dinosaurs, they can outrun or outwit their prey.

Scientists think that in ancient Argentina the biggest predator, *Saurosuchus* (1), ate lumbering plant-eaters like dicynodonts (2). *Herrerasaurus* (3) fed on smaller, crocodile-like animals (4), and *Eoraptor* (5) ate small prey. There was more food for plant-eaters, and their meals were easier to obtain, so they easily outnumbered the meat-eaters.

DAWN OF THE DINOSAURS

For many years, the Valley of the Moon has been known to scientists as the richest source of fossils from the time of the earliest dinosaurs. Remains of *Herrerasaurus*, a predatory dinosaur, were first discovered there in the 1950s. But *Herrerasaurus* and many other creatures from this remote desert became well known only in recent years, after scientists examined the fossils in detail in the laboratory.

No fossil tells as much about the appearance and origins of an animal as its skull. Several bones of *Herrerasaurus* (but no skull) were discovered years ago. In 1988, American paleontologist Dr. Paul Sereno found the first skull of *Herrerasaurus* while he was walking alone in the desert. It was so well preserved that even the bony rings in its eye sockets were still there.

A tiny bone in *Herrerasaurus*'s ears indicates that this dinosaur may have had a keen sense of hearing. Its long claws and sharp-toothed jaws suggest it was a fearsome hunter and killer. *Herrerasaurus*'s upright posture suggests that it was agile and swift for its day.

Remains of a *Herrerasaurus*
The fossilized skull, neck, and forelimb of a *Herrerasaurus* lie in rock in the Valley of the Moon. Next to the fossils, a paleontologist's brush, used for clearing away loose dirt, gives an indication of the size of the bones.

LOST AND FOUND

An aging *Herrerasaurus* breathes its last on the bank of a shallow lake in the Valley of the Moon. All around it, life goes on. But this *Herrerasaurus*, unlike most others, will become a fossil, as shown in this sequence of illustrations.

In shallow water, the dinosaur's carcass bloats with gases produced by microbes as its flesh rots (**1**). Insects, bacteria, and other decomposers eat *Herrerasaurus*'s flesh (**2**). Within weeks of the dinosaur's death, its soft parts are gone. Just the bones and teeth are left. These become buried in sand (**3**).

Minerals from the lake bed enter holes where blood vessels and nerves once ran through *Herrerasaurus*'s bones. The bones turn rock hard.

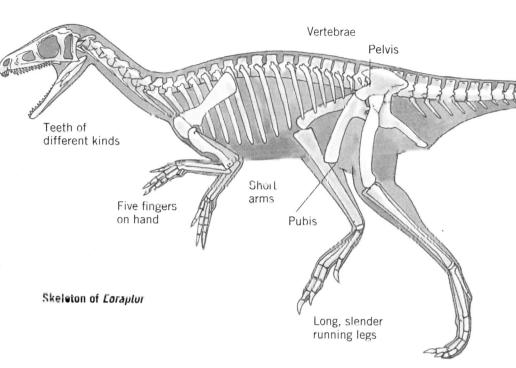

Vertebrae

Pelvis

Teeth of
different kinds

Five fingers
on hand

Short
arms

Pubis

Skeleton of *Eoraptor*

Long, slender
running legs

Eoraptor had several features that
identify it as one of the first
dinosaurs. For example, it had
five fingers. Later meat-eating
dinosaurs had fewer fingers. The
last big meat-eating dinosaurs,
such as *Tyrannosaurus rex*, had
only two fingers. *Eoraptor* had
just three vertebrae (bones of the
back) supporting its tiny pelvis.
As dinosaurs grew bigger, more
vertebrae supported the pelvis.

Eoraptor also lacked an extra
joint in the middle of its jaw and
did not have an especially large
pubis. These were features of
Herrerasaurus and later meat-
eating dinosaurs.

On a second trip to the Valley of the Moon in 1993, Dr. Sereno
and his colleagues uncovered a well-preserved and nearly entire
skeleton of *Eoraptor*. In its skull, the back teeth were grooved
like the steak-knife teeth of other meat-eating dinosaurs. But
its front teeth were leaf-shaped like those of plant-eating
dinosaurs. Perhaps *Eoraptor* ate both plants and meat.

Water levels rise, and iron-rich sand
covers much of the skeleton,
turning the bones dark in
color. Some smaller bones in
the legs and tail are washed
away. Over millions of years,
layers of sand become packed
down and turn to rock above
the fossilized skeleton **(4)**.

As the Valley of the Moon
became a desert in modern
times, winds blew away the layers
of rock. The skull of the dinosaur,
locked in ironstone, was found in
1988 by Dr. Sereno **(5)**.

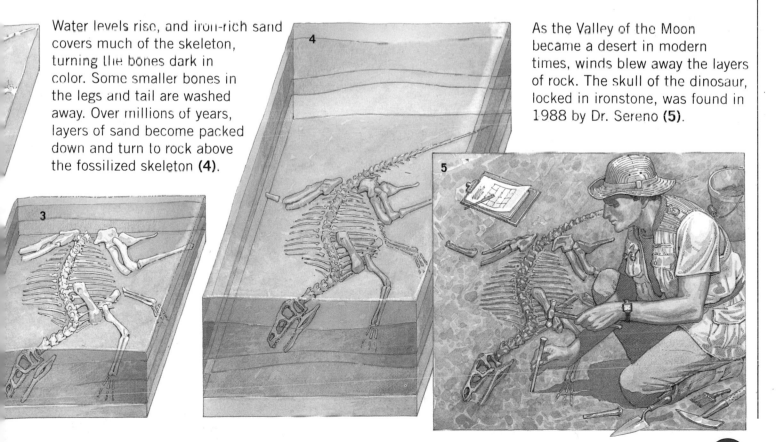

TRAPPED GIANTS

FRICK BRICK QUARRY

Switzerland
215 million years ago

On the bank of a winding river, a plant eating *Plateosaurus* plods into the mud in search of food. It soon sinks to its knees, trapped in the muck. Hungry meat-eating dinosaurs close in to feast on the helpless giant.

FEEDING ON PLANTS

Among the ferns and evergreen trees lining the riverbanks 215 million years ago, plant-eating dinosaurs were thriving. Less than 15 million years before, the first dinosaurs—all small meat-eaters—had appeared. By the Late Triassic the plant-eaters were already giants, the biggest animals in their world. Over the next 100 million years, plant-eating dinosaurs would become bigger still.

Frick Brick Quarry—Today Many partial fossil skeletons of adult *Plateosaurus* have been found here and at several sites in France and Germany.

The first large plant-eating dinosaurs, such as *Plateosaurus*, could walk on all four legs. They could also stand on just their hind legs to feed. They were the first large animals to exploit the food supply found in the treetops and high branches. Like other plant-eaters, these dinosaurs had big bodies with large stomachs.

Meat-eating dinosaurs also lived along the riverbanks. Crocodile-like reptiles, fish, and the first turtles swam in the water. Small flying reptiles soared overhead. In the Late Triassic, the Earth's land was a single continent. The weather was warm and, in most places, dry. In the continent's interior there were desert conditions. At the continent's edges, the effects of the sea made the climate less extreme.

Rivers, lakes, and marshes provided life-giving water in the lowlands. Ferns and horsetails were important parts of the plant community. They reproduced by spores, which need damp places in which to germinate.

In some wet areas, conditions were ideal for animals and plants to fossilize after they died and sank into mud. In several parts of the world, fossil beds from this time have been found. Fossils of similar types of animals have been found in China, South America, Greenland, and southwestern North America. Scientists think the same kinds of creatures lived worldwide because animals could move freely on the single world landmass.

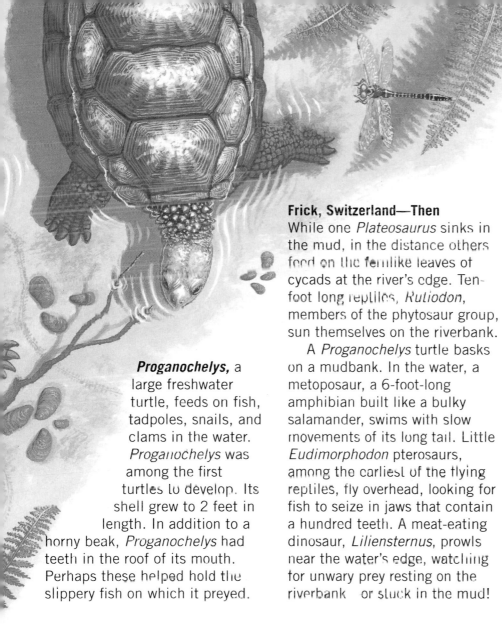

Frick, Switzerland—Then
While one *Plateosaurus* sinks in the mud, in the distance others feed on the fernlike leaves of cycads at the river's edge. Ten-foot long reptiles, *Rutiodon*, members of the phytosaur group, sun themselves on the riverbank.

A *Proganochelys* turtle basks on a mudbank. In the water, a metoposaur, a 6-foot-long amphibian built like a bulky salamander, swims with slow movements of its long tail. Little *Eudimorphodon* pterosaurs, among the earliest of the flying reptiles, fly overhead, looking for fish to seize in jaws that contain a hundred teeth. A meat-eating dinosaur, *Liliensternus*, prowls near the water's edge, watching for unwary prey resting on the riverbank   or stuck in the mud!

Proganochelys, a large freshwater turtle, feeds on fish, tadpoles, snails, and clams in the water. *Proganochelys* was among the first turtles to develop. Its shell grew to 2 feet in length. In addition to a horny beak, *Proganochelys* had teeth in the roof of its mouth. Perhaps these helped hold the slippery fish on which it preyed.

FACT FILE

Switzerland – Then and Now
Today Europe is a mountainous continent with an annual change of seasons. In the Late Triassic, it was mostly underwater, with only a few subtropical islands above sea level.

Globe shows the continents now

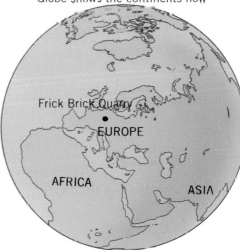

In Europe, Late Triassic animal life featured new types of dinosaurs and other, more ancient kinds of reptiles.

ANIMALS
1. *Eudimorphodon*
   (YOU-die-MORF-o-dahn)
2. *Liliensternus*
   (LIL-ee-en-STIR-nus)
3. Metoposaur
   (meh-TOPE-o-sawr)
4. *Plateosaurus*
   (PLAT-ee-o-SAW-rus)
5. *Proganochelys*
   (pro-GAN-o-KEY-leez)
6. *Rutiodon*
   (ROO-tee-o-dahn)

PLANTS
7. Conifers (KON-ih-furs)
8. Cycads (SY-kads)

ALSO AT THIS SITE:
Calamites (KAL-ah-MY-teez)

GIANTS' ANCESTORS

PLANTS

Calamites, a kind of horsetail, was a common, fast-growing plant along riverbanks. Horsetails grew like reeds, up to 3 inches thick and 15 feet high. Rings of leaves grew out at intervals up the ribbed stems. At the stem tips were reproductive structures, the cones. Modern horsetails are similar but smaller.

CALAMITES

Large long-necked dinosaurs like *Plateosaurus* may have fed on the tips of *Calamites* or on low-growing ferns and cycads and the lower branches of conifer trees. Smaller plant-eaters could not reach up high enough to get food from the trees. Size and sharp thumb claws appear to have been the plateosaur's only defenses against meat-eaters.

Plateosaurs were prosauropod dinosaurs. They relied on large gizzards to help them digest plant material that their small jaws were unable to grind well. Their muscular gizzards may have been bigger than basketballs. The gizzards also may have contained stomach stones to help break down tough plants. Prosauropods later evolved into sauropods, the largest of all land animals.

RUTIODON

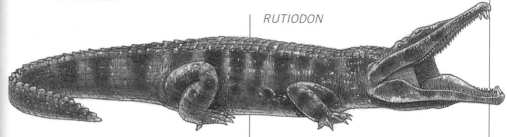

RUTIODON
Meaning of name: "Folded tooth"
Order: Thecodontia
Size, Weight: 10–16 feet long, 500 pounds
Locations: Western Europe, eastern and western North America
Diet: Fish, small reptiles

Rutiodon was a typical phytosaur. It was a heavily armored crocodile-like meat-eater. *Rutiodon* had a long snout filled with sharp teeth for snatching and eating other reptiles and fish. Phytosaurs were common in the Late Triassic and were lords of the water throughout that period.

PLATEOSAURUS

PLATEOSAURUS
Meaning of name: "Broad lizard"
Order: Saurischia
Size, Weight: 20–26 feet long, 1–2 tons
Locations: Western Europe, Greenland
Diet: Plants

Plateosaurus is the best known of all large early plant-eating dinosaurs. The entire skull of *Plateosaurus* was powerfully built. It had many small teeth shaped like leaves with flat sides and serrations. These were good for shredding plants rather than grinding them.

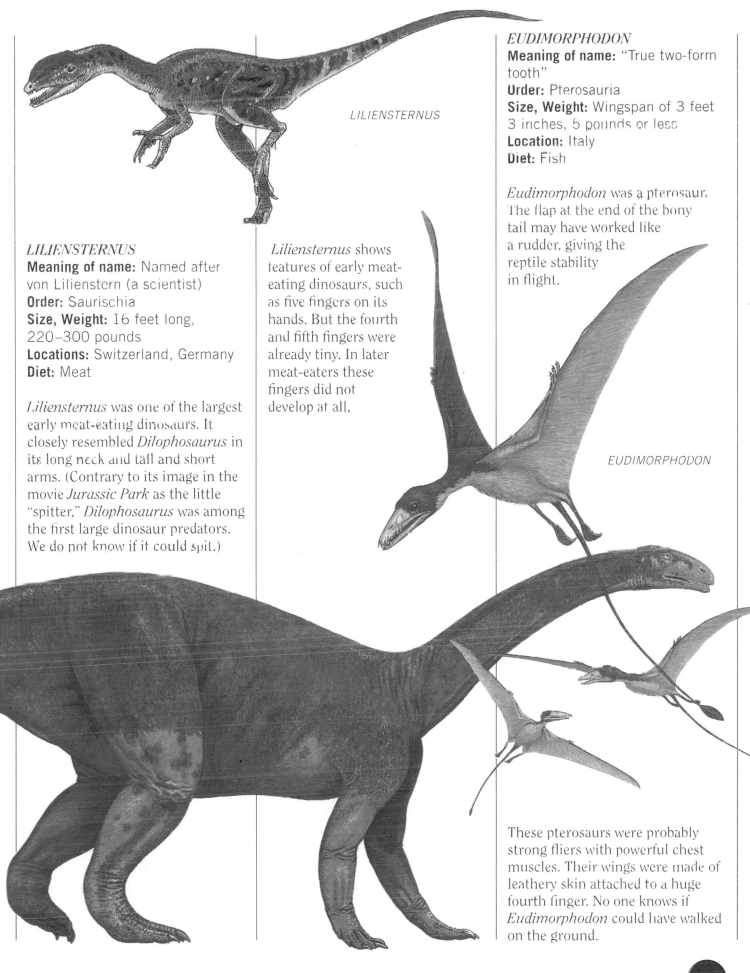

LILIENSTERNUS

EUDIMORPHODON
Meaning of name: "True two-form tooth"
Order: Pterosauria
Size, Weight: Wingspan of 3 feet 3 inches, 5 pounds or less
Location: Italy
Diet: Fish

Eudimorphodon was a pterosaur. The flap at the end of the bony tail may have worked like a rudder, giving the reptile stability in flight.

LILIENSTERNUS
Meaning of name: Named after von Lilienstern (a scientist)
Order: Saurischia
Size, Weight: 16 feet long, 220–300 pounds
Locations: Switzerland, Germany
Diet: Meat

Liliensternus was one of the largest early meat-eating dinosaurs. It closely resembled *Dilophosaurus* in its long neck and tall and short arms. (Contrary to its image in the movie *Jurassic Park* as the little "spitter," *Dilophosaurus* was among the first large dinosaur predators. We do not know if it could spit.)

Liliensternus shows features of early meat-eating dinosaurs, such as five fingers on its hands. But the fourth and fifth fingers were already tiny. In later meat-eaters these fingers did not develop at all.

EUDIMORPHODON

These pterosaurs were probably strong fliers with powerful chest muscles. Their wings were made of leathery skin attached to a huge fourth finger. No one knows if *Eudimorphodon* could have walked on the ground.

RIVER WORLDS

The environment of the center of western Europe in the Late Triassic Period was much like that along the Nile River of Egypt today, though the animals and plants differed greatly. Lush vegetation grew along riverbanks that became flooded after a heavy rain. Farther from the water's edge, the land was generally dry, even desertlike.

The giant reptiles and plant-eating dinosaurs that lived along the riverbanks of Europe 215 million years ago have died out, but some present-day animals in Egypt have lifestyles similar to those of their ancient ancestors.

In the Nile, today's counterparts of the large meat-eating dinosaurs are the crocodiles that patrol the river and its banks in search of prey. Hippopotamuses also live in parts of the Nile River. They come on land to eat large amounts of plants and prefer to feed on the riverbanks. Although adult hippos have no natural predators, their young often fall prey to crocodiles. Fish and reptiles were common then and now. The pterosaurs of the Late Triassic have been replaced by today's wading and fishing birds, such as pelicans.

A cross section of a riverbank in Switzerland 215 million years ago shows a herd of plateosaurs browsing on the plants beside the river **(1)**. A mudslide caused by heavy rains pours over the vegetation **(2)**. One animal has wandered into the sticky mud and is trapped **(3)**. In this scene, a meat-eating *Liliensternus* **(4)** has seen the plateosaurs and is stalking them. Vegetation is most dense along the banks of the river. It thins out away from the water and gives way to a dry landscape.

On the banks of the Nile River, a crocodile attacks a young hippo. Crocodiles are related to ancestors of dinosaurs. Today, crocodiles are among the fiercest of predators.

Two ferocious *Liliensternus* tear at the throat of a thrashing *Plateosaurus*. Like many modern predators, they may have attacked their prey in the water, which slows the movements of large animals and can prevent them from escaping.

Whether in the modern Nile River Valley or in Late Triassic Europe, even large plant-eaters can become prey, especially when they are injured, trapped, or ill. In dry environments like modern Egypt or much of the Late Triassic world, animals gather where food and water are plentiful. When plant-eaters come to feed and drink along the banks of rivers and the shores of lakes, they risk attack from hungry carnivores. A lion, hidden in the grass, waits by a water hole, ready to pounce on any thirsty zebra that comes to drink. In the Late Triassic world, *Liliensternus* probably waited for prey in the same way.

STUCK-IN-THE-MUD DINOSAURS

In quarries across central Europe, dozens of dinosaur skeletons have been found as fossils embedded in Late Triassic rocks. Some of these sites also contain fossils of small plants and small animals. The dinosaur fossils are almost entirely the remains of *Plateosaurus*.

Many plateosaur fossils are preserved with their leg bones intact. The legs are often upright in the rock. This unusual position shows that the dinosaurs were standing when they died and that they stayed in this position after death. Something prevented them from falling. Perhaps they were held in position by stiff mud that later became rock. Scientists think that *Plateosaurus* walked on its back

legs, which were longer and stronger than its front limbs. The back legs supported the weight of the animal, which was up to 2 tons. The head and forelimbs were balanced by the weight of the tail behind. The heavy stomach was close to the balance point.

Plateosaurus's front limbs might have had several purposes. Each thick forelimb had four fingers and a thumb with a large claw, wide and sharp at its tip. Some scientists think the thumb was used for defense. Others think it helped grab food from trees and bushes. Perhaps this thumb had two jobs.

Since plateosaur skeletons are often found in groups, scientists think the animals lived in small herds, as hippos and elephants do today.

Growing bigger and being able to raise their necks allowed prosauropod and sauropod dinosaurs to use new sources of food.

1. *Plateosaurus*
2. *Diplodocus*
3. *Supersaurus*
4. *Brachiosaurus*
5. *Ultrasauros*
6. *Seismosaurus*

Why grow bigger?

Large size is a protection against predators, which prefer to go after the easiest prey to kill. Predators can kill small animals more easily than they can bring down large ones. So small adult animals and the youngsters of large plant-eaters are the main targets. As plant-eating dinosaurs became bigger, they were less likely to be killed by carnivores.

Big animals have to eat large amounts of food to provide the energy their bodies need. But they eat less food for each pound of their mass than a small animal does. Their huge bodies do not lose heat as fast as small animals do. As a result, even low-energy foods like ferns could have provided enough energy for these big dinosaurs to survive.

Without huge energy needs, the giant plant-eaters could travel far on a large stomach full of food. When the plants in one area had been stripped, the herd of giant dinosaurs could trek a great distance to find another food source. Plateosaurs may have traveled long distances between feeding grounds in the way that herding plant-eaters do today.

MASS DEATH

Scientists have discovered more than 140 adult *Plateosaurus* skeletons at one site. A single story may explain how many of the animals died together.

A herd of plateosaurs **(1)** browses on the muddy bank of a river. The animals edge deeper into the thick sticky mud along the riverbank where the stream recently flooded. The herd is soon knee-deep in ooze **(2)**, with individual plateosaurs thrashing to break free.

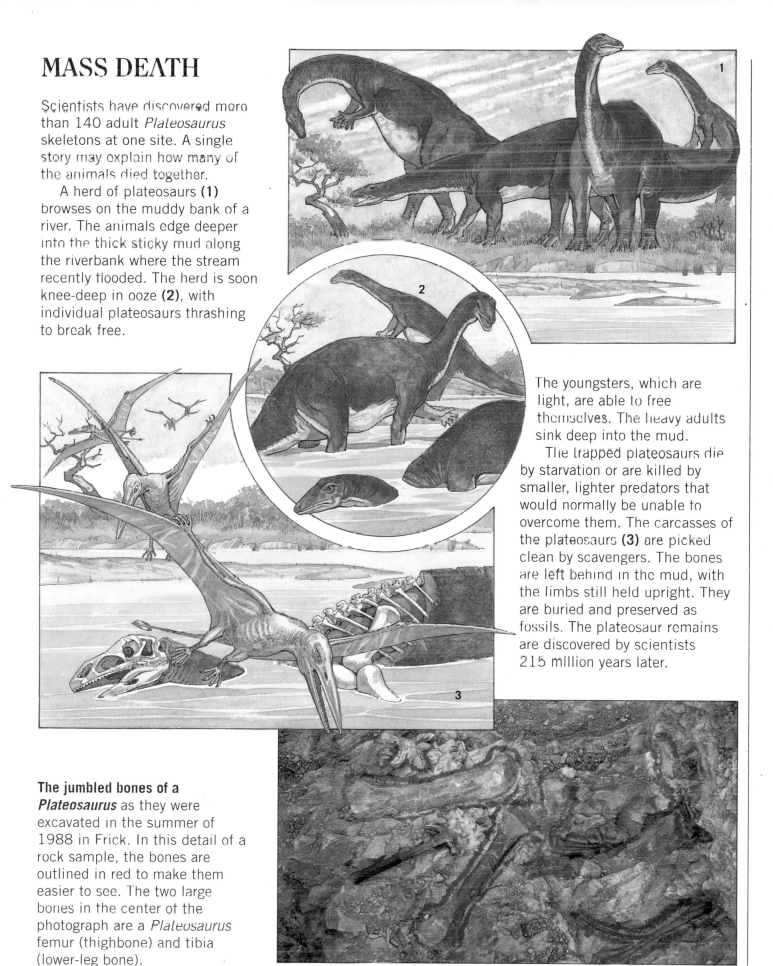

The youngsters, which are light, are able to free themselves. The heavy adults sink deep into the mud.

The trapped plateosaurs die by starvation or are killed by smaller, lighter predators that would normally be unable to overcome them. The carcasses of the plateosaurs **(3)** are picked clean by scavengers. The bones are left behind in the mud, with the limbs still held upright. They are buried and preserved as fossils. The plateosaur remains are discovered by scientists 215 million years later.

The jumbled bones of a *Plateosaurus* as they were excavated in the summer of 1988 in Frick. In this detail of a rock sample, the bones are outlined in red to make them easier to see. The two large bones in the center of the photograph are a *Plateosaurus* femur (thighbone) and tibia (lower-leg bone).

SURVIVAL AND EXTINCTION

BAY OF FUNDY
Nova Scotia
208 million years ago

Panicking reptiles, including small dinosaurs, flee from a forest fire. This disaster is the result of a mysterious worldwide catastrophe that is killing off many species.

DISASTER STRIKES

About 208 million years ago, a mysterious worldwide disaster wiped out many forms of life, ending the Triassic Period and beginning the Jurassic Period. In Nova Scotia and other areas, scientists have found clues about what life was like before and after this mass extinction.

What caused this mass extinction? Scientists have offered several possible explanations. A giant asteroid might have struck the Earth, or changes within the Earth might have triggered a series of volcanic eruptions. Either of these events would have produced drastic changes in the weather. Another possibility is that the slow separation of the world's one landmass into smaller continents would have changed local conditions.

Whatever the cause, small dinosaurs, small land crocodilians, and mammal-like reptiles survived the change, while many larger reptiles died out. The plant life changed, too. Bushes and trees with thick evergreen leaves became the most common types.

Small theropods—meat-eating dinosaurs the size of a small child—feed on procolophonids, fat lizardlike creatures whose closest living relatives may be turtles. The procolophonids died out at the end of the Triassic Period, but dinosaurs lived on.

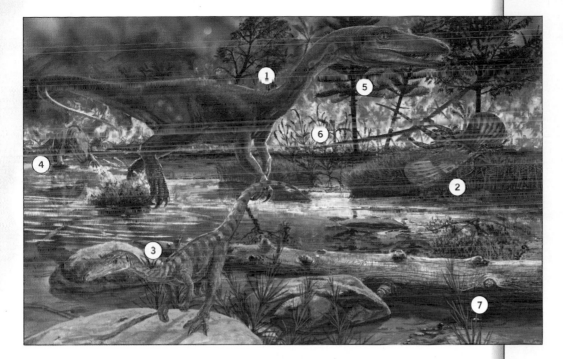

FACT FILE

Only a few of the fossils from Late Triassic and Early Jurassic Nova Scotia have been scientifically described and named. Many of the animals of that time look like small versions of familiar creatures, known from elsewhere

ANIMALS
1. *Coelophysis*-like meat eater (SEE-lo-FY-sis)
2. *Icarosaurus* (ICK-a-ro-SAW-rus)
3. Robin-sized meat-eater
4. Rauisuchian (RAO-y-SOO-key-un)

PLANTS
5. Cheirolepidaceous (KY-ro-LEP-ee-DAY-shus) conifers
6. Cycads and ginkgoes
7. Horsetails

Bay of Fundy—Then Animal and plant life was varied in eastern Canada 208 million years ago, when a great disaster struck the region.

Before the extinction, small meat-eating dinosaurs hunted among such predators as the long-legged rauisuchians. Rauisuchians had also appeared during the Triassic Period, before the dinosaurs. The predatory dinosaurs in Nova Scotia resembled *Coelophysis*, a 10-foot-long carnivore from the American Southwest. Insect-eating reptiles might have included *Icarosaurus*, a lizard that could glide through the air using wings of skin. Ferns, cycads, and conifers grew along the shores of shallow lakes.

Bay of Fundy—Today
Paleontologists hunt for more dinosaur fossils beside the bay, where waves crash against the base of tree-topped cliffs.

Nova Scotia – Then and Now
Now Nova Scotia is a province along the rocky northeastern tip of Canada. At the end of the Triassic Period, it was by a shallow sea, not an ocean. It sat on the great dividing line where Pangaea was beginning to split into two continents.

Globe shows the continents now

Most of the fossils found at the Bay of Fundy are bits and pieces of bone from small animals. Perhaps these creatures survived the disaster because they could hide underground when the climate was harsh. In most extinctions, smaller creatures have survived better than larger ones. At the end of the Permian Era, 245 million years ago, nine out of every ten forms of life were wiped out. Large animals were especially hard-hit.

SMALL WONDERS

UNNAMED THEROPOD

Dinosaurs and other reptiles of the Early Jurassic found in Nova Scotia were tiny. Were most animals there truly small? The conditions at that place and time might have favored small animals. Or small animals might have become fossils more easily there. Usually, small animals are poorly preserved.

UNNAMED THEROPOD
Order: Saurischia
Size, Weight: 1–7 feet long, less than 20 pounds
Location: Nova Scotia
Diet: Meat

A small meat-eating dinosaur is known from scattered fossils and footprints in both the Late Triassic and Early Jurassic rocks of Nova Scotia. It appears to have looked like *Coelophysis*, a larger meat-eater well known from the American Southwest at this time.

Worldwide, the largest land animals of the Late Triassic Period were crocodile-like reptiles. The mass extinction that ended this period killed these creatures and allowed the dinosaurs to thrive. In Late Triassic Nova Scotia, the giants were rauisuchians and a 15-foot-long predator called *Rutiodon*.

Some of the footprints of this as-yet-unnamed theropod were made by an animal no bigger than a robin. The tracks may be those of a youngster. But if they are an adult's, they were made by the smallest dinosaur yet known.

Soon after the extinction at the beginning of the Jurassic Period a variety of dinosaurs lived in Nova Scotia. These dinosaurs included small and large meat-eaters and plant-eaters. Largest of them was a 9-foot-long prosauropod, closely related to the dinosaur *Ammosaurus*—known to have grown to 14 feet elsewhere in North America.

In the Early Jurassic, another small creature living in Nova Scotia was a two-legged ornithischian (bird-hipped) dinosaur that looked like *Lesothosaurus*. The plant-eater *Lesothosaurus* lived in southern Africa and grew to about 3 feet in length. This Nova Scotian relation was no bigger than a turkey. The lizards and crocodilians from Nova Scotia were also small compared to those from other places at this time.

Today, smaller-sized varieties of animals are sometimes found on islands or in places where the environment is difficult to live in. The stresses of everyday life may prevent these animals from reaching their maximum possible size.

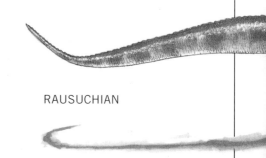

RAUSUCHIAN

ICAROSAURUS

Meaning of name: "Icarus lizard" (Icarus is a flying character in Greek mythology)
Order: Squamata
Size, Weight: 1 foot 8 inches long, 6 ounces or less
Locations: Eastern North America, England
Diet: Insects

This early lizard had very long ribs that could be spread to support a wing of skin used for gliding from branch to branch. The little "flying dragon" lizards of Southeast Asia glide in the same way today.

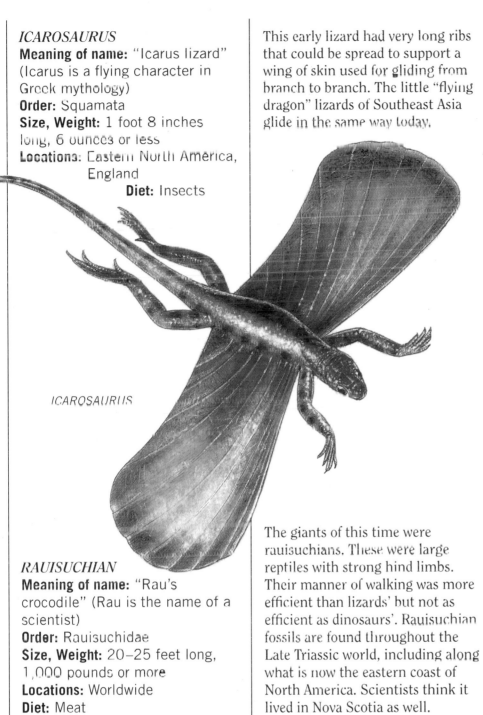

ICAROSAURUS

RAUISUCHIAN

Meaning of name: "Rau's crocodile" (Rau is the name of a scientist)
Order: Rauisuchidae
Size, Weight: 20–25 feet long, 1,000 pounds or more
Locations: Worldwide
Diet: Meat

The giants of this time were rauisuchians. These were large reptiles with strong hind limbs. Their manner of walking was more efficient than lizards' but not as efficient as dinosaurs'. Rauisuchian fossils are found throughout the Late Triassic world, including along what is now the eastern coast of North America. Scientists think it lived in Nova Scotia as well.

PLANTS

Many kinds of nonflowering plants such as ferns, cycads, and evergreen trees lived in Nova Scotia in the Late Triassic Period. But in the Early Jurassic Period of the same area, just a few million years later, most of these plants had disappeared.

Fossil pollen of only one kind of conifer is found here. This conifer, *Classopolis*, grew as both a bush and as a tree. It had very thick needles.

CYCADS

Cycads and cycadeoids were common in dinosaur times. These plants bore cones and had thick trunks with flat scales. A fan of leaves spread from their crowns. Cycadeoids are extinct, but cycads are still common in warmer climates today.

TRIASSIC EXTINCTION

After a disaster, life goes on, though many kinds of animals and plants can be wiped out forever. Fast-growing plants, small animals, and animals with less specialized needs in diet or habitat are the most likely to survive.

Exploding volcanoes, like the 1982 eruption of Mount St. Helens in Oregon in the United States, have both local and worldwide effects. For miles around the volcano, fiery lava and thick layers of hot ash kill living things on the ground. High in the atmosphere, gases and ash are blown around the world by winds, causing hazy skies and warmer temperatures.

But not all life is killed around the disaster site. The Mount St. Helens eruption did not kill the roots of trees, and new growth soon sprouted from the trunks. Mice and other small burrowing mammals, insects, and worms emerged from underground hiding places. More insects, spiders, and the seeds of fast-growing plants were blown onto the mountainsides by winds. As insects and plants began to multiply, birds flew in and larger animals returned to the area.

In Nova Scotia at the end of the Triassic Period, a similar pattern of regrowth would have brought back abundant life.

Mount St. Helens volcano in Oregon erupted in 1982, with far-reaching damage. The blast was seen and heard over an area of hundreds of square miles, and it affected weather worldwide. Life has already returned to the site.

In the Late Triassic, Nova Scotia was a dry area. Animal and plant life was richest along the shores of lakes and rivers. But many shallow lakes were drying up. Dinosaurs and other reptiles, such as the aetosaurs and large phytosaurs shown here, lived in the lush valleys. Reptiles swam in the waters and flew in the skies. Amphibians, fish, insects, and mammals lived in this area, too.

At the end of the Triassic Period, many plants and animals became extinct. For the most part, larger animals died. Survivors included many smaller creatures. Their ability to find shelter may have

These fast-growing, spreading herb plants were among the first forms of vegetation to return to the slopes of Mount St. Helens following the eruption. This photo was taken about two years after the disaster.

An asteroid, a chunk of rock orbiting the Sun, hurtles to the Earth. Its impact causes changes worldwide, some disastrous for life. Such a disaster is the likely cause of some of the sudden mass extinctions of animals and plants in Earth's history.

Perhaps the impact of a large asteroid killed off many kinds of animals at the end of the Triassic Period. A cloud of smoke and ash, much the same as a volcanic eruption produces, would have been thrown up into the air. The dust would have blocked the sunlight. This could have led to a drop in temperature worldwide and to the death of those plants that could no longer use the Sun's energy to make food. The effect on plant-eating animals, and on those meat-eaters that fed on them, would have been catastrophic.

helped them survive. Small crocodilians and a variety of fish, little dinosaurs, mammal-like reptiles, and *Clevosaurus* (a little broad-headed reptile) lived on in Nova Scotia.

In the Early Jurassic Period in Nova Scotia, a new group of plants and animals settled in a very changed land. The environment was moister, yet there were far fewer kinds of plants and animals.

Plant-eating dinosaurs, from small ornithischians to larger prosauropods, were the most abundant animals. Meat-eating dinosaurs, large and small, were also present.

SEARCHING FOR THE REASON

The Bay of Fundy, Nova Scotia, is where fossils best show the drastic change in life across the boundary of the Triassic and Jurassic Periods. From 1988 to 1993, Drs. Paul Olsen, Neil Shubin, and Hans Sues, three of the world's leading scientific experts on the animals of this time, explored the Bay of Fundy and excavated the fossils.

Their finds and others at the Nova Scotia site include several partial skeletons and thousands of fossil fragments. The fossil animals range in size from reptiles 25 feet long to amphibians only inches in length. Triassic fossils in this part of Canada date from as far back as 225 million years ago. Other fossils found by the bay date from shortly after the start of the Jurassic Period, 208 million years ago.

Close to the changeover in geological periods, the fossil animals and plants show smaller-sized individuals and fewer varieties. This change in fossil types reflects a shift in the environment that must have been drastic and relatively sudden. Footprints and skeletons from Nova Scotia show that in the Jurassic Period, the dinosaurs prospered as plant-eaters and meat-eaters that grew much larger than before.

These footprints show the three-toed anatomy typical of meat-eating dinosaurs. The unusual thing about them is that they were made by a robin-sized animal—the smallest dinosaur known. About 208 million years ago in Nova Scotia, small animals flourished and bigger ones died out. Although scientists can make suggestions about why this should be, no one really knows.

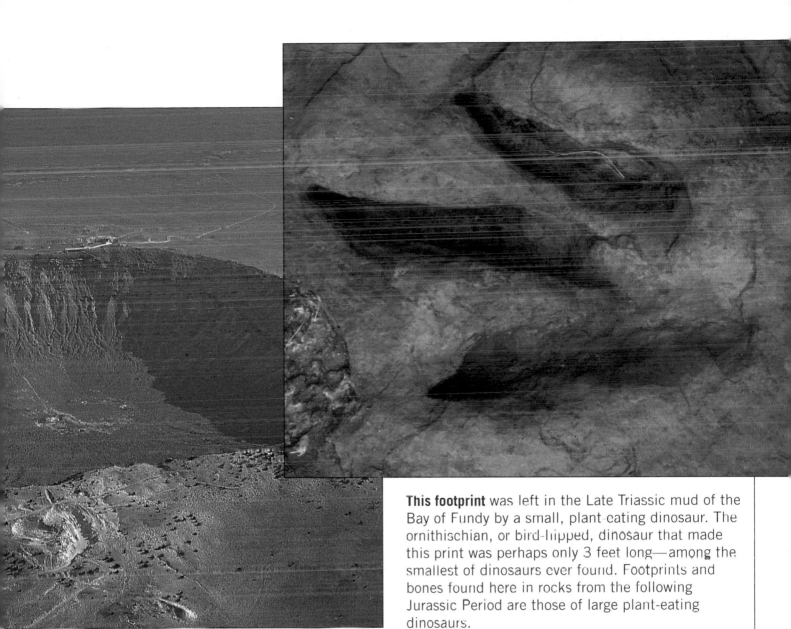

This footprint was left in the Late Triassic mud of the Bay of Fundy by a small, plant-eating dinosaur. The ornithischian, or bird-hipped, dinosaur that made this print was perhaps only 3 feet long—among the smallest of dinosaurs ever found. Footprints and bones found here in rocks from the following Jurassic Period are those of large plant-eating dinosaurs.

Meteorite Crater in Arizona is nearly a mile wide and 560 feet deep. It was formed when a fragment of rock from space struck the Earth long after dinosaurs became extinct. Scientists search for much larger craters in the hope of explaining mass extinctions. No such crater has yet been linked to the disaster that ended the Triassic Period.

Good scientific theories are based on evidence. Did an asteroid collide with the Earth at Nova Scotia at the end of the Triassic Period and cause weather changes that killed many kinds of plants and animals? So far, the evidence for such an event at the Bay of Fundy fossil site is slight.

Elsewhere in the world, though, scientists have found a variety of clues and evidence for a major disaster at this time. For example, in Europe they have found "shocked quartz," a type of rock usually formed by enormous impacts, such as an asteroid striking the Earth. In Europe, Africa, and America, fossils of ancient sea creatures show that almost ninety percent of species alive in Triassic times had disappeared by the Early Jurassic Period.

Just as the pieces of a jigsaw puzzle interlock to make a single image, so geological information from various fossil sites has combined to reveal the geological changes in Nova Scotia at the end of the Triassic.

A NEW WORLD
MANA PARK GAME
RESERVE
Zimbabwe
200 million years ago

46

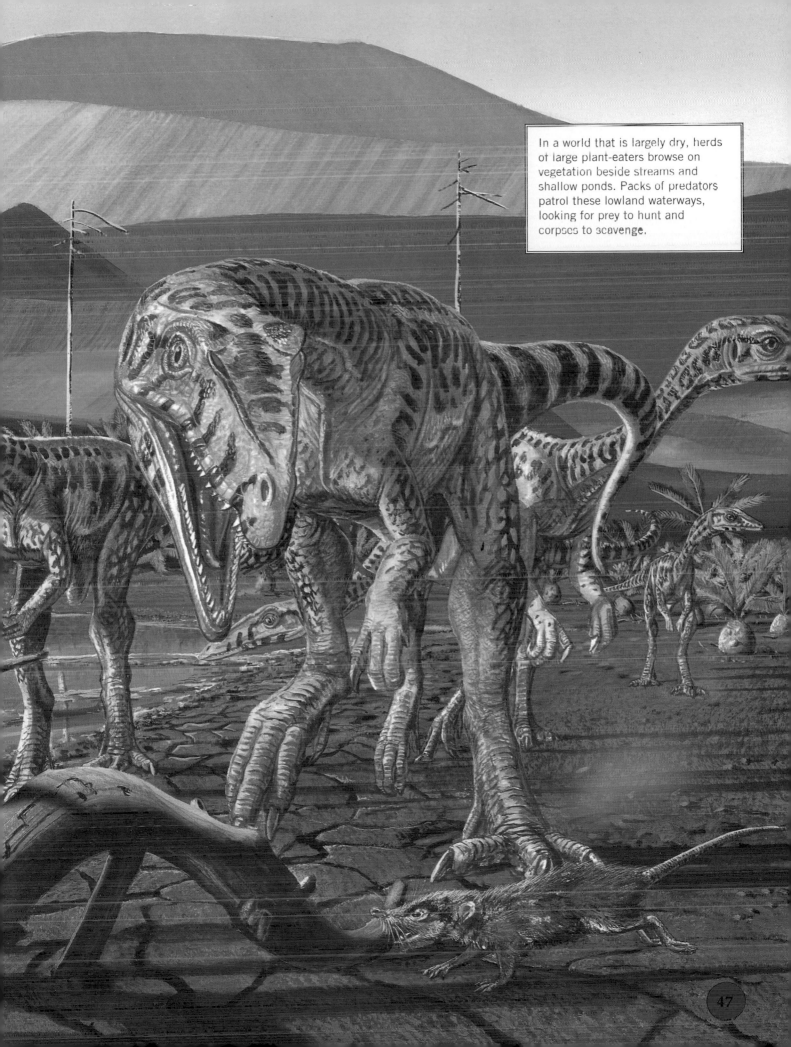

In a world that is largely dry, herds of large plant-eaters browse on vegetation beside streams and shallow ponds. Packs of predators patrol these lowland waterways, looking for prey to hunt and corpses to scavenge.

WATERSIDE FORESTS

The landscape of what is now southern Africa was nearly desert 200 million years ago. Bare sand dunes covered many areas. Yet a wide range of plants, from small ferns to large conifer trees, survived in this harsh environment. Animal life included sturdy fish and primitive mammals. But the rulers of this new period were dinosaurs of many sizes and forms.

The dinosaurs are divided into two groups—bird-hipped and lizard-hipped. All of the bird-hipped dinosaurs were plant-eaters. The lizard-hipped dinosaurs included all of the meat-eaters and still more plant-eaters.

Scientists say birds evolved from dinosaurs. It seems to make sense that these modern animals would have come from bird-hipped dinosaurs. But two clues suggest that birds grew out of a family of lizard-hipped meat-eaters. The first piece of evidence comes from the earliest bird, *Archaeopteryx*, which had lizard hips. The second clue comes from the most birdlike dinosaurs, which were small lizard-hipped carnivores.

The mammals of ancient Zimbabwe were shrewlike in size. Scientists think that some of their habits and body features were also shrewlike. They spent a long time on the ground.

A *Massospondylus* walks beneath spreading araucarian conifers. These trees grew worldwide in the early Jurassic and still survive in the Southern Hemisphere. We call them monkey puzzle trees. A tiny *Megazostrodon* mammal high in a tree snatches a beetle in its sharp front teeth. Scientists think *Megazostrodon* might have moved up and down among the trees.

Mana Park Game Reserve—Today
Paleontologist Mike Raath walks with his camera beside the fossil site in Mana Park Game Reserve. The soft sandstone banks of the Zambesi River hold fossils, including those of dinosaurs, from 200 million years ago.

48

Fossils from Early Jurassic Mana Park show that the mammals had one set of milk teeth and then one set of permanent teeth—as we do. (Reptiles keep changing their teeth throughout life.) These shrewlike mammals were probably active at night, or in twilight, when they would be less vulnerable to carnivorous dinosaurs and other predators. The high branches of the araucarian trees would have also provided safety from predators. The tiny mammals probably scrambled up the tree trunks when they felt threatened.

FACT FILE

By the Early Jurassic Period, dinosaurs were the largest animals on land. The first mammals had evolved from cynodont reptiles. Plants were slower to change. Many types survived from the Triassic.

ANIMALS
1. *Erythrotherium* (eh-RITH-ro-THEER-ee-um)
2. *Lesothosaurus* (leh-SOO-too-SAW-rus)
3. *Massospondylus* (MASS-o-SPON-duh-lus)
4. *Megazostrodon* (MEG-a-ZOSS-tro-dahn)
5. *Semionotus* (SEM-ee-o-NO-tus)
6. *Syntarsus* (sin-TAR-sus)

PLANTS
7. Cycads (SY-kads)
8. Cycadeoid (sy-KAD-ee-oyd)

ALSO AT THIS SITE:
Dicroidium ferns (DIE-crow-ID-ee-um)

Mana Park Game Reserve—Then
A *Syntarsus* dinosaur pack prowls the shore of a shallow lake. In the background, high sand dunes stretch into the distance. Where the dinosaurs' feet disturb the ground, the tiny mammals called *Megazostrodon* and *Erythrotherium* scurry underfoot looking for insects to eat. Plant-eating dinosaurs, the little *Lesothosaurus* and the larger *Massospondylus,* nervously watch the predators from a safe distance. *Semionotus* fish swim in the lake. Vegetation crowds the shore, including ferns, squat cycadeoids, taller cycads called *Dicroidium*, and towering araucarian trees.

Zimbabwe, Then and Now
Today, Zimbabwe lies in hot, humid southeastern Africa. In the Early Jurassic, it was hotter and drier as part of the southern continent, Gondwana.

Globe shows the continents now

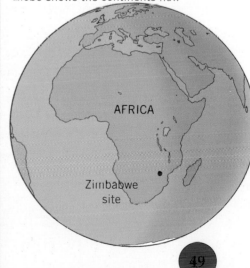

AFRICA

Zimbabwe site

DINOSAURS DOMINATE

PLANTS

Because humans belong in the mammal group, even scientists have sometimes thought of mammals as the "best" animals. But for 135 million years, the dinosaurs formed the more important group. It is doubtful that dinosaurs even noticed the mammals in their world, except as an occasional snack.

MEGAZOSTRODON
Meaning of name: "Large girdle tooth"
Order: Triconodonta
Size, Weight: 5 inches long, under 8 ounces
Location: Lesotho, southern Africa
Diet: Insects and other invertebrates

Megazostrodon belongs to one of the earliest groups of mammals, the triconodonts, which were named for the three points on each of their back teeth. *Megazostrodon*'s body shape is known from a complete skeleton. It looks like some other early mammals from China and Britain, which somewhat resemble a modern shrew.

Beneath majestic conifer trees, cycads and ferns grew in moist areas in the Early Jurassic. Cycads had thick trunks with flat, scaly surfaces like the outsides of pineapples. Fernlike leaves fanned out from their tops. These leaves had holes to let air in and out, unlike the leaves of the closely related cycadeoids.

Ferns came in many forms. Seed ferns had large seeds, trunks like trees, and big roots at their bases. These large plants had been growing in wetlands even before there were dinosaurs. Smaller ferns formed a ground cover.

Sphenophyllum lay close to the ground and spread into a circle of triangular leaves from a single, central stalk. Grass did not yet exist.

MEGAZOSTRODON

The first mammals appeared at the very end of the Triassic Period, but they were different from mammals of today. Most modern mammals bear live young. But scientists think the first mammals laid eggs, like their reptilian ancestors and like monotreme mammals of today, such as the echidnas.

How can scientists tell that a prehistoric animal was a mammal? They discovered that some extinct animals had teeth, jawbones, and ear bones like those of modern mammals. These animals had biting teeth (incisors) in the front, sharp canine teeth for tearing, and premolar and molar teeth for chewing. The lower jaws of these creatures were formed from a single bone, like mammals' jaws. A reptile's lower jaw has several bones. And these animals had a mammal-like combination of three hearing bones. Reptiles have only one.

DICROIDIUM

50

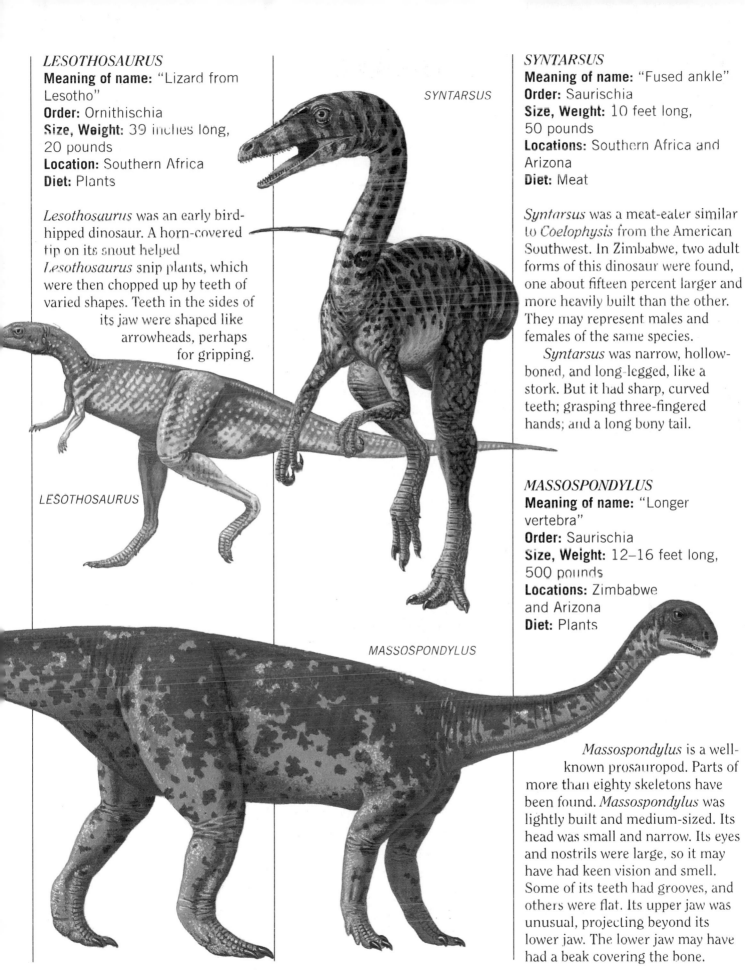

LESOTHOSAURUS

Meaning of name: "Lizard from Lesotho"
Order: Ornithischia
Size, Weight: 39 inches long, 20 pounds
Location: Southern Africa
Diet: Plants

Lesothosaurus was an early bird-hipped dinosaur. A horn-covered tip on its snout helped *Lesothosaurus* snip plants, which were then chopped up by teeth of varied shapes. Teeth in the sides of its jaw were shaped like arrowheads, perhaps for gripping.

LESOTHOSAURUS

SYNTARSUS

SYNTARSUS

Meaning of name: "Fused ankle"
Order: Saurischia
Size, Weight: 10 feet long, 50 pounds
Locations: Southern Africa and Arizona
Diet: Meat

Syntarsus was a meat-eater similar to *Coelophysis* from the American Southwest. In Zimbabwe, two adult forms of this dinosaur were found, one about fifteen percent larger and more heavily built than the other. They may represent males and females of the same species.

Syntarsus was narrow, hollow-boned, and long-legged, like a stork. But it had sharp, curved teeth; grasping three-fingered hands; and a long bony tail.

MASSOSPONDYLUS

Meaning of name: "Longer vertebra"
Order: Saurischia
Size, Weight: 12–16 feet long, 500 pounds
Locations: Zimbabwe and Arizona
Diet: Plants

MASSOSPONDYLUS

Massospondylus is a well-known prosauropod. Parts of more than eighty skeletons have been found. *Massospondylus* was lightly built and medium-sized. Its head was small and narrow. Its eyes and nostrils were large, so it may have had keen vision and smell. Some of its teeth had grooves, and others were flat. Its upper jaw was unusual, projecting beyond its lower jaw. The lower jaw may have had a beak covering the bone.

AFRICAN WATER HOLES

In dry regions of the world, animals gather in lowlands, where water is more often found. In the valleys of the Serengeti Plain of East Africa today, the need for water during dry seasons forces animals to visit watering holes. Some visit infrequently. Other kinds have to drink every day. The same thirst drove plant-eating and meat-eating dinosaurs to gather in the valleys of southern Africa during the Early Jurassic Period. Here they could find the lakes and water holes that were vital for life.

Whatever the climate, smaller carnivores may form groups to hunt together. Coordinated pack hunting enables these animals to take down prey much larger than themselves. Lions in modern southern Africa gather where game is plentiful. They combine to pull down zebras and wildebeests, tearing at them until they are too weakened to resist. Usually the females do the hunting; the males live off their kills. Using the same strategy, packs of *Syntarsus* dinosaurs may have killed *Massospondylus*, even though these herbivores were quite large.

A lion and lioness feast on an African buffalo at a water hole in Serengeti National Park in East Africa. Buffalo are fierce, but they are no match for lions working as a team. Predators have evolved greater speeds, higher intelligence, and keener senses to give them an advantage in their battles of wits and their struggles with prey.

pubis

"boot"

Lizard-hipped

pubis

Bird-hipped

Lesothosaurs drink from a watering hole in the dry valleys of southern Africa 200 million years ago. Footprints along the water's edge show that other animals came to drink here, too. Lesothosaurs were bird-hipped dinosaurs. With their balance and agility, they were well suited for life in an environment where limited resources and nimble predators were constant threats.

In dry areas, a sudden rain may pour down so heavily that the water is not absorbed by the hard ground. Instead, deadly walls of water rush down the valleys, threatening wildlife. Entire herds may be wiped out as a flash flood sweeps across them. Such disasters sometimes kill caribou in Canada and wildebeests in the Serengeti Plain of East Africa. In southern Africa 200 million years ago, floods may have overtaken herds of dinosaurs when rivers quickly swelled with rain. Their bodies rotted away, and the bones of some of them became fossilized.

Bird hips and lizard hips
All but the very first dinosaurs belong to one of two groups, the ornithischian (bird-hipped) dinosaurs or the saurischian (lizard-hipped) dinosaurs.
Saurischians had a pelvis in which the pubis protruded forward. Meat-eaters and giant sauropods like *Brachiosaurus* were saurischians. Many meat-eating saurischians had a broad lump—a "boot"—at the end of the pubis.
Ornithischians had a pelvis in which the pubis slanted back parallel to another hipbone, the ischium. Early ornithischians were small two-legged plant-eaters. Later ones included large duckbills and many four-legged plant-eaters. Their hips gave these animals a lower center of gravity, helping them to hold their balance in spite of their big stomachs.

MASS DROWNING

In 1972, paleontologist Dr. Michael Raath was walking along an elephant track to a river in the Zambesi Valley when he saw something that, in his words, made his hair stand up. Ahead of him was a treasure trove of dinosaur bones, remains of a catastrophe 200 million years ago. The bones of many *Syntarsus* meat-eaters were exposed there. The remains included complete skeletons of both adults and juveniles.

THE KILLER FLOOD

A pack of *Syntarsus*, young and old, walks across a sandy plain **(1)**. Sudden torrential rains produce a flash flood from the hills **(2)**. In panic, the dinosaurs scatter. They swim well, but the flood is so strong that the entire pack is swept under and drowned **(3)**. The flood recedes, leaving decaying bodies covered by sand. Minerals seep into the bones and preserve them in detail for 200 million years.

The fossils were embedded in fine-grained sandstone that showed the dinosaurs had died among sand dunes. Dr. Raath concluded that they died suddenly, in a flash flood.

The bones were so well preserved that Dr. Raath could see the grooves where blood vessels once ran through them and the places where muscle tendons had been attached. Another South African scientist, Dr. Anusuya Chinsamy, studied these fossils under a microscope and added new evidence in many areas of dinosaur research—from how dinosaurs grew, moved, and used energy to how they died and became fossils.

Studies of many specimens of *Syntarsus* and *Massospondylus* have also added new evidence to a long, continuing debate: Were some dinosaurs warm-blooded? The bones of these dinosaurs have growth rings like those seen in trees. Among animals, growth rings are usually marks of cold-blooded animals like reptiles.

COLD- OR WARM-BLOODED?

Cross sections of the bones of cold-blooded animals show distinct rings of growth. Bone growth is not constant. It slows and speeds up in regular cycles, perhaps by year or season.

1. The bones of the plant-eating dinosaur *Massospondylus* show growth rings (seen here in close-up as lines), like those of a cold-blooded animal. But the bones of some dinosaurs show no rings of growth when viewed in cross section.

2. The bones of warm-blooded animals show no growth rings as in this section of a bird's bone. These animals grow faster than do cold-blooded animals and at a more even speed as they reach adulthood.

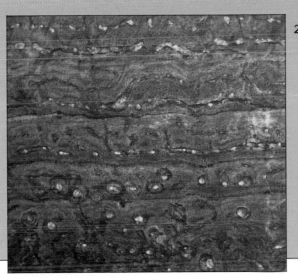

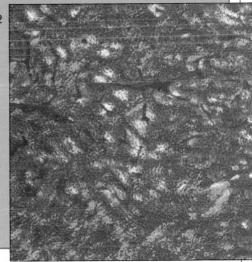

A worker on Dr. Raath's team chisels away at rock in the Zambesi River Valley, looking for more *Syntarsus* fossils. The gentle covering of fine sand kept the bones in position after the animals drowned and their flesh rotted away.

How might a warm-blooded or cold blooded dinosaur have behaved? Warm-blooded animals like mammals and birds have a built-in control that keeps their body temperatures constant. A warm-blooded dinosaur might have had the endurance to move quickly for long periods of time. But it would have also needed vast amounts of food to fill its energy needs. Cold-blooded animals manage their body temperatures by their activity and by moving between sunlight and shade. A cold-blooded dinosaur would have had much lower energy needs.

Warm-blooded or not, dinosaurs thrived. Some of them evolved into enormous species, and new kinds of dinosaurs replaced other animals, filling many different roles in their environments. From the Early Jurassic until their extinction 65 million years ago, the dinosaurs truly ruled the Earth.

THE JURASSIC PERIOD

The Jurassic Period was the central time in dinosaur evolution. During this span of about 60 million years, dinosaurs became the dominant animals on Earth. By the Late Jurassic, some plant-eating dinosaurs, the brachiosaurs, grew bigger than any other land animals before them. Flying reptiles (pterosaurs) and sea reptiles (such as the ichthyosaurs and plesiosaurs) evolved into many new forms. The first butterflies, moths, and birds appeared in the Jurassic. Small mammals lived in the shadows of the giant dinosaurs.

In much of the world, the climate of the Jurassic Period was dry. Lowland valleys were the wettest places and had the thickest vegetation. Many of the plants were similar to those of the Triassic Period.

In a museum workroom, a paleontologist puts some finishing touches to dinosaur fossils about to be displayed. Enormous plant-eaters lived in the Jurassic Period. Many of them had huge leg bones like those shown here.

The skeleton of an animal rebuilt from its bones or from casts of the bones is known as a reconstruction.

In the Jurassic Period, ferns were common in the clearings. Cycads and related plants, such as the bennettitaleans, thrived as shrubs and low-growing plants. New kinds of trees included a deciduous tree related to the conifers, and the ginkgo, which is still alive today

The sky was filling with life. The many kinds of small, long-tailed rhamphorhynchid pterosaurs still flourished. The shorter-tailed pterodactyls evolved in the Late Jurassic. The first birds arose from dinosaurs in the Jurassic.

New kinds of dinosaurs included stegosaurs, sauropods, and *Allosaurus*, one of the largest of all carnivores. Bony fishes became more common in the sea. They were preyed upon by marine reptiles such as *Ichthyosaurus*.

JURASSIC FOSSIL FINDS AROUND THE WORLD
The four sites featured in this section are shown in red.

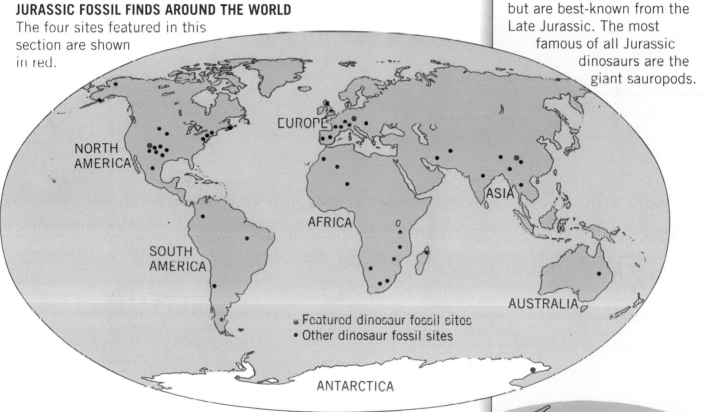

- Featured dinosaur fossil sites
- Other dinosaur fossil sites

NORTH AMERICA

EUROPE

ASIA

AFRICA

SOUTH AMERICA

AUSTRALIA

ANTARCTICA

Early Jurassic dinosaurs lived on many continents. Prosauropod dinosaurs and new predatory dinosaurs spread across the globe, even to **Antarctica**. At the time, Antarctica was not frozen, but cool and moist.

The Middle Jurassic provides few dinosaur fossils. But a quarry in **China** has produced a collection of nearly intact skeletons, including large sauropod dinosaurs.

Late Jurassic Period dinosaurs are known from the **American West** and **Eichstätt, Germany.** They include plant-eaters 100 feet long and meat-eaters as long as school buses.

The shape of the land changed greatly in the Jurassic Period. The single landmass, Pangaea, began to break up. The northern part, Laurasia, moved away from the southern part, Gondwana. A shallow but widening sea formed between the supercontinents.

Dinosaur fossils have been found from the Early, Middle, and Late Jurassic Periods, but are best-known from the Late Jurassic. The most famous of all Jurassic dinosaurs are the giant sauropods.

Black lines show the outlines of the present-day continents.

SOUTHERN
JUNGLE
MT. KIRKPATRICK
Antarctica

200 million years ago

The sun rises over a seashore beside a forest of conifers swathed in mist. Meat-eating dinosaurs share a feast in the waves while a bigger carnivore approaches.

ANTARCTIC JUNGLE

Dinosaurs lived on every continent, including what is now Antarctica. During the Early Jurassic, Antarctica was farther north than it is today, and it had warm, moist weather. The bones of dinosaurs found in the frozen mountains of Antarctica offer new clues about the appearance and behavior of predatory dinosaurs.

In 1991, scientists exploring just 400 miles from the South Pole discovered the remains of a large and unfamiliar meat-eating dinosaur in rocks from this time. This carnivore, which has been named *Cryolophosaurus*, was remarkable because of the unusual crest on its head. It might have been the Early Jurassic's biggest meat-eater. Two other dinosaurs were also found on Antarctica. The first resembled *Coelophysis*, a smaller carnivore that lived in western North America. The second seemed to be related to *Dilophosaurus*, another Early Jurassic meat-eater of western North America.

CRYOLOPHOSAURUS

DILOPHOSAURUS

Mount Kirkpatrick— Today The Antarctic is colder than a deep freeze, even in summer. On the slopes of this mountain, geologists found dinosaur bones.

In the Early Jurassic, predatory dinosaurs evolved into larger and more elaborate forms. The crests of *Cryolophosaurus* and *Dilophosaurus* might have served as displays used to attract mates or frighten rivals. As in modern animals, it might have been that only male dinosaurs had these display features. Crests could also have frightened enemies.

FACT FILE

ANIMALS
1. Ammonites (AM-uh-nights)
2. *Coelophysis*-like carnivore (SEE-lo-FY-sis)
3. *Cryolophosaurus* (CRY-o-LO-fo-SAW-rus)
4. *Nautilus* (NOUGT-ih-lus)
5. Rhamphorhynchid pterosaur (RAM-fo-RING-kid)

PLANTS
6. *Brachyphyllum* conifer (BRACK-ee-FY-lum)
7. Podocarp conifer (POE-doe-karp)

ALSO AT THIS SITE:
Dilophosaurus-like carnivore (die-LO-fo-SAW-rus)
Oreochima-like fish (ORE-ee-o KY-muh)
Prosauropod plant-eater (pro-SAW-ruh-pod)
Tritylodon (try-TIE-lo-dahn)
Seed ferns

Mount Kirkpatrick—Then The dawn light is misty and dim in a seaside forest. It is early in the Jurassic, the first period in which the largest plant- and meat-eaters on land were dinosaurs.

Between the sea and the forest, *Cryolophosaurus*, a 25-foot-long predatory dinosaur, searches for its next meal. Behind this killer, the forest is home to such animals as tritylodonts—mammal-like reptiles the size of a beaver—that might make a meal. In front of *Cryolophosaurus*, one of its own kind is being eaten in the shallows by a *Coelophysis*-like dinosaur and its young. Overhead, a pterosaur, the size of a crow, flaps toward the water.

It looks down at a school of *Oreochima*, which are minnow-sized fish.

COELOPHYSIS

Not all predatory dinosaurs had crests. *Coelophysis* might have used changing skin-color patterns to communicate during courtship displays. Some dinosaurs might have communicated with calls.

Antarctica, Then and Now
About 200 million years ago Antarctica was the most southerly part of the world, just as it is today. But then it was still part of the world's single continent and much closer to the equator.

The globe shows the position of the continents now.

NEW DISCOVERIES IN THE ICE

Because dinosaur remains had been found all over the world, scientists believed that dinosaurs must have lived in Antarctica, too. But it was not until 1986 that fossil evidence of dinosaurs was discovered there. Among the most dramatic of the discoveries was the accidental find of the meat-eater *Cryolophosaurus*.

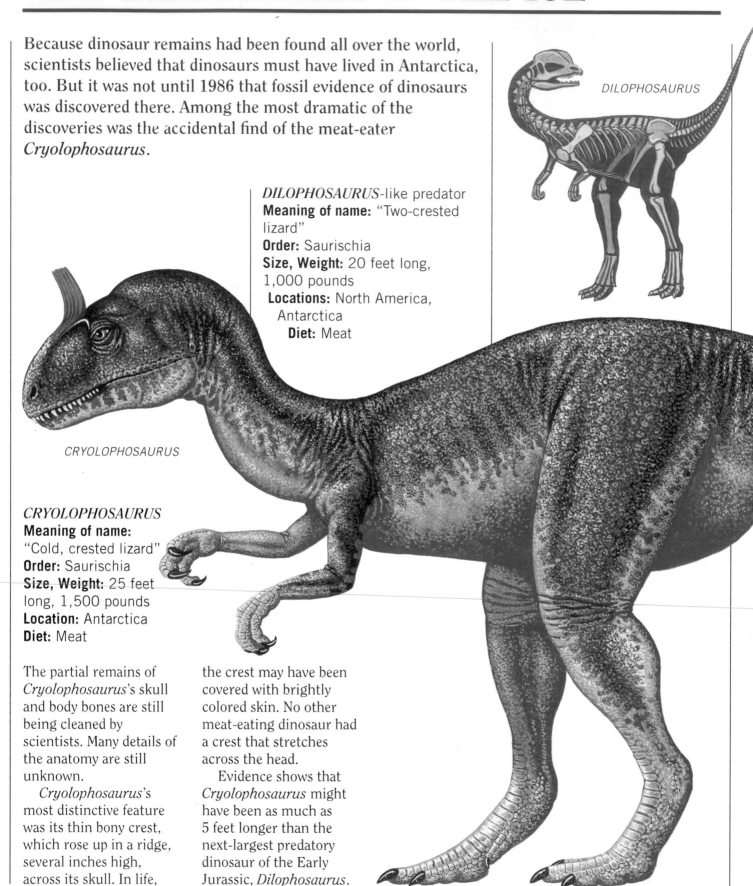

DILOPHOSAURUS

DILOPHOSAURUS-like predator
Meaning of name: "Two-crested lizard"
Order: Saurischia
Size, Weight: 20 feet long, 1,000 pounds
Locations: North America, Antarctica
Diet: Meat

CRYOLOPHOSAURUS

CRYOLOPHOSAURUS
Meaning of name: "Cold, crested lizard"
Order: Saurischia
Size, Weight: 25 feet long, 1,500 pounds
Location: Antarctica
Diet: Meat

The partial remains of *Cryolophosaurus*'s skull and body bones are still being cleaned by scientists. Many details of the anatomy are still unknown.

Cryolophosaurus's most distinctive feature was its thin bony crest, which rose up in a ridge, several inches high, across its skull. In life, the crest may have been covered with brightly colored skin. No other meat-eating dinosaur had a crest that stretches across the head.

Evidence shows that *Cryolophosaurus* might have been as much as 5 feet longer than the next-largest predatory dinosaur of the Early Jurassic, *Dilophosaurus*.

TRITYLODONT

TRITYLODONT
Meaning of name: "Three-knobbed tooth"
Order: Therapsida
Size, Weight: 4 feet long, 30 pounds
Locations: England, western North America, China, South Africa, Antarctica
Diet: Plants

Tritylodonts were mammal-like reptiles with unusual teeth. They had large fangs in the front of their jaws with a toothless gap on either side. At the back of the jaws were seven square cheek teeth on each side. Each upper tooth had three knobs. Lower teeth had two knobs. Tritylodonts ground up plants by sliding their lower jaws back and forth.

PLANTS

The plant life of Antarctica in the Early Jurassic is not well known. Scientists think that it was like that of the rest of the world. On other lands, there were forests of nonflowering evergreen trees, such as the podocarp conifers. These grew tall, with small leaves on their branches. Seed ferns and palmlike cycads were also common. The cycads *Antarcticycas* had inch-thick stems spreading along the ground and upright fronds.

OREOCHIMA
Meaning of name: "Mountain winter storm"
Order: Teleostei
Size, Weight: 1 inch long, 1 ounce or less
Location: Antarctica
Diet: Aquatic plants and insects

OREOCHIMA

GYMNOSPERM TREE

Worldwide, during the Late Triassic and the Early Jurassic Periods, many new creatures inhabited the sea as well as the air and land. Along with giant sea reptiles and the first turtles, new kinds of fish lived at this time.

The teleosts became one of the most successful groups of fish. They evolved in the Late Triassic Period 220 million years ago. By the end of dinosaur time, 65 million years ago, they had become the most common bony fishes in the world. They still are. They began as small fish resembling herring. These early teleosts had flexible upper and lower jaws, and upper and lower tail fins that were similar in shape.

FISHING AS A WAY OF LIFE

Two hundred million years ago in what is now Antarctica, forests by the seaside would have been damp, sometimes cool, but never freezing. In many ways they were like the rain forests of the American Northwest today. And as in modern temperate rain forests, the big trees in the forests of Early Jurassic Antarctica were conifers.

These trees supported many kinds of insect and other animal life, though the identity and habits of many of those creatures remain a mystery. It is likely that the highest branches of the trees nearest the water were roosting places for the only flying backboned animals of the time, pterosaurs. The pterosaurs of the Early Jurassic were known as rhamphorhynchids.

Rhamphorhynchids were relatively small, usually less than 4 feet wide in wingspan. They had large lightweight skulls and many sharp teeth. This suggests that they were fish-eaters. Rhamphorhynchids were strong fliers, with powerful chest muscles. They had long tails that ended in diamond-shaped flaps. These tail flaps may have helped them steer in flight.

Scientists disagree about how rhamphorhynchids and other pterosaurs flew. They even disagree about how these creatures took flight. Some scientists think pterosaur wing flaps were attached high on the animals' legs. If so, pterosaurs might have had a birdlike posture and could have walked and run.

Other scientists think that the wings of pterosaurs were attached at the ankles. If so, the animals would have sprawled awkwardly on the ground, as bats do. They would have launched themselves from tree branches or cliffs.

64

Today, forests offer homes for life at many heights or levels. Some creatures live on the dark forest floor. Others thrive in the canopy, the leafy treetops. A few creatures live only on the emergent level, where the sunny tops of the tallest trees poke out of the forest canopy.

Scientists think that creatures in the evergreen forests of Early Jurassic Antarctica also lived at many levels. On the ground and among the low-growing cycads, amphibians and lizards scurried, preying upon insects and one another. Mammal-like reptiles might have lived in the branches of cycads and taller tree ferns. Near the water, in the tops of towering conifer trees, pterosaurs roosted.

The modern counterparts of the small pterosaurs in Early Jurassic Antarctica may be the ospreys and pelicans of North American lakes and seaside forests. Pterosaurs used their strong chest muscles to flap their broad wings, as do present-day ospreys. Like these birds, pterosaurs might have roosted and nested high in trees.

Two *Cryolophosaurus* (1) hunt in a clearing by a stream where thirsty herbivores are likely to gather. High above the trees **(2)** of this Early Jurassic forest pterosaurs **(3)** look for roosts. Carnivores rely on herbivores for their food. Meat-eaters do not take their energy directly from plants. They get it by eating other animals. Scientists have not yet found fossils of the plant-eaters from this place and time.

A white pelican scoops fish from the water with its beak. Two hundred million years ago, pterosaurs would have fed in a similar way. They might have swooped and dived to pick fish from the water with their beaks.

BONES FROM THE FREEZER

American researcher Dr. William Hammer and his colleagues spent three Antarctic summers excavating fossils on the cold and windy slopes of Mount Kirkpatrick. They found parts of the skull and limbs of *Cryolophosaurus*, teeth of a small meat-eating dinosaur, remains of a large prosauropod dinosaur, a *Dilophosaurus*-like dinosaur, and a tritylodont.

The idea that dinosaurs like *Cryolophosaurus* and *Dilophosaurus* might have used their head crests to communicate comes from observations of many modern animals. Display features that have no other obvious purpose are common among animals today. For example, fiddler crabs have one claw larger than the other and wave it about in ritual courtship dances on the beach. Male deer have large elaborate antlers, which they show off as they raise their heads and call out to win the favor of female deer.

Dr. Hammer uses a gas-powered saw to penetrate frozen ground and thick, fossil-rich rock in Antarctica. He and the other members of the dig team must have their tools flown in by helicopter. Even in summer, they struggle to stay warm as they work in temperatures of -30 degrees Fahrenheit.

CREST AND HORNS

In addition to *Cryolophosaurus* and *Dilophosaurus*, several large carnivorous dinosaurs had unusual skulls. *Monolophosaurus* (China, 170 million years ago) had a single crest down the middle of its skull. *Allosaurus* (United States, 145 million years ago) had bony knobs near its eyes. *Carnotaurus* (Argentina, 97 million years ago) had bull-like horns. In addition to using these projections as displays, some of these creatures might have used them in sparring matches with rivals for territory or mates.

Cryolophosaurus

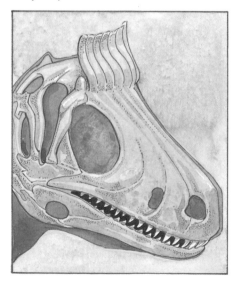

Dilophosaurus

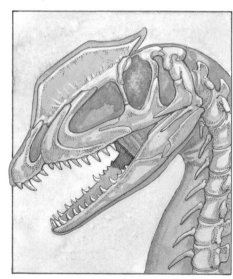

Living birds, the closest relatives of dinosaurs, have many colorful display features and behaviors. For instance, peacocks fan and wave their brilliantly colored tail feathers as they prance about to draw the attention of peahens. *Cryolophosaurus* may have pushed its head forward to show off its crest in disputes with rivals over territory, as blue jays do today.

Many living species of reptiles also have colorful displays. Male and female lizards often look very different. This makes it easy for the sexes to recognize each other at mating time. Usually the males are more colorful or than the females.

Male anole lizards have a flap of skin under the chin that can be expanded in a flash of color. Male plumed basilisks have colorful crests.

Dr. William Hammer, the scientist who found *Cryolophosaurus,* compares its crest to Elvis Presley's haircut, one of the rock musician's own prominent display features. Dr. Hammer jokingly calls the dinosaur "Elvisaurus."

Monolophosaurus

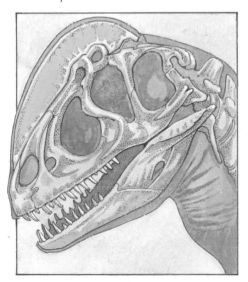

Allosaurus

Carnotaurus

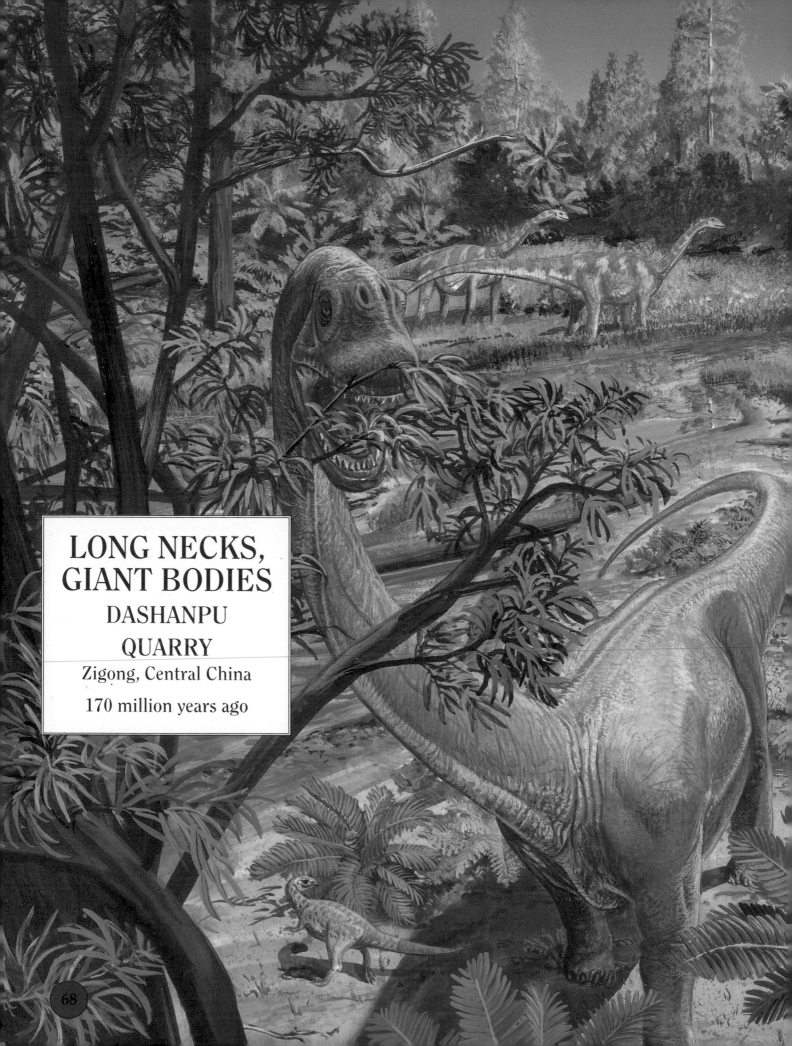

LONG NECKS, GIANT BODIES

DASHANPU QUARRY

Zigong, Central China

170 million years ago

Plant-eating dinosaurs are munching their way through a lush forest amid streams and lakes. Four-legged herbivores, some big, others enormous, feed at different levels of the forest. A pterosaur flies overhead.

69

CHINESE DINOSAURS

The Middle Jurassic is the mysterious heart of dinosaur time. Around the world, only very few rocks from this time have been found, so dinosaurs and their environments are little known. But in central China, Middle Jurassic plants and animals are preserved in spectacular completeness.

The rock formations here contain entire skeletons of plant-eating dinosaurs as well as fossilized trunks of huge conifer trees. The fossils reveal a hitherto unknown population of large dinosaurs, especially large, four-legged plant-eaters. They lived in a well-watered lowland forest and grew to truly enormous sizes. Some had especially long necks, giving them access to a higher level of the treetops than any other animals had ever reached. The earliest known spike- and plate-backed stegosaurs lived here.

Dashanpu Quarry—Today
In the mudstone of Zigong region of Sichuan Province in central China, paleontologists are digging up some of the world's best-preserved dinosaur fossils.

More than 50 feet long,
Datousaurus was a huge and solidly built early sauropod. Sauropod skulls are rare. But complete *Datousaurus* skulls were found in Dashanpu Quarry.

FEEDING LEVELS

Several different large plant-eaters could share the same environment by feeding at different heights.

Omeisaurus, at more than 66 feet long, was the largest plant-eater in this world. With its long neck it could stretch to the treetops. At half the height of *Omeisaurus*, *Shunosaurus* could feed from branches well above ground level. *Huayangosaurus* stood low on all fours and could nibble plants on the forest floor.

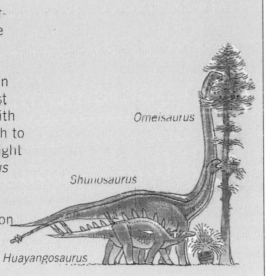

Omeisaurus

Shunosaurus

Huayangosaurus

Dashanpu Quarry—Then

Huge plant-eaters traveled through the forests of central China 170 million years ago. The largest of all, *Omeisaurus*, towered over even the 50-foot-long *Datousaurus* and the 40-foot-long club-tailed *Shunosaurus*. Other plant-eating dinosaurs included the spike-backed *Huayangosaurus* and the little two-legged *Xiaosaurus*.

Gasosaurus, a long-legged meat-eater 15 feet long, is ready to pounce on any animal it can overcome. Above, a big-toothed pterosaur, *Angustinaripterus*, soars in search of fish. An amphibian, a flat-bodied labyrinthodont, lies quietly in the stream. The forest trees are huge evergreen conifers. Seed ferns and cycads are abundant in the understory and forest clearings.

FACT FILE

By the Middle Jurassic dinosaurs had replaced other reptiles as the most important land animals.

China, Then and Now

China is now a part of the vast continent of Asia. During the middle of the Jurassic Period, its land may have been divided into two or more landmasses.

Globe shows the continents now

ANIMALS

1. *Angustinaripterus*
   (AN-gus-TEEN-ah-RIP-tch-rus)
2. *Gasosaurus*
   (GAS-o-SAW-rus)
3. Labyrinthodont
   (LAB-uh-RIN-tho-dahnt)
4. *Omeisaurus*
   (O-mee-SAW-rus)
5. *Shunosaurus*
   (SHOO-no-SAW-rus)
6. *Xiaosaurus*
   (ZHOW-o-SAW-rus)

PLANTS

7. Conifers
8. Cycads
9. Seed ferns

ALSO AT THIS SITE:
Datousaurus (DAT-oo-SAW-rus)
Huayangosaurus
   (hwi-YANG-o-SAW-rus)

KEEP ON GROWING

The enormous increase in body size shown by the sauropods of Middle Jurassic China was not matched by a similar growth in brain size. These giant dinosaurs, some as long as a tennis court, had brains smaller than table-tennis balls. Small brain size does not necessarily indicate stupidity, but these animals probably were limited in the range of behavior. They probably spent most of the day walking, feeding, and producing waste.

Scientists think that spoon-shaped dinosaur teeth, like those of the sauropods of Middle Jurassic China, were good for cutting tough plants. The pencil-shaped teeth of diplodocids and other, later sauropods were better suited for nipping soft plants, such as those that grow near water. All sauropods had tiny heads and big stomachs. These dinosaurs digested plants with the aid of stones, which they swallowed. The stones helped grind food in their stomachs.

OMEISAURUS

DATOUSAURUS

SHUNOSAURUS

OMEISAURUS
Meaning of name: "Sacred mountain lizard"
Order: Saurischia
Size, Weight: 54 to 68 feet long, up to 20 tons
Location: China
Diet: Plants

Omeisaurus was the largest of the sauropods known from Sichuan. Its small skull sat atop an enormously long and slender neck. The skull had nostrils near the top and teeth shaped like spoons. Most likely, *Omeisaurus* fed from the trees and digested the rough vegetation in its huge stomach vat.

Spoon-shaped tooth

All three of these sauropod dinosaurs lived in Middle Jurassic China, although scientists are not sure that all were present in the same area at the same time. If they did share this habitat, they probably had different food preferences.

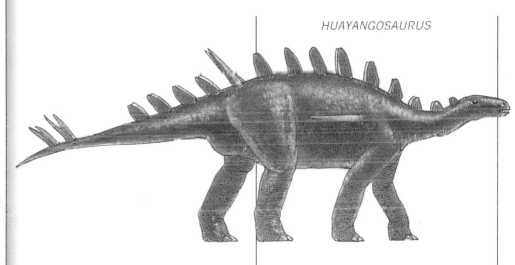

PLANTS

Classopolis was a type of conifer that grew 40 feet tall in Jurassic times. Scientists have found pollen grains from this tree among the fossils at Dashanpu Quarry.

CLASSOPOLIS

SHUNOSAURUS
Meaning of name: "Lizard from Sichuan" (formerly Shuo)
Order: Saurischia
Size, Weight: 40 feet long, 10 tons
Location: China
Diet: Plants

Shunosaurus seems to have been the most common dinosaur in China at this time. It was "small" — only as long as a moving van. Its remains were very complete. Scientists were surprised to find that it had a clublike tail.

HUAYANGOSAURUS
Meaning of name: "Lizard from Sichuan" (Huayang = Sichuan)
Order: Ornithischia
Size, Weight: 13 feet, 1 to 4 tons
Location: China
Diet: Plants

Huayangosaurus was an early stegosaur with long spikes. Along its back were pairs of heart-shaped plates. Later stegosaurs featured a double row of spikes on their backs.

DATOUSAURUS
Meaning of name: "Lizard from Datou"
Order: Saurischia
Size, Weight: 50 feet long, 20 tons
Location: China
Diet: Plants

Datousaurus's skeleton suggests it was related to lightly built sauropods like *Diplodocus*. But its skull is like that of a bulky sauropod, such as *Omeisaurus*.

Since the *Datousaurus* skull and skeleton were found apart, they may come from different kinds of dinosaurs.

DEFENSE AGAINST PREDATORS

Plant-eaters' defenses against attack included such weapons as horns, spikes, and armor in the form of a thick skin. In Middle Jurassic China, *Gasosaurus* and other predators hunted the plant-eating dinosaurs. Among the giant herbivores, only *Shunosaurus* had a weapon — a pineapple-like tail club. By swiping its tail, *Shunosaurus* could give a lethal blow, as a giraffe or kangaroo does with a kick of its leg. The small plant-eaters found here had either armor or spikes for protection.

In the warm, watery regions of East Africa today, crocodiles are terrifying predators in and near the water. But large plant-eaters like the hippopotamus have defenses against these hunters. A full-grown hippopotamus has sharp tusks and big powerful jaws. Snapping its jaws, a hippopotamus can bite a crocodile in half!

Like the hippopotamus, large plant-eating dinosaurs might have used their size to protect themselves and their young. The young, the old, the small, and the weak are the favorite targets of predators because frail and small individuals are the least able to defend themselves. So the meat-eater has the best chance of a successful hunt, with least risk to itself. Yet even lions, the most fearsome of modern predators, fail in their hunting efforts nine times out of ten.

In Middle Jurassic China, some large plant-eaters traveled in herds for protection, helping one another. Later in dinosaur evolution, plant-eaters such as *Iguanodon* were equipped with huge thumb spikes as weapons. *Triceratops* had long horns like those of rhinoceroses today as well as a frill of bone protecting its neck and shoulders.

In the North American wilderness, a young moose stays close to its mother. While the youngster is capable of walking from nearly the moment of birth, it is small and vulnerable to predators such as wolves. By staying close to a healthy and full-sized adult, the young moose has added protection against attack. In a similar way, individual and herding adult sauropods in Middle Jurassic China would have protected their young.

An adult *Huayangosaurus* (1) **defends its young** against attack from hungry *Gasosaurus* (2). The sharp spikes on the *Huayangosaurus*'s back point toward the predators, and it lashes out with its long-spiked tail. These weapons are not powerful enough to disable or kill big predators, but they might discourage hunters from pursuing their prey. It would not be worth risking injury, so the hunters look for an easier meal.

Huayangosaurus **had spikes** running from its shoulders to the middle of its tail. Its legs were of nearly equal length, whereas later stegosaurs had shorter forelimbs in proportion to the hind legs.

A *Huayangosaurus* and its young feed in the thick foliage around a river. Using their small grinding and nipping teeth, these plant-eaters nibble cycads and ferns growing in forest clearings.

In these clearings the young *Huayangosaurus* are easily visible to predators such as *Gasosaurus*. But the predator will not attack as long as the young dinosaur stays near its parent.

A FANTASTIC FIND

Fossils of land animals of the Middle Jurassic Period are not well known, although *Cetiosaurus*, the first sauropod dinosaur ever discovered, was found in England in Middle Jurassic rocks. But one Chinese site has produced not just a good dinosaur record from this time, but some of the most complete dinosaur fossils ever found. This site was discovered in the early 1960s in Dashanpu, China, by a construction crew. When dinosaurs were discovered, the construction project was halted, and scientists moved in to supervise the excavation.

Chinese paleontologists uncover dinosaur bones at Dashanpu Quarry (below right). The workers were led by Dr. Dong Zhiming of Beijing, China's leading dinosaur scientist. He has excavated more dinosaurs than anyone in history. Dr. Dong named Dashanpu's big meat-eater *Gasosaurus* in honor of the gas company that began the excavation.

This spectacular skull of the oldest and most primitive member of the stegosaur family yet found was discovered at Dashanpu Quarry in 1992. Scientists have named the dinosaur *Huayangosaurus*. Unlike later plated dinosaurs, *Huayangosaurus* had teeth in the front of its jaw.

Among the large plant-eating dinosaurs found in southwestern China, *Mamenchisaurus* is known from the Late Jurassic, *Shunosaurus* from the Middle Jurassic, and *Yunnanosaurus* from the Early Jurassic. This region of China is one of the few on Earth that preserves dinosaurs from such a wide range of time—more than 50 million years.

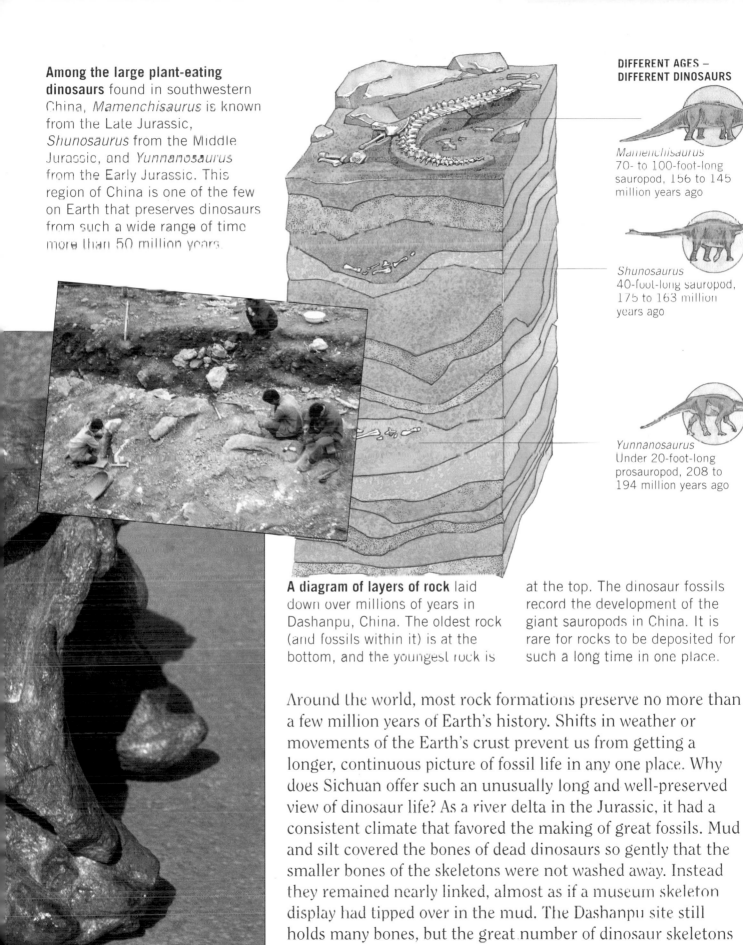

Mamenchisaurus
70- to 100-foot-long sauropod, 156 to 145 million years ago

Shunosaurus
40-foot-long sauropod, 175 to 163 million years ago

Yunnanosaurus
Under 20-foot-long prosauropod, 208 to 194 million years ago

A diagram of layers of rock laid down over millions of years in Dashanpu, China. The oldest rock (and fossils within it) is at the bottom, and the youngest rock is at the top. The dinosaur fossils record the development of the giant sauropods in China. It is rare for rocks to be deposited for such a long time in one place.

Around the world, most rock formations preserve no more than a few million years of Earth's history. Shifts in weather or movements of the Earth's crust prevent us from getting a longer, continuous picture of fossil life in any one place. Why does Sichuan offer such an unusually long and well-preserved view of dinosaur life? As a river delta in the Jurassic, it had a consistent climate that favored the making of great fossils. Mud and silt covered the bones of dead dinosaurs so gently that the smaller bones of the skeletons were not washed away. Instead they remained nearly linked, almost as if a museum skeleton display had tipped over in the mud. The Dashanpu site still holds many bones, but the great number of dinosaur skeletons and their huge size make their excavation time-consuming.

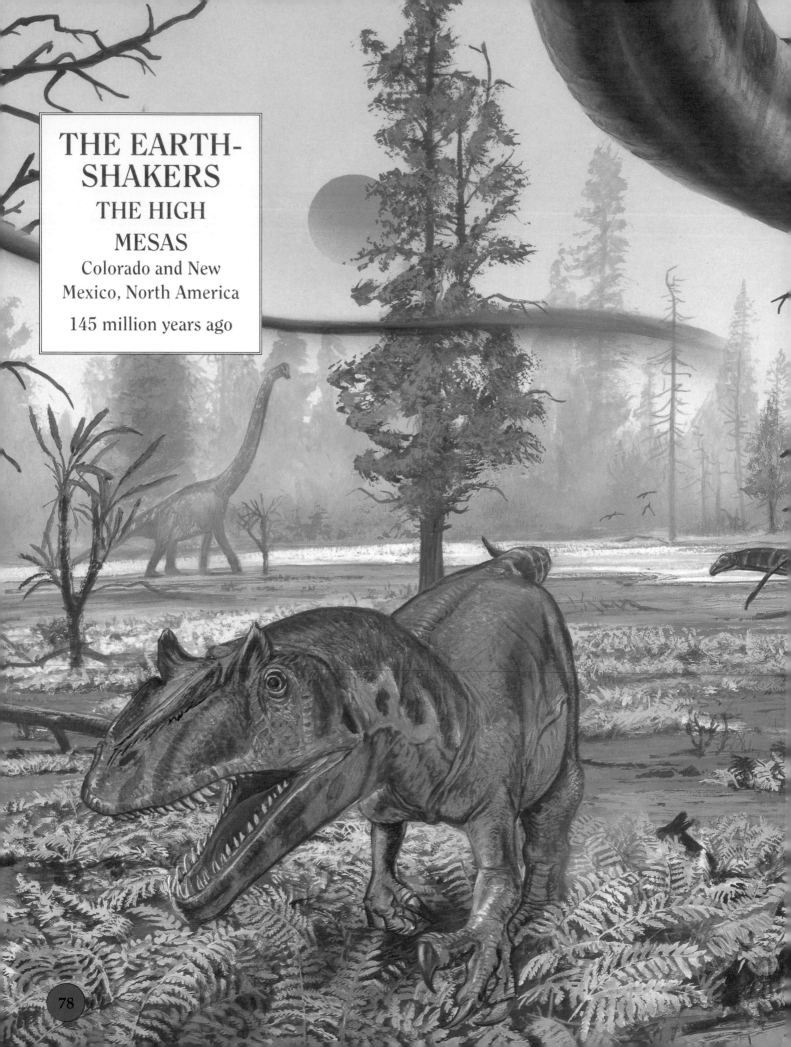

THE EARTH-SHAKERS

THE HIGH MESAS

Colorado and New Mexico, North America

145 million years ago

A warm, dry climate allows the growth of tall conifer trees and low-growing plants. Here, tall dinosaurs live a peaceful life, feeding most of the day. They tower over the smaller dinosaurs, even the large meat-eaters, that roam in their area.

WHY WERE THEY GIANTS?

The ground shook with the footsteps of some of the largest animals ever to walk the Earth—plant-eaters nearly 60 feet tall and more than 100 feet long. The weak and frail among these giant plant-eaters were food for some of the largest of all predatory dinosaurs. As well as the giants, there were many other animals. Small meat-eating dinosaurs preyed on little plant-eating dinosaurs, and other reptiles and small mammals hid in the undergrowth and preyed on one another.

Nilssonia **was a low-growing cycadeoid** plant. It grew in clearings created by fires, as weeds do today. Many hairy leaves up to 3 feet long sprouted from its narrow stem. Its small seeds grew on hairlike stems. The hairs may have discouraged large plant-eaters, but not insects. Many insects like those of today—such as shield bugs, thrips, leaf bugs, and plant-hoppers—lived in and around plants like *Nilssonia*.

It is a mystery why Late Jurassic dinosaurs reached sizes never seen before in any land animal. Their environment was not very lush. The climate was warm, but dry. Shallow lakes dotted the forests and clearings. Jurassic trees were neither fast-growing nor packed with foliage. Thick-stemmed cycads and their close relatives, cycadeoids, were some of the most common plants. Their modern relatives have poisonous leaves. Perhaps these Late Jurassic plants were not suitable food for plant-eaters of the *Stegosaurus* type, which ate off low-growing vegetation. But clearly, the giant plant-eaters, stretching upward, found sufficient food among the evergreens.

High Mesas—Today

Supersaurus bones are embedded in rock at Dry Mesa, in western Colorado. The fossil site in this dry region has been excavated for two decades. It has revealed the fossils of two of the largest plant-eaters known, *Supersaurus*, as here, and *Ultrasauros*.

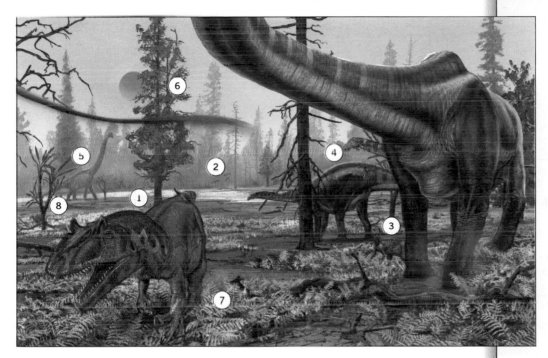

Many giant sauropods are found in the American West. These plant-eaters might have lived together or at different times. Big predators like *Allosaurus* were less common.

ANIMALS
1. *Allosaurus*
   (AL-o-SAW-rus)
2. *Dermodactylus*
   (DERM-o-DACK-till-us)
3. *Othnielia*
   (oth-NEE-lee-uh))
4. *Seismosaurus*
   (SIZE-mo-SAW-rus)
5. *Ultrasauros*
   (UL-trah-SAW-ross)

PLANTS
6. Conifers
7. Ferns
8. *Nilssonia*
   (nil-SONE-ee-uh)

ALSO AT THIS SITE:
Supersaurus
   (SOO-pur-SAW-rus)
Cycads
Ginkgoes

Globe shows the continents now

High Mesas—Then

Near the shore of a shallow lake, where *Nilssonia* plants and ferns spread along the ground, a large *Allosaurus* roars and charges forward, lunging at its prey. A small dinosaurian plant-eater, *Othnielia*, looks on. It stands in the shadow of a giant sauropod, a *Seismosaurus*, which sweeps its whiplike tail over the predator.

This and another *Seismosaurus* in front of it are too large to be frightened, even of a 40-foot *Allosaurus*. In the distance, the even bulkier *Ultrasauros* can reach high into the evergreens to nibble and gulp down leaves and twigs. A group of pterosaurs, *Dermodactylus*, fly overhead, looking for fish in the clear water of the lake.

The supergiant dinosaurs of the American West 145 million years ago were part of an animal community in which many smaller dinosaurs prospered. The smallest meat-eaters, like *Ornitholestes*, were under 7 feet long. The "bird-hipped" plant-eater *Othnielia*, only 5 feet long, ran on slender hind legs.

American West, Then and Now

Colorado and New Mexico were once dry lowlands. Now they are dry but mountainous.

81

HIGH AND HEAVY

ULTRASAUROS

SEISMOSAURUS

The many sauropods of the American West in the Late Jurassic belonged to two groups: the giraffe-necked brachiosaurids and the slimmer, long-tailed diplodocids. Their size is almost beyond belief. Ten bull elephants—the largest modern land animals—might not equal the weight of one of these "super" sauropods. If *Ultrasauros* were alive today, it could look into the sixth-story window of a building.

ULTRASAUROS

Meaning of name: "Beyond lizard"
Order: Saurischia
Size, Weight: 100 feet, 50 tons or more
Location: Colorado
Diet: Plants

Ultrasauros is known from only a few bones of a single animal found in Dry Mesa, Colorado. The best-preserved fossil is a massive 9-foot-long shoulder blade. Some scientists think this brachiosaurid might actually be an especially large specimen of *Brachiosaurus*. For years, *Ultrasauros* was considered the largest dinosaur, but it was recently overshadowed by another sauropod found in Argentina.

SEISMOSAURUS

Meaning of name: "Earth-shaker lizard"
Order: Saurischia
Size, Weight: 100 to 120 feet long, 40 tons or more
Location: New Mexico
Diet: Plants

Only the back end of a single *Seismosaurus* has been found, but it shows the whole animal must have been more than 100 feet long, making this the longest dinosaur yet found. Its body was slim and had short legs. Since it was a member of the diplodocid family of giant plant-eating dinosaurs, scientists think it had a very long neck that matched its lengthy tail. Some scientists have speculated that the only known specimen may be a particularly large *Diplodocus*.

GIGANOTOSAURUS

EORAPTOR

CRYOLOPHOSAURUS

OMEISAURUS

(O-mee-SAW-rus)
"Sacred Mountain Lizard"

Year named: 1939
Size: 54 to 68 feet long
Weight: Up to 40 tons
Location: Central China
Time: 170 million years ago
Diet: Plants

The earliest huge, four-legged plant-eating dinosaurs that are known were discovered in China. *Omeisaurus* was the biggest of the three giants found there.

From **Dinosaur Worlds**, ISBN: 1-56397-597-1
by Don Lessem
Boyds Mills Press • 1-800-949-7777
At your bookseller
Illustration by Steve Kirk
Copyright © 1996 Boyds Mills Press

ARGENTINOSAURUS

(ARE-jen-TEEN-o-SAW-rus)
"Argentina Lizard"

Year named: 1993
Size: 110 feet long
Weight: 100 tons or more
Location: Argentina
Time: 100 million years ago
Diet: Plants

This giant was possibly the largest animal ever to walk the Earth. It was even bigger than *Brachiosaurus* and *Seismosaurus*.

From **Dinosaur Worlds**, ISBN: 1-56397-597-1
by Don Lessem
Boyds Mills Press • 1-800-949-7777
At your bookseller
Illustration by Steve Kirk
Copyright © 1996 Boyds Mills Press

TYRANNOSAURUS REX

(tie-RAN-uh-SAW-rus rex)
"Tyrant Lizard King"

Year named: 1905
Size: 40 feet long
Weight: 7 tons or more
Location: Western North America
Time: 67 to 65 million years ago
Diet: Meat

Fourteen *T. rex* skeletons have been unearthed in the past six years—more than were found in the previous century.

From **Dinosaur Worlds**, ISBN: 1-56397-597-1
by Don Lessem
Boyds Mills Press • 1-800-949-7777
At your bookseller
Illustration by Steve Kirk
Copyright © 1996 Boyds Mills Press

ONISAURUS

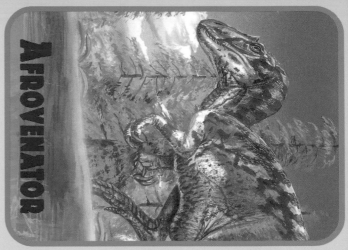

AFROVENATOR

ARGENTINOSAURUS

UTAHRAPTOR

TYRANNOSAURUS REX

LESOTHOSAURUS

PLANTS

Plants were slower to change than animals. Many Jurassic plants were similar to those of the Triassic Period. Some remain largely the same today, such as ginkgoes, or maidenhair trees. They are native only to China now, although planted worldwide as ornamental trees. Ginkgoes date back to the Triassic. Their pollen and unique fan-shaped leaves are found in rocks throughout dinosaur time.

Close-up photo of modern ginkgo leaves

DERMODACTYLUS
Meaning of name: "Skin-finger"
Order: Pterosauria
Size, Weight: 3-foot wingspan, less than 2 pounds
Location: Montana
Diet: Fish

This pterodactyl is known from a wing bone found in 1878.

STEGOSAURUS
Meaning of name: "Roof lizard"
Order: Ornithischia
Size, Weight: 25 feet long, 4 to 7 tons
Location: Western North America
Diet: Plants

Stegosaurus was a "bird-hipped" dinosaur, unrelated to the giant "lizard-hipped" sauropods.

Did *Stegosaurus* have one or two rows of plates on its back? This has been a subject of scientists' debates for many decades. *Stegosaurus* was found in the late 1870s in both Wyoming and Colorado. But the most complete discovery, made in Colorado in the early 1990s, revealed that *Stegosaurus* had two rows of pointed plates after all. An as-yet unnamed stegosaur, recently discovered in Utah, had rounder plates on its back.

The function of the plates is also debated. Were they for defense? Were they display features used to frighten predators or to impress mates? Perhaps the best suggestion is that they were body-temperature regulators, since they were full of blood vessels. By positioning the plates toward the morning sun, the stegosaurs could warm themselves. Wind blowing around the plates might have helped cool down an overheated *Stegosaurus*.

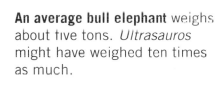

An average bull elephant weighs about five tons. *Ultrasauros* might have weighed ten times as much.

HERDS ON THE MOVE

The landscape of the American West 145 million years ago was very similar to modern East Africa. Most areas during the Late Jurassic were warm and dry, like the modern African savannah. (But there was none of the savannah's grass in dinosaur times.) Herds of huge plant-eaters moved across the plains and drank from watering holes and shallow lakes, just as elephants, wildebeests, and African buffalo do on the savannah now.

In many ways, the lifestyle of these dinosaurs is a mystery. How could they find enough food to eat in a dry environment? In the Late Jurassic, the giant plant-eating dinosaurs probably migrated across the landscape of western North America. By keeping on the move, they found enough food to fuel their enormous bodies, and they would not have stripped the landscape of plant life. If these dinosaurs were not warm-blooded, they would have needed far less food to function than a mammal would at their size. Instead, their bulk and the warm weather would have helped keep their body temperatures high. Moving slowly, they would not have burned much fuel.

As a herd of brachiosaurs traveled, the adults sheltered the young ones by keeping them in the center of the group, as African elephants do today. Scientists have concluded that herds moved in this way because fossil tracks of a whole herd of these dinosaurs on the move have been found, with small footprints surrounded by larger ones.

The footprints that the herd made in mud show that the animals were walking slowly. But they may have been able to travel more quickly when the need arose. Some of the meat-eaters, large and small, may have traveled with their prey, just as hyenas follow herds of wildebeests, capturing any that fall behind the herd.

(Photo above) A herd of African elephants migrates. The herd is led by an old female, while the youngsters keep in the center of the group.

Like the sauropods unearthed in China, North America's giant plant-eaters might have fed on plants at different levels. This split of resources can be seen in present-day African plant-eaters. Giraffes, with their long legs and necks, feed from the trees. Gerenuk antelopes rear on their hind legs to feed from bushes. Zebras, bending their heads down, feed on plants at ground level. The high-shouldered brachiosaurs probably fed from the treetops at least some of the time. The diplodocids, with their short front legs, probably fed closer to the ground.

It may have been hard for diplodocids to keep their giraffe-like necks up for long periods of time. Sometimes, perhaps, they used their necks like the flexible pipe on a vacuum cleaner, allowing their heads to sweep from side to side along the ground or among the vegetation in bushes. Enormous pressure (more than in any living animal) was required to send blood to a head 60 feet in the air. Maybe brachiosaurs, like giraffes today, had contracting valves in their neck arteries to help pump the blood to their heads.

LIFE OF A GIANT PLANT-EATER

FOOD REQUIREMENTS

Even if *Seismosaurus* and other large dinosaurs were cold-blooded (warmed by their surroundings), they would have had to consume huge amounts of food. An elephant eats 500 pounds of plant food each day. For a huge dinosaur to take in enough protein for growth and carbohydrates for energy, the animal would have had to eat more than this.

How could dinosaurs as large as apartment buildings find enough food to survive? How could they mash it up with a head only as big as a horse's and with little pencil-shaped teeth? Part of the answer lies in the stones they swallowed to help grind food. A cluster of these stones was found near what had been the stomach of *Seismosaurus*, the longest dinosaur.

Large sauropods could not afford to be fussy eaters. They lived in a dry environment, where plants were not plentiful. Their diet of conifers, cycads, ferns, and horsetails was high in fiber but low in nutrients. These dinosaurs probably needed to eat nearly all their waking hours to meet their energy needs.

1. Digestion was a long process for a sauropod dinosaur. Here a *Seismosaurus* stops to swallow hard stones. The creature carries them in its stomach to aid digestion. Scientists call stomach stones gastroliths. At times they are rocks made up of minerals that are not typically found where the animal died, evidence that they were carried in the belly of the dinosaur.

2. The *Seismosaurus* reaches a well-watered region with many plants. It reaches out its neck to sweep the area, nipping off many branches with its teeth.

Sauropod teeth were spoon-shaped or pencil-shaped, and set in weak-jawed skulls only a few feet long. Sauropods raked or snipped off plants with their teeth, but must have swallowed their food without chewing.

Details of dinosaur digestion are not known, since soft parts of dinosaurs are not preserved. But somewhere in their guts, dinosaurs used stones and acids to break down plants. When *Seismosaurus* was excavated in New Mexico in the 1980s, a pile of gastroliths, or stomach stones, was found in the area that was once the animal's stomach. Perhaps, as in present-day plant-eaters, bacteria in the cecum (a pouch joined to the large intestine) digested the plants further. Finally, undigested material emerged as dung. Fossil dung is known, but none can be definitely identified as having come from sauropods. Most likely, dung was produced in big lumps, like an elephant's.

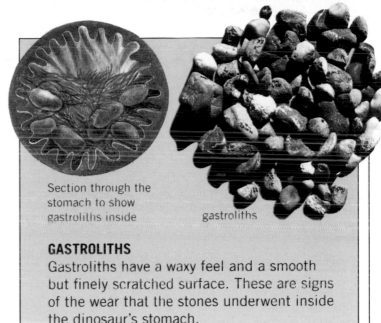

Section through the stomach to show gastroliths inside

gastroliths

GASTROLITHS
Gastroliths have a waxy feel and a smooth but finely scratched surface. These are signs of the wear that the stones underwent inside the dinosaur's stomach.

3. In the vast vat that is the animal's stomach, the stones and stomach acid churn about with the plant food. The food breaks into smaller pieces and digestion begins. Some nutrients may be absorbed in the stomach, others in the large intestine. A large proportion of the tough food may not get broken down at all, ending up as waste that gets passed out from the animal.

4. The *Seismosaurus* walks on, feeding and digesting. As food is digested, the animal drops dung. Dung beetles scurry into the waste to deposit their eggs, as they do in elephants' dung today.

Each day, far more than 500 pounds of plant material may have been eaten by a giant sauropod. Hundreds of pounds of dung passed out of the giant, fertilizing the surroundings.

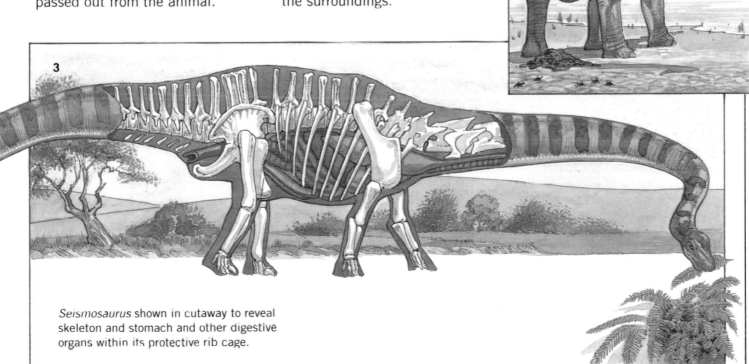

Seismosaurus shown in cutaway to reveal skeleton and stomach and other digestive organs within its protective rib cage.

THE POISON
LAGOONS
EICHSTÄTT

Bavaria, Germany

145 million years ago

Under a subtropical sky, pterosaurs and a primitive bird soar above a poisoned lagoon. Below, islands formed by coral are homes for plant and animal life.

LIFE IN LAGOONS

In the heart of dinosaur time, Europe was dotted with coral islands and subtropical lagoons. Pterosaurs glided along the shoreline. When fish appeared, the flying reptiles dived into the shallow, salty water to catch them. A few birds were on the wing, searching for insects to snatch, just as the smaller pterosaurs were doing. On dry land, small dinosaurs hunted lizards. In the water, marine reptiles swam after their prey.

Solnhofen Quarry—Today
A stoneworker cuts up a fine-grained block of limestone.

While splitting the slabs, quarrymen have discovered thousands of spectacularly well preserved fossils. These fossils are the skeletons and impressions of creatures that were buried in the soft bottoms of lagoons 145 million years ago.

During the Late Jurassic, an ichthyosaur glides among coral islands and reefs in search of fish. Also living in these waters are ammonites, horseshoe crabs, jellyfish, and squid.

The Late Jurassic world had many different habitats and a rich variety of life in the sea and the air as well as on land. Reptiles dominated oceans and skies as dinosaurs ruled dry land, but there were many other successful animals around.

Several animals we would recognize today—horseshoe crabs, nautilus-like ammonites, bony fish, squid, and jellyfish—lived off the shores of what is now Europe. But the main predators of the ancient seas were creatures now extinct. They included ichthyosaurs, strong-swimming reptiles that resembled modern dolphins in shape and size.

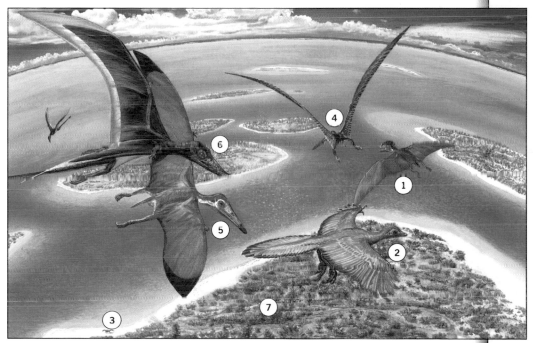

(Left) An underwater view of life in the sea at Eichstätt 145 million years ago. Above the surface of the water, pterosaurs fly overhead. In the distance is the mainland.

Solnhofen Quarry—Then
Pterosaurs and an early bird fly over coral islands, which are known as atolls. A *Pterodactylus* and *Rhamphorhynchus* soar in search of fish.

The hawk-sized *Anurognathus* catches mayflies in flight, while a bird, *Archaeopteryx*, also hunts insects.

Below, the atolls are sandy and dotted with vegetation, such as low-growing club mosses, ginkgoes, bennettitaleans, and horsetails. The sea is rich in life, but the poisonous bottom waters of the lagoon between atoll and land are as still as death.

FACT FILE

While some of the largest dinosaurs ever known were walking the Earth at this time, those at Eichstätt were small.

ANIMALS
1. *Anurognathus* (an-YOUR-og-NAY-thus)
2. *Archaeopteryx* (ARE-kee-AWP tair-icks)
3. *Compsognathus* (KOMP-sog-NAY-thus)
4. *Pterodactylus antiquus* (TAIR-o-DACK-till-us AN-ti-kwus)
5. *Pterodactylus kochi* (TAIR-o-DACK-till-us KO-chee)
6. *Rhamphorhynchus* (RAM-fo-RING-kus)

PLANTS
7. Club mosses, ginkgoes

ALSO AT THIS SITE:
Ardeosaurus (are-DEE-o-SAW-rus)
Ichthyosaurus (ICK-thee-oh-SAW-rus)
Mayflies
Bennettitaleans (beh-NET-tih-TAY-lee-uns)
Horsetails

Germany, Then and Now What is now central Europe was on the edge of the Atlantic and closer to the equator than it is today.

Globe shows the continents now

THE EARLY CRETACEOUS PERIOD

During the Early Cretaceous, lands separated, creating isolated populations of animals that evolved in different ways. Many new dinosaurs evolved, including efficient plant-eaters and deadly meat-eaters. Climates varied greatly, from the cool darkness of polar lands to the humid tropical swamps. Most plants were similar to those from earlier times, but among them were also the first flowering plants—weedy little herbs. Fish, birds, and the tiny mammals became more varied and sophisticated.

Fossil finds worldwide indicate that the Early Cretaceous was a period when dinosaurs grew to record lengths and developed more advanced types of teeth and claws.

Paleontologist Dr. Paul Sereno cleans rock debris from the fossilized upper-arm bone of a large plant-eating dinosaur. The bone was discovered in the Sahara Desert in Niger, West Africa, in 1987. In that year and on a return journey in 1993, Sereno's team found the remains of both large plant-eaters and meat-eaters.

In Early Cretaceous North America, the giant four-legged plant-eaters called sauropods had died out, but similar forms still lived in North Africa. Other giant plant-eaters survived in South America, and still others lived on in Asia. A new type of large plant-eater with teeth adapted for grinding plants appeared and succeeded worldwide. These dinosaurs, the iguanodontids, may have been well suited for eating the new plants that were appearing—flowering herbs.

Other new dinosaurs were savage hunters, including giant large-clawed predators. Armored dinosaurs and small bird-hipped dinosaurs also became more common in the Early Cretaceous Period.

EARLY CRETACEOUS FOSSIL FINDS AROUND THE WORLD
The four sites featured in this section are shown in red.

EUROPE
NORTH AMERICA
ASIA
AFRICA
SOUTH AMERICA
AUSTRALIA
• Featured dinosaur fossil sites
• Other dinosaur fossil sites
ANTARCTICA

In the Early Cretaceous, **North Africa** was close to the equator. All year round it was a hot and swampy region. **Utah** 125 million years ago was mostly arid plain, with life concentrated in rivers and nearby forests. New dinosaurs have been discovered here recently, including *Utahraptor*, a vicious meat-eater.

Australia was farther south, and part of it was within the Antarctic Circle. Some dinosaurs might have lived there through months of darkness. Early Cretaceous **England** was a lowland of forest and marshes. Its dinosaurs included a big fish-eater called *Baryonyx* and *Iguanodon*, which was a big herbivore.

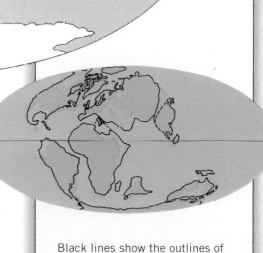

AN ANCIENT
SWAMPLAND
SAHARA DESERT,
NIGER

North Africa

130 million years ago

Near the equator, the climate is hot and wet. A 50-foot-long crocodile lurks in a coastal river, and a shark preys on other fish in the warm water. On the riverbank, large predatory dinosaurs close in on a huge plant-eater.

NEW SOUTHERN ANIMALS

In Early Cretaceous North Africa, some very odd-looking new dinosaurs appeared. In this region there was a fascinating mixture of newer dinosaur types living among creatures that resembled giants of an earlier time.

During the Cretaceous Period, each part of the world was beginning to develop its own particular dinosaur community. Throughout most of Gondwana, new kinds of big plant-eaters and meat-eaters became the dominant dinosaurs.

But in North Africa, there were dinosaurs that resembled the big meat-eaters and plant-eaters of Jurassic North America. Examples of these creatures were *Afrovenator*, which is like *Allosaurus*, and a recently discovered sauropod similar to North America's *Camarasaurus*. How did these creatures come to live in North Africa? Perhaps North Africa still had some land linking it to the northern supercontinent, Laurasia, and animals used this land bridge to move between the two areas.

Some of the new North African dinosaurs had sail-fins on their backs, meat-eaters and plant-eaters alike. The sail-backed plant-eaters included a large *Iguanodon*-like bird-hipped dinosaur called *Ouranosaurus*. Scientists think the fins might have worked like radiators to help these dinosaurs lose excess body heat.

Many other new life-forms besides dinosaurs are found in North Africa during the Early Cretaceous Period. They include many early examples of the types of fish and reptiles alive today.

By the Early Cretaceous, a group of fish called "ray-fins" greatly outnumbered all others (below). Two ray-fins of ancient Niger were *Lepidotes* and a pycnodont. They are called ray-fins because their fins are stiffened by slender, bony rods, or rays. Most modern fish are ray-fins.

Many "lobe-fins," which have lobes formed of bone and muscle in their fins, were disappearing. The lungfish *Ceratodus* and the coelacanth *Mawsonia* were lobe-fins of that time. Today, lungfish and coelacanths are the only known survivors of this group.

Also swimming in these waters were "cartilaginous" fish, which include sharks, rays, and other fish with skeletons of cartilage instead of bone. *Hybodus* was an Early Cretaceous shark.

CERATODUS

MAWSONIA

LEPIDOTES

Niger—Today
A convoy of vehicles carrying paleontologists drives along the edge of the Sahara Desert in Niger. The scientists found tons of jumbled dinosaur bones in the remains of a river bottom from 130 million years ago. These Early Cretaceous graveyards held fossils of huge plant-eating dinosaurs and a big carnivorous dinosaur.

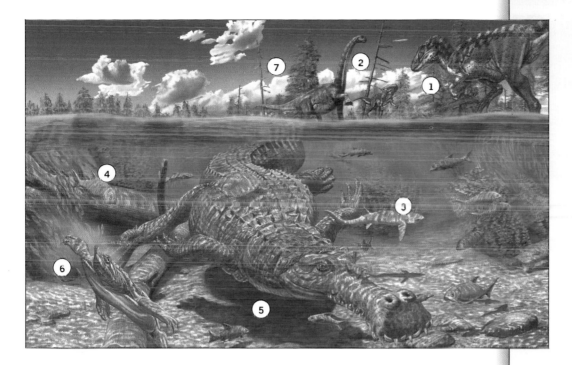

FACT FILE

ANIMALS
1. *Afrovenator*
   (AF-ro-vuh-NAY tur)
2. *Camarasaurus*-like
   sauropod
   (KAM-uh-ruh-SAW-rus)
3. *Hybodus* (hy-BOW-dus)
4. *Lepidotes*
   (LEH-pih-DOH-tees)
5. *Sarcosuchus*
   (SAR-ko-SOO-kus)
6. *Trionyx* (try-AW-nicks)

PLANTS
7. *Brachyphyllum* conifer
   (BRACK-ee-FY-lum)

ALSO AT THIS SITE:
Ceratodus (sair-AH-toe-dus)
Mawsonia
Pycnodonts (PICK-no-dahnts)
Cedar trees
Ferns
Ginkgoes

Sahara Desert, Niger—Then

In the hot, wet conditions of 130 million years ago, ferns and ginkgo plants thrive. In these watery lowland forests, the larger trees are *Brachyphyllum* and other conifers. In these woods there is danger. Two *Afrovenator*, 30-foot-long predators, attack their sauropod prey.

Sarcosuchus, longer than any killer dinosaur from any time, hunts in the river. So do 6-foot-long *Hybodus* sharks. *Trionyx* turtles, just 2 feet 6 inches long, feed on plants and insects in the water. The many-finned coelacanth, *Mawsonia,* and the various ray-finned fish are likely victims of the large predators.

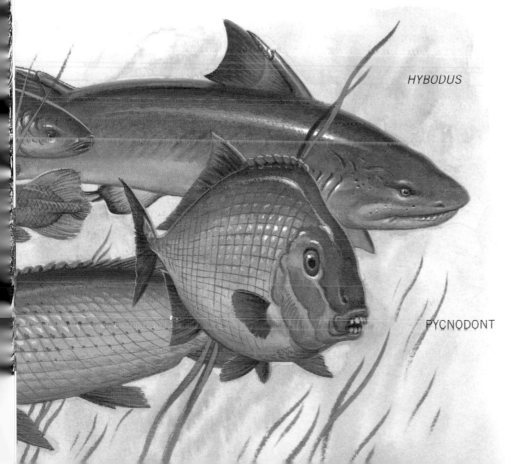

HYBODUS

PYCNODONT

Niger, Then and Now Today, the place where these Early Cretaceous plants and animals lived is more than 1,000 miles north of the equator, and it is mostly desert. As part of Laurasia 130 million years ago, this region was wetter and closer to the equator.

The globe shows the continents now

103

RISE OF THE RAPTORS
CEDAR MOUNTAINS
Utah, North America
125 million years ago

In a savage attack, a pack of giant "raptor" predators pounces on a sauropod. The hunters slash forward with the claws on their hands and feet. As strikes of these blades weaken the herbivore, the hunters move closer and bite their victim with sharp teeth.

KILLER CLAWS

New discoveries in Utah reveal a giant breed of the familiar "raptor" predators. Raptor dinosaurs are named from a Latin word meaning "robber." In addition to the sharp, saw-edged teeth of most predatory dinosaurs, these raptors had a curved claw more than 10 inches long on each hand and foot.

As a raptor dinosaur attacked its prey, it was able to slash with its claws in a slicing arc. The first raptors ever discovered were small animals from later times, but new finds in Utah, Japan, and Mongolia show that raptors could grow to 20 feet long.

Armored plant-eaters (from 125 million years ago) are found in Utah. Perhaps the armor of these tanklike creatures helped protect them from the threat from the new hunters. Some sauropods were still living, but they were not so big as those 20 million years earlier. But new large plant-eaters, the iguanodontids, were emerging.

Cedar Mountains—Today

Dr. James Kirkland visits the site in eastern Utah where a giant-clawed hunter and various plant-eaters were discovered. Sandstones here date from 125 million years ago, when this region was a swampy lowland, warm all year. Now it is a place with hot, dry summers and long, snowy winters.

Utahraptor **slashes** at the plant-eater "Gastonia." Too slow to run from the hunter, the armored dinosaur crouches, protecting its delicate underbelly as a porcupine does when attacked.

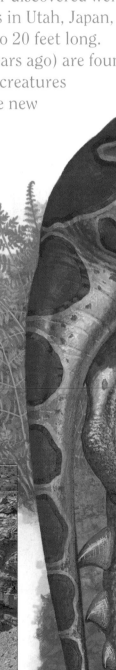

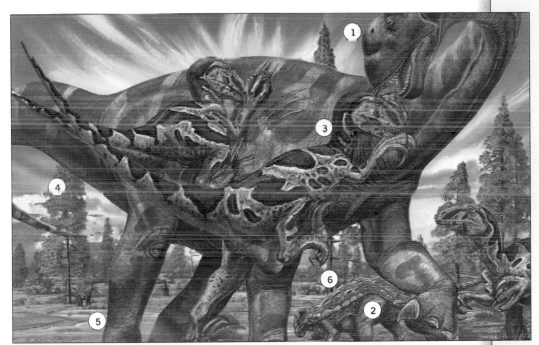

ANIMALS
1. *Camarasaurus* -like sauropod (KAM-uh-ruh-SAW-rus)
2. "Gastonia" (gas-TOE-nee uh)
3. *Utahraptor* (YOU-tah-RAP-tur)

PLANTS
4. *Brachyphyllum* conifer (BRACK-ee-FY-lum)
5. *Clatophlebis* ferns (KLAT-o-FLEE-bis)
6. Cycads

ALSO AT THIS SITE:
Mormon tea plants

Utah—Then

In this scene in Early Cretaceous North America, both predators and prey are large. A pack of *Utahraptor*, each a ton in weight, attacks a *Camarasaurus*-like sauropod. Various small predators scavenge on the leftovers of the *Utahraptor* hunt. Other plant eaters pictured here include an armored dinosaur called "Gastonia."

Large conifers shade ferns and 2-foot-tall cycads in a moist lowland region. In more open areas, bushy Mormon tea plants spread close to shallow pale blue alkaline pools.

Utah, Then and Now

Today, the area where *Utahraptor*, "Gastonia," and these other creatures lived is a high plateau about 150 miles from the Rocky Mountains. During the Early Cretaceous, it was a dry lowland dotted with ponds. The Rocky Mountains had not yet formed.

The globe shows the continents now

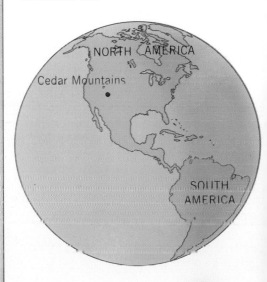

Utahraptor was heavily built for a raptor dinosaur, yet it was far less bulky than meat-eaters like *Allosaurus*, which preceded it in the American West. Its trim but muscular build suggests to scientists that it could run faster than these earlier predators. *Utahraptor* was probably faster-moving than its prey. These might have included a more heavily built armored dinosaur called "Gastonia" and various *Iguanodon*-like plant-eaters with sails on their backs.

NEW KILLERS UNEARTHED

Raptor dinosaurs, the dromaeosaurids, were among the best equipped of meat-eating dinosaurs. Their most terrifying weapons were their enormous sharp toe and hand claws. The new discovery of *Utahraptor* and other giant raptors from Mongolia and Japan suggests that this line of killer dinosaurs began as large animals in the Early Cretaceous.

Utahraptor **was far larger** than those later raptors we know well, such as *Deinonychus* (western United States, 110 million years ago), *Velociraptor* (Mongolia, 80 million years ago), and *Dromaeosaurus* (North America, 74 million years ago).

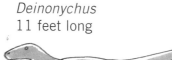

Deinonychus
11 feet long

Velociraptor 6 feet long

Dromaeosaurus
6 feet long

UTAHRAPTOR
Meaning of name: "Utah thief"
Order: Saurischia
Size, Weight: 20 feet long, 1 ton
Location: Utah
Diet: Meat

Utahraptor was named in 1993. Fragments of this animal, including its giant claws, had been found over preceding summers. Parts of a jaw with short but sharp and powerful teeth were found, too. Pieces of upper-leg bone show that *Utahraptor* was heavily built.

Among raptors, *Utahraptor* is the earliest and largest of its kind yet found. Most types of dinosaurs grew bigger as time passed. But raptors appear to have become smaller.

The bladelike claws on the second digits of *Utahraptor*'s hands and feet were nearly 12 inches long. *Utahraptor* also had two other large claws on each hand. Powering these claws were strongly muscled arms and legs. The leg bones are almost twice the thickness of leg bones from an *Allosaurus*, even though *Allosaurus* grew nearly twice the length of *Utahraptor*. The thick legs and tail of *Utahraptor* led some scientists to wonder if it hopped like a kangaroo rather than ran. Other scientists say this hopping would be unlikely in any dinosaur.

UTAHRAPTOR

CAMARASAURUS-LIKE SAUROPOD
Order: Saurischia
Size, Weight: 50 feet long, 10 tons or more
Location: Utah
Diet: Plants

Parts of two different sauropod dinosaurs have been found near *Utahraptor*. Neither is named yet. They have large spoon-shaped teeth like those of the blunt-headed medium-sized *Camarasaurus* of the Jurassic Period. There are also similarities to *Eucamerotus*, an English sauropod of the Early Cretaceous, known for more than 100 years from fossil fragments. One of the recently discovered sauropods has tailbones linked by ball-and-socket joints, normally seen only in sauropods called titanosaurs.

CAMARASAURUS-LIKE SAUROPOD

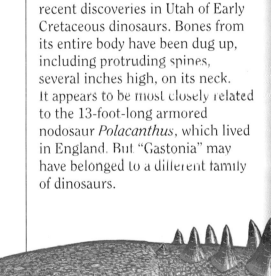

"GASTONIA"
Meaning of name: "Gaston's animal"
Order: Ornithischia
Size, Weight: 18 feet long, 1 to 2 tons
Location: Utah
Diet: Plants

"Gastonia" has yet to be formally named but will likely become an official dinosaur in 1996 or 1997.

"GASTONIA"

It is the best known of all the recent discoveries in Utah of Early Cretaceous dinosaurs. Bones from its entire body have been dug up, including protruding spines, several inches high, on its neck. It appears to be most closely related to the 13-foot-long armored nodosaur *Polacanthus*, which lived in England. But "Gastonia" may have belonged to a different family of dinosaurs.

"Gastonia" had thick legs and was built low to the ground. Clearly, it was not equipped to run quickly. Plates and spikes covered its entire upper body, and this heavy armor might have discouraged most predators.

INSECTS

Insect fossils are not commonly found in these rocks. In Nebraska, in rocks of similar age, fossil evergreen leaves show tunnels made by caterpillars of primitive moths. Relatives of these moths (Phyllocristinae) are alive today, and their caterpillars feed on sycamore trees.

PLANTS
Forests of tall evergreens grew, as did cycads and bushy Mormon tea plants.

EVERGREEN TREE

115

SAVANNA WITH SAUROPODS

Though there was no grass in dinosaur times, the open land of Early Cretaceous Utah resembled, in many ways, the East African savanna of today in the dry season. Tall trees grew by pools and watering holes. Scrubby vegetation grew elsewhere, with ferns, cycads, and bushy plants abundant in more open areas. Large animals gathered by the watering holes—both thirsty plant-eaters and carnivores looking for prey.

Utah in the Early Cretaceous was a moister area than it had been in the Late Jurassic. The land was still mostly arid, but now there were more pools and lakes. Turtles, bony fish (including lungfish), and crocodiles inhabited the water. The climate was warm year-round.

Interestingly, many dinosaur types of this time were able to live in a variety of habitats. In Utah, the same animals probably lived in forests and open lands. Animals similar to *Utahraptor* lived in dry environments in Asia. Plant-eaters like those of Utah at the same time lived in a wetter environment in England.

In East Africa today, game animals like these wildebeests spread across the savanna in the rainy season. In the dry season, they move to wetter land or gather around watering holes. About 125 million years ago, dinosaurs in Utah probably migrated in the same way.

A *Utahraptor* (1) stalks plant-eaters gathered around a pool. The herbivores include sauropods **(2)** and the armored Gastonia **(3)**. The predator will choose its prey based partly on which plant-eater it prefers to eat and partly on which is the more likely to be an easy kill. Smaller predators are present, too.

How did so many plant-eaters share one environment? They probably had different feeding niches. Iguanodontids stood on their hind legs to feed from the middle levels of trees. Sauropods stretched higher still. The ankylosaur browsed at ground level.

Like savanna animals today, plant-eating dinosaurs may have moved in herds, never staying in one place so long that they ate all of the plants. This is a way of sharing food resources.

***Utahraptor* on the run—** perhaps chasing a theropod dinosaur. The little meat eaters found in this environment are similar to the small predator *Ornitholestes* from the American West in the Late Jurassic.

Scientists can only guess whether *Utahraptor* ever ran down small predators. It is likely that, unless surprised, little meat-eaters were too quick for the heavy-legged *Utahraptor*.

How did *Utahraptor* hunt? It might have prowled in packs, as lions do. Using their scythe claws, a pack of these one-ton monsters would have been able to cut down even the largest sauropods in their world. Or perhaps *Utahraptor* hunted alone. It might have had a camouflage skin color that allowed it to ambush a passing *Iguanodon*. Then *Utahraptor* might have leaped on *Iguanodon*, holding and tearing its victim's flesh with its claws, as a solitary tiger attacks a deer or antelope today.

CLAW CLUE

The claw of *Utahraptor* is one of the most effective killing weapons of any animal. Discovered in 1991, the hand claw of *Utahraptor* was the first clue to the identity of this giant raptor dinosaur. It is similar in shape to claws of the small raptor dinosaurs known for more than fifty years, but it is bigger than any other raptor claw.

Shown twice its actual size here, the hand claw of *Utahraptor* was a thin blade, only one-half inch thick at its widest point.

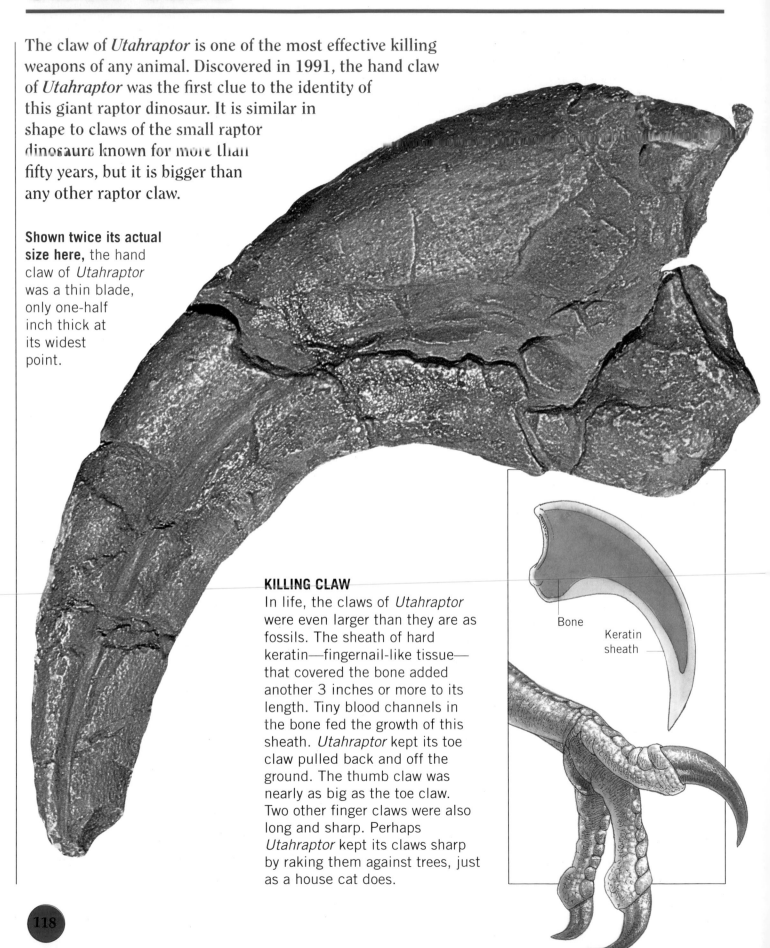

KILLING CLAW
In life, the claws of *Utahraptor* were even larger than they are as fossils. The sheath of hard keratin—fingernail-like tissue— that covered the bone added another 3 inches or more to its length. Tiny blood channels in the bone fed the growth of this sheath. *Utahraptor* kept its toe claw pulled back and off the ground. The thumb claw was nearly as big as the toe claw. Two other finger claws were also long and sharp. Perhaps *Utahraptor* kept its claws sharp by raking them against trees, just as a house cat does.

Bone

Keratin sheath

118

RAPTOR ATTACK

Utahraptor eyes a "Gastonia" **(1)**. Before the plant-eater sees that it is being stalked, the *Utahraptor* rushes in toward the slower-moving prey. The armored dinosaur turns its back toward the *Utahraptor* to protect its vital organs and belly.

Although its claws can slash through hide an inch thick, *Utahraptor* cannot penetrate the thick armor and sharp spikes that cover the plant-eater's back **(2)**. The raptor's bladelike claws are so narrow that a careless blow might snap one. Frustrated by its lack of success, the predator moves on, leaving the plant-eater unharmed.

The *Utahraptor* is joined by another. Together, they overpower a young sauropod **(3)** that they have successfully maneuvered away from its herd. They slash at the sides and belly of the giant plant-eater, striking with the blades on their toes and hands.

While the weapons of *Utahraptor* are now well known, the way in which it used them is still a mystery. The powerful hind legs of *Utahraptor* were ideal for kicking but not for fast running. But most of the large herbivores it might have hunted were not built to move quickly either, and a predator needs only to be faster than its prey to succeed. If fossil footprints are ever found, they could solve the debate about how *Utahraptor* moved. Footprints might also reveal whether *Utahraptor* traveled and hunted alone or in packs.

As with most fossil meat-eaters, there is no direct evidence of *Utahraptor* as a hunter, but its weapons indicate that it was a killer.

Like many predators, *Utahraptor* might have scavenged when possible. This lifestyle saves an animal injury from prey that fight back. Scavenging also uses less energy than hunting does. Most hunts end unsuccessfully for predators of today, and the same was probably true in the past.

Utahraptor's habits are not known, but we know something about the lifestyle of its relative *Deinonychus*. In Montana, bones from several *Deinonychus* skeletons have been found among the scattered fossils of a *Tenontosaurus*. Scientists think a pack of raptors tore apart the plant-eater, which killed several of the raptors before it died.

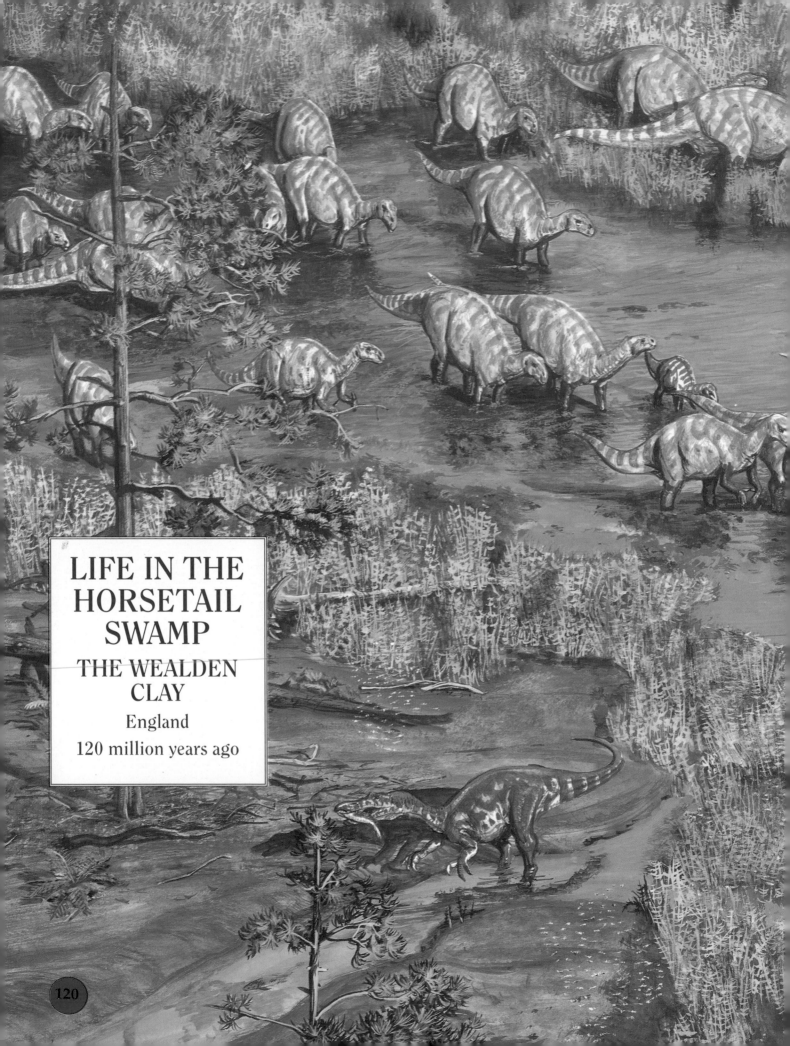

LIFE IN THE HORSETAIL SWAMP

THE WEALDEN CLAY

England

120 million years ago

At the mouth of a river, herds of dinosaurs wade into the shallows to feed on horsetail plants. Nearby, on the water's edge, a large carnivorous dinosaur eats a fish it has caught with its huge sickle-shaped thumb claws. Dragonflies flit overhead.

IGUANODON PARADISE

About 120 million years ago, southern England was a region of lakes and marshes, full of life. The dinosaur *Baryonyx*, with its narrow crocodile-like jaws, caught fish at the water's edge. Other dinosaurs, reptiles, and fish were plentiful. The wide variety of plants included some of the first flowering plants.

In England 120 million years ago
Iguanodon fed on shrubs with little flowers that grew in the marshes. *Baryonyx*, a carnivore, fed on fish.

Flowering plants were greatly outnumbered by more ancient evergreen plants. Ferns flourished in the damp areas. Horsetails, which are large reedy plants, were the most common plants of all. Trees included cone-shaped ancestors of redwoods and the bald cypress trees still seen in warm swamps today. Butterflies, bees, and wasps were among the insects that pollinated the early flowering plants.

The Wealden—Today
Southern England now is a cool environment and receives only about 30 inches of rain a year. Here, paleontologists search in the sandstone and clay for more dinosaur fossils from 120 million years ago.

122

The plant-eaters of Early Cretaceous southern England are particularly well known. They include many new kinds of bird-hipped dinosaurs. Tiny plant-eaters ran on slim hind legs. Twelve-foot-long armored dinosaurs nibbled at ground-level plants. But the most common dinosaur was *Iguanodon*. This large animal sometimes walked on two legs and other times on all fours. It had more advanced jaws than the sauropods.

The front of its jaw had a wide toothless beak. Nipping off plants with its beak, *Iguanodon* would then mash the plants with the 100 teeth in its jaws. The tooth rows were good grinding surfaces. The jaw muscles were very strong. When *Iguanodon* brought its jaws together, the upper jaws flexed and slid outside the lower jaws, grinding food between upper and lower teeth. Cheek pouches helped keep food in the mouth. *Iguanodon* had the best chewing mechanism dinosaurs had yet evolved—a big advantage in dealing with tough plant food.

The Wealden—Then A herd of *Iguanodon* grazes on horsetails and other plants in shallow waters where a river meets the sea. *Iguanodon* adults are two different sizes, probably male and female. Other smaller bird-hipped dinosaurs called *Hypsilophodon* also feed on plants. *Baryonyx* dips its claws into the water to snare fish.

Horsetail plants grow several feet high. *Clatophlebis* ferns flourish in the warm, wet conditions. Away from the water, taxodioid trees (related to modern redwoods) and araucarian conifers grow. Shrublike flowering plants grow in the clearings. The many kinds of insects include termites, dragonflies, flies, moths, beetles, and ants.

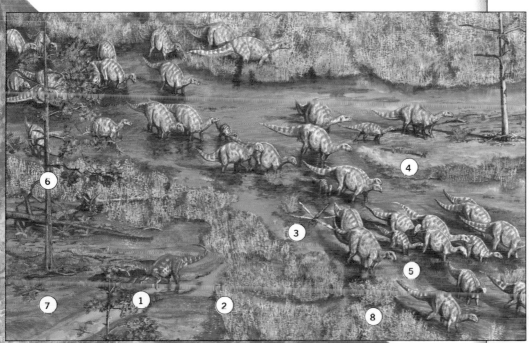

LAND OF REEDS

Southern England 120 million years ago was a fertile lowland with rivers and streams flowing across the region. When rains were heavy and water levels high, the area was marshy. As the rains ceased, the land became drier and there were many lakes. In time, vegetation filled the lakes and created new land.

For the most part, the ancient Wealden region was warm and moist year-round, much like subtropical marshes today. The river deltas of the Middle East—such as the Tigris-Euphrates Valley, where the first human civilizations dawned thousands of years ago—resemble the marshes of Early Cretaceous England.

In the ancient marshes, *Iguanodon* probably used its spike-thumbed hands to grip the reeds and tear off the most edible portions. Many modern plant-eaters are also adapted to live on a limited choice of foods. Koalas, for example, have nimble hands for pulling at the eucalyptus leaves of Australian forests. The giant panda of China is descended from meat-eating bears. But it has evolved grinding teeth and a digestive system for eating only the bamboo plants of its forest habitat.

Marshes become land
Iguanodon feed on weeds **(1)** in a wet lowland. One of the dinosaurs dies at the water's edge as the water level rises in a rainy period. This *Iguanodon*'s body decomposes, leaving only the skeleton **(2)**.

Plants grow thickly as water levels drop. Soon, layers of dead plants cover the bones and prevent more water from entering the lake **(3)**. This section of earth sinks below sea level. Over many millions of years, the marshes become rock.

The koala is one of the most specialized animals in Australia. Its diet is almost entirely eucalyptus leaves. Some of these leaves contain poisonous chemicals, but the koala's digestive system renders them harmless.

In the Early Cretaceous Wealden region, fast-growing reeds, cycads, ferns, and flowers were excellent food sources for herds of *Iguanodon* and other dinosaurs. *Iguanodon* probably had padded feet that spread their body weight as they waded in the soft marshes. Their grasping hands could hold the swaying marsh plants in order to eat the plants' nutritious and tender new growth. *Iguanodon*'s jaws could process enough plants to provide the energy for an active 3- to 7-ton animal.

In the midst of a wet lowland, *Iguanodon* graze. They grasp horsetail reeds, pulling them to their mouths to be cropped off by their wide horny beaks.

Dragonflies hover near the dinosaurs. Beetles, flies, and other insects pollinate the flowering plants in the marsh.

FIRST DISCOVERY

Iguanodon and the meat-eater *Megalosaurus* were the first dinosaur fossils found and identified by scientists. (*Megalosaurus* lived during the Middle Jurassic Period.) The story of *Iguanodon*'s discovery in 1822 by Dr. Gideon Algernon Mantell has become legendary. However, scientists today draw a different picture of *Iguanodon* and its life from that suggested by Dr. Mantell.

This jumbled partial skeleton of an *Iguanodon* was found in a quarry in Kent, England. Dr. Mantell's friends bought it for him for a price that was equal to a month's salary for a scientist at that time.

In Dr. Mantell's first restoration of *Iguanodon*, he showed the animal as a squat four-legged creature with a horn (really one of its claws) on its snout. He first described *Iguanodon* in 1825 on the basis of the teeth he had found. Dr. Mantell believed *Iguanodon* to be a 40-foot-long plant-eating fossil lizard.

At the time, dinosaurs were not known. The term *dinosaur* ("terrible lizard") was not used to describe large extinct reptiles until the year 1842, when the word was invented by British scientist Sir Richard Owen.

Dr. Mantell was a family doctor in Sussex, southern England, who collected rocks and fossils. In 1822, he acquired several large mysterious teeth from a nearby rock quarry. Unable to identify them, he showed them to leading scientists in England and France. He believed that the teeth belonged to an extinct creature buried in ancient rock. Scientists doubted the rock's age and thought the teeth belonged to a large fish or mammal.

Dr. Mantell felt certain the rocks were very old, but he could not date them accurately. And he was sure that the teeth must belong to an extinct reptile. Comparisons to other teeth suggested to him that these were most like the teeth of the modern iguana lizard, so he called the fossil animal *Iguanodon*, "iguana tooth." Some of Dr. Mantell's ideas were proved wrong when more discoveries were made, but his ideas were excellent science for their time.

A CHANCE FIND

An often-told story, in which Dr. Mantell's wife, Mary Ann, found the first dinosaur fossil, is now considered a fable. According to this tale, she went with Dr. Mantell on a house call in 1822. While he was inside, Mary Ann stayed outside and looked at rocks near the road (1). She saw an object resembling a large tooth (2). Knowing her husband's interest in natural objects for the little museum he had at home, she picked up the tooth and gave it to him. Struck by its unusual appearance, Dr. Mantell studied the fossil and concluded that it was the tooth of an extinct reptile.

The truth is that quarry workers in nearby Tilgate Forest found unusual fossils. They brought these to Dr. Mantell. He came to the quarry to try to tell the age of the rocks (3).

Back at his museum, Dr. Mantell chopped away the rock around the *Iguanodon* fossil bought for him by his friends (4).

In the 1850s, Waterhouse Hawkins, a British painter and sculptor, created a life-sized *Iguanodon* sculpture for the Crystal Palace Exhibition in London. Hawkins's dinosaur sculptures still stand in Sydenham Park in South London.

Just before the sculpture was finished in 1854, Hawkins and his scientific expert, Sir Richard Owen, celebrated with a New Year's Eve dinner party for twenty-one people inside the mold of the body of *Iguanodon* (5). A huge meal was served.

129

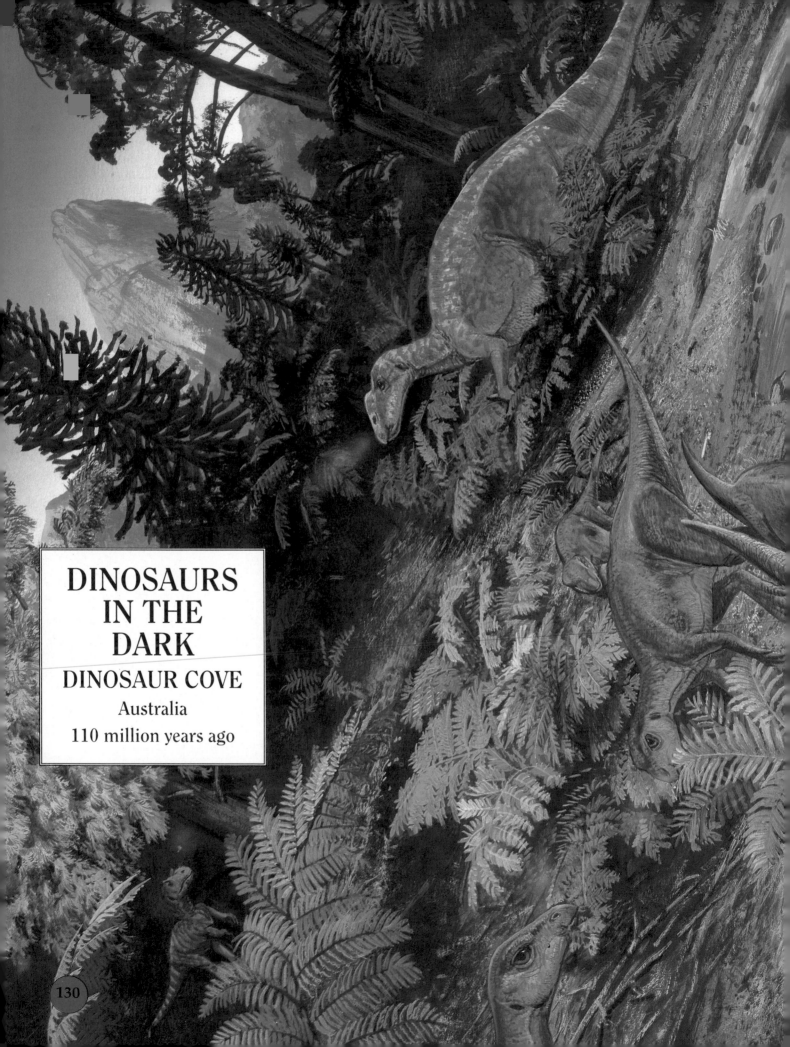

DINOSAURS
IN THE
DARK

DINOSAUR COVE

Australia

110 million years ago

Little dinosaurs with keen eyes find their way along a lakeshore in the daylong twilight of Antarctic early winter. The weather is cool and moist, and a thin layer of ice crackles beneath the feet of the little plant-eaters. Many other animals lurk in the dim light of a long dark season.

DARKNESS DOWN UNDER

In Early Cretaceous times, Australia was much farther south than it is today. As a result, the climate was cooler than in present-day Australia. During this warmer era there was no permanent ice, even at the Poles, but Australian dinosaurs and other animals might have sometimes seen snow.

This area offers a glimpse of lifestyles that are far-removed from the usual notions of dinosaur life. The landscape was home to two kinds of small two-legged, sharp-eyed plant-eaters found nowhere else. Also lurking in the dim light was a small solidly built predator stalking its prey. Another meat-eating dinosaur darted like an ostrich through the fern underbrush in search of small mammals or hatchling dinosaurs. A large herbivore, a relative of *Iguanodon* with a large bump on its snout, also lived here. A small armored dinosaur snipped at low-growing plants.

The plant-eaters had many food sources to choose from—ferns, cycads, evergreens of many sizes, and even a few of the newly evolved flowering plants.

Dinosaur Cove—Today At this site in southeastern Australia, thousands of fragments from dinosaurs of 110 million years ago lie in the sandstone cliffs. The land is dry and cool in winter, hot in summer.

Little *Leaellynasaura* plant-eaters huddle together as a dusting of snow falls. Scientists think Antarctic temperatures in the Early Cretaceous rarely dipped below freezing, even on the coldest days.

Lush vegetation grows in southern Australia. Huge Wollemi pines and araucarian conifers are the tallest trees. Small herbivores eat lower-growing deciduous plants such as ferns, bennettitaleans, and Koonwarra plants (small, scrambling, flowering vines that cover the ground in open places between the trees).

Dinosaur Cove—Then
Small hypsilophodontids—two-legged bird hipped species—are the most common dinosaurs. Among them are little *Leaellynasaura* and the slightly larger *Atlascopcosaurus*, both of which have large brains and keen eyes to see in the darkness of the polar winter. Bigger still is *Muttaburrasaurus*, a plant eater similar in body shape and lifestyle to *Iguanodon*. This damp and sometimes cool environment is home to an armored dinosaur, too. This animal is so recently discovered that scientists have not yet given it a name.

Meat-eating dinosaurs are represented by a stocky predator, no bigger than a person, which was possibly related to *Allosaurus*, the giant North American predator of the Jurassic. Labyrinthodonts—large amphibians—inhabit rivers.

Plant life is varied in this moist environment. Ferns and deciduous cycadeoids are among the low growing plants. In the forest grow huge Wollemi pines, ginkgoes, and araucarian trees.

FACT FILE

Australia, Then and Now Today, Dinosaur Cove is on the southeastern coast of Australia. This part of the continent is about 2,000 miles north of the Antarctic Circle. During the Early Cretaceous, Australia was joined to Antarctica, and Dinosaur Cove was within the Antarctic Circle. Although the weather around the world was generally warmer than it is today, the climate in Australia was actually cooler.

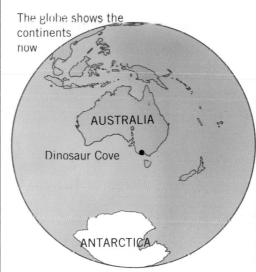

The globe shows the continents now

ANIMALS
1. *Allosaurus* -like therapod (AL-o-SAW-rus)
2. *Leaellynasaura* (lay-EL-in-ah-SAW-rah)
3. *Muttaburrasaurus* (MUT-uh-BUR-uh-SAW-rus)

PLANTS
4. Araucarian conifer cone (AIR-ah-CARE-ee-un)
5. Cycadeoid
6. Ferns
7. Ginkgo
8. Wollemi pine

ALSO AT THIS SITE:
Atlascopcosaurus (AT-lus-KOP ko-SAW-rus)
Labyrinthodonts
Minmi -like ankylosaur (MIN-mee)
Timimus (tih-MY-mus)

SMALL AND ODD

Australian dinosaurs of 110 million years ago are mostly small compared to those known from elsewhere. They might have been primitive holdovers, descendants of dinosaurs that were already extinct elsewhere in the world. Or, as Australian researchers speculate, they might have been pioneers—the first of new forms of dinosaurs that would spread across the world.

LEAELLYNASAURA
Meaning of name: "Leaellyn's lizard"
Order: Ornithischia
Size, Weight: 6.5 to 10 feet long, 15 to 22 pounds
Location: Australia
Diet: Plants

This little plant-eater was no bigger than a young kangaroo. It was a member of the hypsilophodont family of small, lightly built two-legged herbivores that lived around the world in the Cretaceous. Fossils of its braincase show that it had a big brain compared to its body size, and that it might have been among the smartest of dinosaurs. The area of the brain that controls vision, the optic lobe, is particularly large. This suggests that *Leaellynasaura* might have seen particularly well, even in the near-darkness of the polar winters. It had unusual ridges on both sides of its upper teeth.

LEAELLYNASAURA

UNNAMED ANKYLOSAUR
Order: Ornithischia
Size, Weight: Up to 10 feet long, 500 pounds
Location: Australia
Diet: Plants

Fragments of a small ankylosaur found at Dinosaur Cove resemble the fossils of *Minmi*, a small ankylosaur found in later rocks of Early Cretaceous northern Australia. *Minmi* lacked a clubbed tail. Unlike any other dinosaur, it had armor plates on its belly and under the skin of its back. The belly plates were thin and probably not noticeable. The back plates might have supported the backbone or helped move the outside armor.

UNNAMED ANKYLOSAUR

PLANTS

Fossil leaves and pollen from Australia 110 million years ago show some of the plants that lived there at the time. In 1995, scientists in northeastern Australia announced a surprising discovery. They had found living trees previously known only from fossils that are 200 million years old. Named Wollemi pines, the trees are tall, with dense branches of narrow waxy leaves. Their bark is knobby and chocolate brown in color. Only a single grove of a few hundred of these trees is known, in Queensland, Australia. They would certainly have grown in Early Cretaceous Australia.

WOLLEMI
PINE

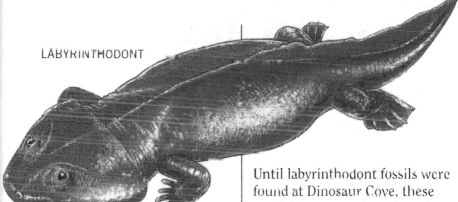

LABYRINTHODONT

LABYRINTHODONT
Meaning of name: "Folded tooth"
Order: Temnospondyli
Size, Weight: 10 feet long, 250 pounds
Location: Southeastern Australia
Diet: Small fish, insects, reptiles

Labyrinthodonts were amphibians that were named for their complex teeth. Each tooth was folded in an elaborate pattern. The coelacanth-like lobe-finned fish that were probably their ancestors had very similar teeth.

ALLOSAURUS-LIKE THEROPOD
Order: Saurischia
Size, Weight: (Australian form) 10 feet long, 100 to 300 pounds
Locations: Southeastern Australia, North America, Africa
Diet: Meat

Allosaurus is well known in North America as the largest carnivorous dinosaur of the Late Jurassic, growing more than 40 feet long. The only fossil found in Australia is a single ankle bone. This bone seems to be from an animal that is smaller than all but three of the fifty-five known specimens of *Allosaurus* from North America. Perhaps *Allosaurus* survived into the Cretaceous in Australia, but in a stunted form. Or the bone may be from a new kind of dinosaur.

Until labyrinthodont fossils were found at Dinosaur Cove, these amphibians were thought to have become extinct nearly 200 million years ago. In dinosaur time, labyrinthodonts were replaced by crocodiles in most of the world. But the waters of Early Cretaceous Australia might have been too cool for crocodiles. Some amphibians today can tolerate colder temperatures than crocodiles can. In the cool waters of the south, the labyrinthodonts might have survived much longer than they did elsewhere because there were no crocodiles to push them out. They are now known to have lived on Earth for 250 million years.

ALLOSAURUS LIKE
THEROPOD

APART, FOR ALL TIMES

Millions of years ago in Australia, marsupials—the family of pouched mammals—triumphed over all other mammals. Except for opossums, marsupials became extinct almost everywhere else on Earth. But on Australia, marsupials evolved into a range of successful species, such as the kangaroo and the koala.

A similar process might have been underway among dinosaurs in Australia during the Early Cretaceous. Australia was still linked to Antarctica but was isolated by valleys and mountains.

Some scientists think that Australia's small allosaurs and ankylosaurs were runty survivors of animals that had disappeared in less sheltered places long before. In this same protected Australian environment, an ancient amphibian—a labyrinthodont—survived 90 million years longer than its relatives elsewhere. But fragments of bones from Early Cretaceous Australia suggest to other scientists that advanced kinds of dinosaurs first appeared here at this time. These species included the earliest ostrich-like and horned dinosaurs.

Leaellynasaura and **Atlascopcosaurus** **plant-eating dinosaurs** browse in the lush environment of Early Cretaceous southern Australia. They feed on low-growing ferns and cycads and occasional flowering plants. Wollemi pines tower in the background.

Atlascopcosaurus grew to 10 feet long and are named for a drilling company that lent equipment to paleontologists. *Atlascopcosaurus* was similar to dinosaurs in other parts of the world at this time.

Marsupials, like this kangaroo, keep their babies in pouches. Their young are born at an early stage of development and stay in the mother's pouch until they can fend for themselves. "Placental" mammals, including humans, give birth to young that have developed more fully inside the mother's womb, or "uterus."

The earliest mammals laid eggs and fed their young with milk from specialized glands on the underbelly. Mammals of this type are known as "monotremes." Echidnas and platypuses are the only living examples of monotremes.

How did Australian dinosaurs cope with the cool of winter? Unlike mammals, they had no fur to warm them, and they might not have been warm-blooded. Perhaps they sought shelter in caves or burrows, or they hibernated. They could not have migrated far because of their isolation. Youngsters might have grown fast to adult size, which would have helped them become strong enough to survive.

Separation of Australia and Antarctica due to movements in the Earth's crust.

ANTARCTICA

Dinosaur Cove

AUSTRALIA

LABYRINTHODONT

LEFTOVERS OR PIONEERS?

Some animals found at Dinosaur Cove, such as the labyrinthodont amphibian, are unusually primitive. They died out in other regions 100 million years before; they seem to be "leftovers" from an earlier age. Dinosaurs such as *Leaellynasaura* may have been "pioneers"—advanced forms compared to the rest of the world. *Leaellynasaura*, with its big brain, might have been an ancestor of the smart dinosaurs, which lived elsewhere during later times.

As Australia separated from Antarctica, dinosaurs might have been isolated in Australia's lush valleys. Did this make the continent a breeding ground for new dinosaur forms? Australian scientists have suggested this idea. Other dinosaur researchers think that this polar land was home to evolutionary leftovers. Island and isolated animals are often stunted in size. A cool climate as well as geography might have contributed to the unusual nature of the animals of Early Cretaceous Australia.

137

TINY TREASURES

Dinosaur fossils from any time are rare in Australia. The country's richest supply of them has been excavated from Dinosaur Cove. There are hundreds of fossil fragments, all of which fit into two museum cabinets. Incomplete as these fossils are, they provide a record of a wide variety of unusual dinosaurs and other animals in Australia.

Prospecting paleontologists discovered fossils along the granite and sandstone cliffs of southeastern Australia in the early 1980s. Intense digging, drilling, and dynamiting of the cliff faces was done over several hot summers.

Leading the excavations were husband-and-wife scientists Thomas Rich and Pat Vickers-Rich. Many volunteers were needed to help haul rocks up from the wave-swept base of the cliffs and then sift through the rocks for fossils. Two caves were dynamited into the cliff face, leaving a column of stone between the caves. The rock richest in fossils proved to be within that column! No complete skeletons were found, but the remains of two kinds of hypsilophodont dinosaurs and a small meat-eating dinosaur were discovered.

The Riches named the smaller plant-eating dinosaur *Leaellynasaura* after their daughter, Leaellyn, and the meat-eater *Timimus* after their son, Tim.

The digs at Dinosaur Cove were made along a rough, rocky coast. The paleontologists used a range of drilling equipment, as here, along with rope pulleys called "flying foxes" to haul loads of rock to the top of the cliff. After several seasons of intense exploration, the quarries at Dinosaur Cove have been closed. Researchers are now investigating other fossil sites nearby.

LIFE IN THE DARK

Skull bones of *Leaellynasaura* indicate it had a big brain and keen eyes. It used its sharp senses to cope with life in the months of gloom and weeks of darkness in ancient polar Australia. Perhaps it used its ability to see in the dark to avoid competitors and predators year-round by doing much of its feeding at twilight and at night.

Embryos of a related dinosaur found in Montana in the United States suggest that a young *Leaellynasaura* was self-sufficient from the time it hatched. Here, a young *Leaellynasaura* hides and rests (1). Meanwhile, one of its parents forages for food in a valley in the dim moonlight (2).

The *Leaellynasaura* skull was one of the best fossil finds from Dinosaur Cove. Here, seen from above at half the actual size, the skull preserves a cast of the upper surface of the brain. The animal was less than 4 feet tall.

The face of *Leaellynasaura* shows its large eyes and its small beak for cutting vegetation. Here, the dinosaur is pictured with the pupil (the black center of the eye) wide open to let in as much light as possible.

2

The story of Australia's Early Cretaceous dinosaurs is one of strange little creatures in a cool, dark, and changing land. During the next and final stage of dinosaur time, the Late Cretaceous, the land and climate continued to change. And dinosaurs became more varied than ever, before they and many other life forms vanished in a mysterious extinction.

THE LATE CRETACEOUS PERIOD

The last and most powerful dinosaurs appeared in the Late Cretaceous Period. We know these dinosaurs far better than those from any other time. More than half of all known dinosaurs come from these last 20 million years (85 million to 65 million years ago) of the dinosaur era. They include familiar favorites like *Tyrannosaurus rex*, the horned dinosaurs such as *Triceratops*, and the duck-billed dinosaurs. Recent finds are even more exciting, including the largest dinosaur of all and a meat-eater even longer than *Tyrannosaurus*.

During the Late Cretaceous, sea levels were dropping again after reaching their highest point ever 100 million years ago. The environments of the Cretaceous continued to change, and the climate was more varied than in the Triassic or Jurassic Periods. Conditions became far more like those we would recognize today. Grass had yet to evolve, but flowering plants grew in size and number until, by the end of the Cretaceous, they were the most common plants in some habitats. Dinosaurs were widespread and numerous, living not only in the Arctic, where winters were cool, but also in the hot, dry lands of Central Asia.

Nests containing eggs of the Late Cretaceous dinosaur *Oviraptor* have been found throughout the Gobi Desert in Mongolia. When first discovered, these eggs were wrongly thought to be those of *Protoceratops*. *Oviraptor* was named "egg thief" because scientists thought it was preying on these eggs. New finds of *Oviraptor* embryos in the eggs and four *Oviraptor* adults on top of the nest show that this dinosaur was the parent, not a predator, of these eggs.

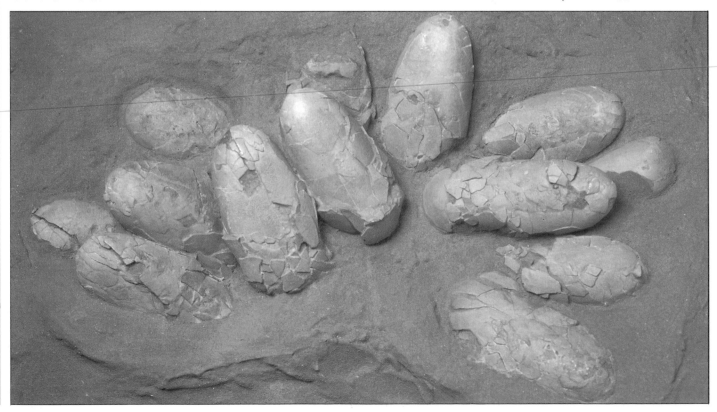

In the Late Cretaceous, mammals were still generally smaller than house cats. The first primates (squirrel-sized mammals that scientists think were the ancestors of humans) scurried about in trees. The first bees and ants appeared—and started to pollinate the flowers.

The dinosaurs that were best-equipped for chewing plants, the duckbills, appeared at this time. They were named for their spoon-shaped bills, which resemble those of duck-billed platypuses. Armored dinosaurs reached their largest size. So did meat-eaters. Fossils show that birds became more common. Pterosaurs grew to record sizes, as big as fighter planes.

CONTINENTS—THEN AND NOW

The continents were taking their modern shape in the Late Cretaceous. India had moved north from Africa to its present position. North America and Asia were joined at a narrow northern connection during much of this period. South America and North America were still separated until the very end of the Cretaceous.

Although temperatures rarely dipped below freezing, there was more seasonal variation in temperature and rainfall than earlier in the Mesozoic.

LATE CRETACEOUS FOSSIL FINDS FROM AROUND THE WORLD
The four sites featured in this section are shown in red.

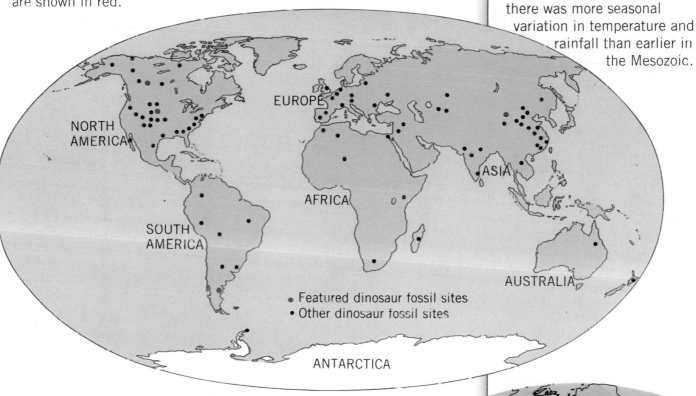

• Featured dinosaur fossil sites
• Other dinosaur fossil sites

Argentina was home to a plant-eater larger than any known land animal before or since. Also living there was a meat-eater larger than *T.rex.*

Dinosaurs of the Gobi Desert of **Mongolia** included some peculiar meat eaters seen nowhere else on Earth. At least thirty-seven kinds of dinosaurs are known from

Alberta, Canada. Among them are the tyrannosaur *Albertosaurus* and duck-billed and horned dinosaurs.

In **Montana** in the United States 65 million years ago lived *Tyrannosaurus* and herds of plant-eating dinosaurs. Here, too, the rocks show the very time when dinosaurs died out.

Black lines show the outlines of the present day continents.

BIGGEST OF THE BIG
PATAGONIA
Argentina
90 million years ago

The footsteps of some of the largest dinosaurs ever to walk the Earth thud and echo in the South American forests. Huge plant-eaters browse high in the branches of the tall evergreens. They are alert, even as they feed, to the approach of a fierce predatory dinosaur, a meat-eater more than 40 feet long.

WHERE GIANTS WALKED

The largest animals that ever walked the Earth are known only from fragments. Scientists suspect that these huge plant-eaters were herding animals, like elephants today. We do not know why these animals grew so enormous. Perhaps a lack of competition from other dinosaurs or the moist and warm climate may have helped these dinosaurs attain huge sizes.

But by the end of dinosaur time, the isolated dinosaurs of South America were far smaller and more peculiar. Some plant-eaters had spiny backs or armored sides, and some meat-eaters had bulldog-like faces and arms even runtier than *T. rex*'s.

Patagonia—Today Here, in two sites about 100 miles apart, the world's biggest meat-eating and plant-eating dinosaurs were recently discovered. Above, scientists excavate an *Argentinosaurus* vertebra.

Burrowing insects, worms, and mammals make their homes among roots of huge araucarian conifer trees in the lush forests of Patagonia 90 million years ago. Such creatures were widespread in Late Cretaceous Argentina.

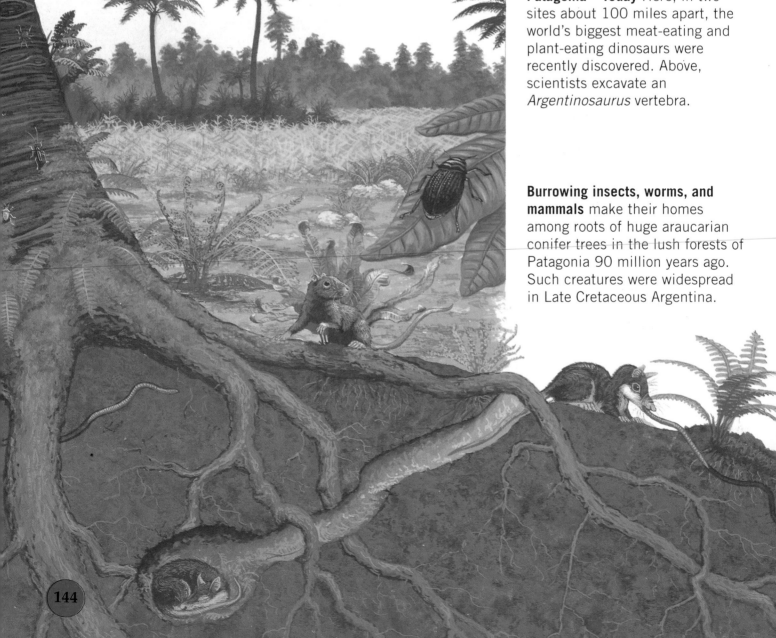

South America was an island continent for much of the Cretaceous Period. As a result, the dinosaurs of that continent went their own peculiar direction in evolution. In the Northern Hemisphere, by the Late Cretaceous, horned and duck-billed dinosaurs had replaced the giant plant-eating sauropods of the Jurassic Period. But in South America the giant sauropods were still thriving. They were members of a large and stocky group known as the titanosaurs.

Predators were also huge in South America about 100 million years ago. In the Northern Hemisphere, small raptor dinosaurs were widespread, and bigger hunters, the tyrannosaurs, were soon to appear. But in South America, the killer giants that have just been discovered were even larger than *Tyrannosaurus*. They were bulkier than *Tyrannosaurus* but had less powerful jaws.

Patagonia—Then
Several *Argentinosaurus*—the largest known dinosaur—nibble at the branches of the towering araucarian trees, deep in the well-watered evergreen forests of central Argentina. Huge but more lightly built sauropods, possibly relatives of *Diplodocus*, fed here, too. The plant eaters' diet includes ferns and the leaves of flowering plants like *Gunnera*.

Suddenly, a meat eater—perhaps a descendant of the huge killer *Giganotosaurus*—darts out from the thick vegetation. With large bladelike teeth suitable for slicing flesh (not crushing bone), it homes in on one of the herbivores as a target. Small mammals lurk in the distance among ferns, out of harm's way. A pterosaur glides overhead, on its way to the coast in search of fish.

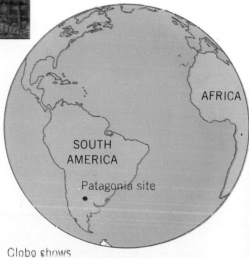

Globe shows the position of the continents now

145

THE BIGGEST EVER

These record-setting dinosaurs are truly awe-inspiring. Imagine a plant-eater as long as three school buses and taller than a house. And picture a meat-eater as long as a moving van, with a head bigger than a whole human!

The giant dinosaurs of Patagonia showed several features that were unknown on other dinosaurs. The enormous plant-eaters had an extra set of supports on each of their vertebrae, which were as tall as a grown human and as wide as a refrigerator. These bony braces would have helped contain their huge guts.

Twenty million years after the giant plant- and meat-eaters ruled South America, the continent was home to dinosaurs half as large but very strange. The spiny manes on some of these huge plant-eaters and the large horns over the eyes of the meat-eaters may have been developed for display. These prominent bones could have been used to attract the attention of possible mates or to inspire fear in rivals.

GIGANOTOSAURUS
Meaning of name: "Giant southern reptile"
Order: Saurischia
Size, Weight: 45 feet long, 8 tons or more
Location: Argentina
Diet: Meat

Giganotosaurus was named in 1995. It is known from a single specimen, more than three-fourths complete. This dinosaur was a terrifying hunter, probably faster and more alert than the plant-eaters in its world. It was narrower in the shoulders than *Tyrannosaurus* but longer and more heavily built.

Giganotosaurus was succeeded by smaller but still impressive meat-eating dinosaurs which ruled Late Cretaceous South America.

GIGANOTOSAURUS

Giganotosaurus (shown in light blue in this comparison) was bigger than *Tyrannosaurus rex* (shown in dark blue) but it was not so powerful. It had a smaller brain, less powerful jaws, and narrower teeth than *T. rex* had.

T. rex was long considered by paleontologists as the all-time king of predators. For killing power, it still is unrivaled. But *Giganotosaurus* is now the largest carnivorous dinosaur known. It was a long as four cars.

146

PLANTS

Gunnera is a modern plant with leaves 6 feet long. These leaves are fan-shaped like those of a rhubarb plant. But in Argentina, in the Late Cretaceous, these flowering plants grew far smaller, with leaves just 4 inches across. Most prominent among the flowering plants of the time were shrubs with magnolia-like flowers like those shown below.

Late Cretaceous flowers

ARGENTINOSAURUS
Meaning of name: "Argentina lizard"
Order: Saurischia
Size, Weight: 110 feet long, 100 tons or more
Location: Argentina
Diet: Plants

Argentinosaurus may be the heaviest animal ever to walk the Earth, three times heavier than *Seismosaurus* (although not as long). Scientists discovered only a few fossils of *Argentinosaurus*, including one shin and bits of the hips, backbone, and ribs. This dinosaur was very solidly built and designed to support great weight. Its vertebrae, each 5 feet long and 5 feet wide, had extra bony struts linking them. Most dinosaur ribs are flattened, but *Argentinosaurus*'s were stout and rounded.

ARGENTINOSAURUS

BULLDOZING THE HABITAT

Soft mudstone around the fossilized *Giganotosaurus* suggests that its habitat was a lush river delta. The nearby *Argentinosaurus* site is harder sandstone, with pebbles surrounding the bones. These fossils indicate that by *Argentinosaurus*'s time, just a few million years later, this nearby area was one of faster-flowing rivers.

1

2

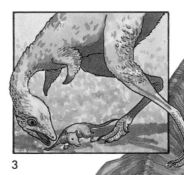

3

4

FOOD CHAIN
Plants are consumed by plant-eating insects, reptiles, and mammals. Mammals and lizards **(1)** feed on insects.

A small mammal kills and eats the lizard **(2)**. The mammal, in turn, is preyed on by a bird **(3)** while its rests after its meal.

5

In all environments, life-forms survive by eating other organisms. The link among living things that eat one another is known as a food chain. In Patagonia, as in other Late Cretaceous lands, dinosaurs were at the top of these food chains. But the length of the food chains varied greatly. The giant plant-eating dinosaurs like *Argentinosaurus* were probably in a very short chain: they ate plants, and usually died of disease, injury, or old age.

Of course, the plant-eating dinosaurs were part of a larger web of interlinked food chains. Some food chains in this web (as the one pictured above) had more links.

In the savannas of modern Africa, elephants are part of a food chain that can be as short as that involving *Argentinosaurus*. Elephants eat leaves and branches of trees. Eventually they die, or occasionally they are the victims of large predators such as lions.

Surprised on the land, the small bird is no match for the agile meat-eating dinosaur **(4)** that overpowers it.

Giganotosaurus **(5)** snaps up the smaller meat-eater. It would also have fed on the flesh of plant-eaters.

Although they return many nutrients to the soil through their waste and their decaying corpses, big plant-eaters can also cause great damage to plant life as they feed. Unless elephants roam widely, they can quickly destroy all the trees in an area. The same was probably true of giant plant-eating dinosaurs.

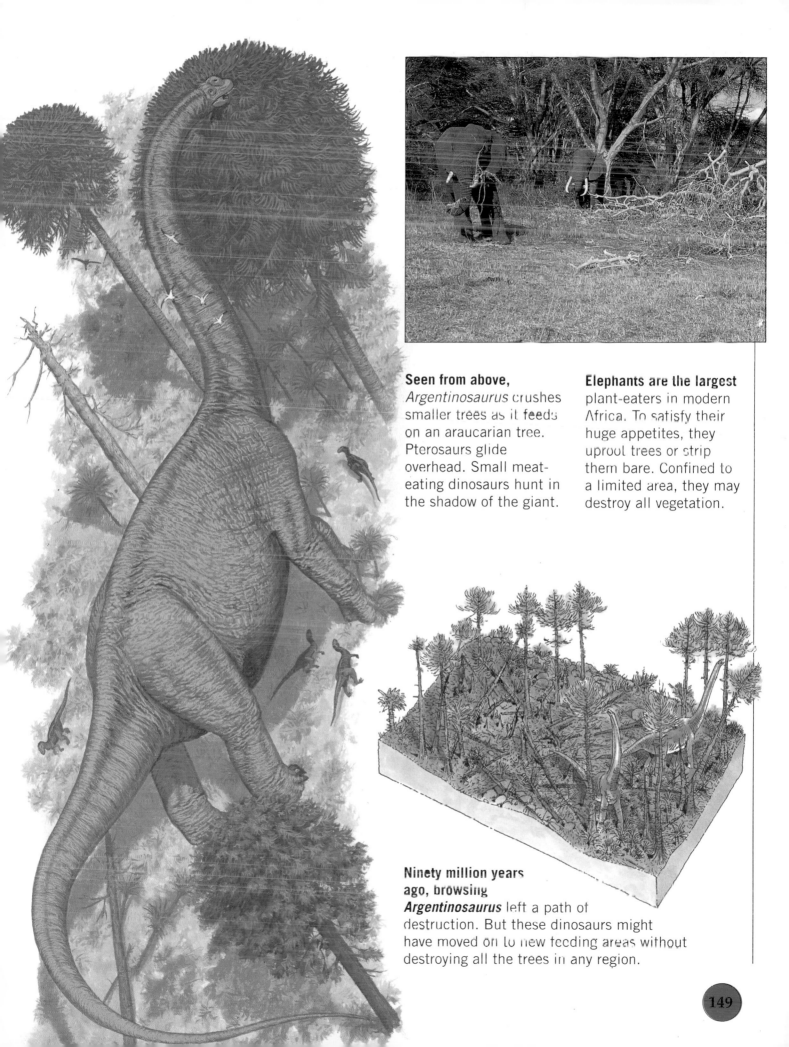

Seen from above, *Argentinosaurus* crushes smaller trees as it feeds on an araucarian tree. Pterosaurs glide overhead. Small meat-eating dinosaurs hunt in the shadow of the giant.

Elephants are the largest plant-eaters in modern Africa. To satisfy their huge appetites, they uproot trees or strip them bare. Confined to a limited area, they may destroy all vegetation.

Ninety million years ago, browsing *Argentinosaurus* left a path of destruction. But these dinosaurs might have moved on to new feeding areas without destroying all the trees in any region.

DIFFICULT DIGGING

The discoveries of the largest meat-eating and plant-eating dinosaurs ever known were made by amateur fossil-hunters in northern Patagonia. Much remains to be learned about these creatures and their habitats. Excavation of the largest of them all, *Argentinosaurus*, has been going on during several recent summers.

Left: Professor Rodolfo Coria (on the right) and an assistant clean the fossil skull of a big meat-eater. **Below:** Working at one site, Coria's team has excavated several huge bones of *Argentinosaurus* - pelvis, backbones, and leg bone, as shown. They recently discovered more of this dinosaur's fossils nearby.

DEATH OF *ARGENTINOSAURUS*

Argentinosaurus dies **(1)** and falls into a fast-flowing river. Sand from the stream bottom, along with many pebbles, builds up quickly around the body.

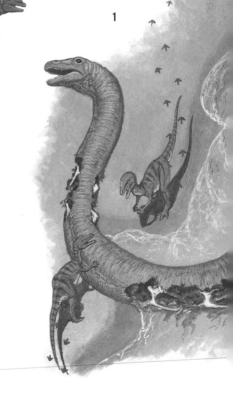

A rancher found the 5-foot-long shinbone of *Argentinosaurus* in 1987. It was beside a highway near his home in Plaza Huincul. At first he guessed it was a petrified tree log and showed it to local scientists. They reasoned from its shape and porous internal structure that it was a dinosaur bone. They called in fossil experts from Argentina's capital, Buenos Aires. José Bonaparte, a paleontologist from the national science museum, led a full-scale excavation.

The dig at the site uncovered 5-foot-long vertebrae and parts of *Argentinosaurus*'s hip. Professor Bonaparte's assistant, Rodolfo Coria, stayed on in Plaza Huincul to continue the work. He has found more bones of *Argentinosaurus*, including a small portion of its skull. Professor Coria has also excavated many other dinosaur fossils in the region, including *Giganotosaurus*.

The bones of the *Argentinosaurus* are picked clean by small scavenging dinosaurs **(2)**. The bone heap causes a sandbank to form in the riverbed. The swift-flowing water carries down more rocks, which wedge in the sandbank. The current washes away many of the smaller bones and scatters even the largest bones along the riverbed.

150

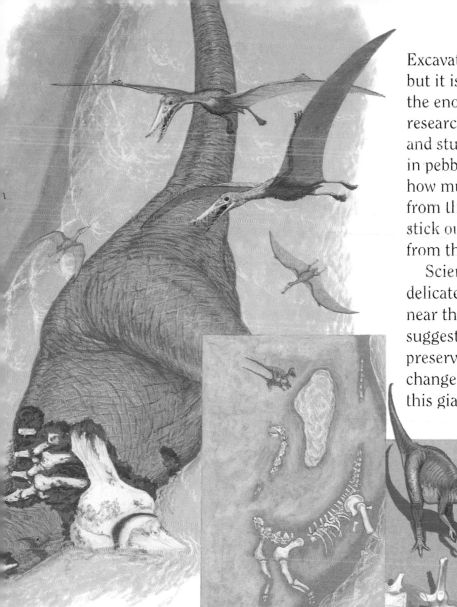

Excavation of *Argentinosaurus* began in 1988, but it is far from finished. Lack of funds and the enormous labor involved have slowed researchers from completing their search for, and study of, the bones. Each vertebra, covered in pebbly sandstone, weighs nearly a ton. Just how much of the dinosaur will be recovered from the site is not yet known. Pieces of bone stick out of the ground as much as 200 yards from the site of the first discoveries.

Scientists were surprised to discover small, delicate pieces of jawbone of *Argentinosaurus* near the larger bones in 1995. This discovery suggests that much of the dinosaur is still preserved at the site. New finds may well change scientists' image and understanding of this giant prehistoric animal.

In 1988, Argentine scientists excavate the *Argentinosaurus* site **(4)**. Air-powered drills are used to expose the bones. Other fossils can be seen in the ground, but the work is so difficult and slow that many bones have yet to be excavated.

2

At the original spot where the dinosaur died, only the heaviest bones **(3)** remain after just a few years of battering from the river current. The largest vertebrae and the sacrum (hipbones) are so heavy that even the fast waters do not tumble them downstream. In a year or two, the bones are completely covered with sediment. The bones become fossils as minerals enter into them and harden them. A small theropod dinosaur looks in the shallow river for the last bits of decaying flesh on the bones of

3

Argentinosaurus before sand and pebbles cover them. Over millions of years, the fossilized bones become buried deeper in the rocks.

4

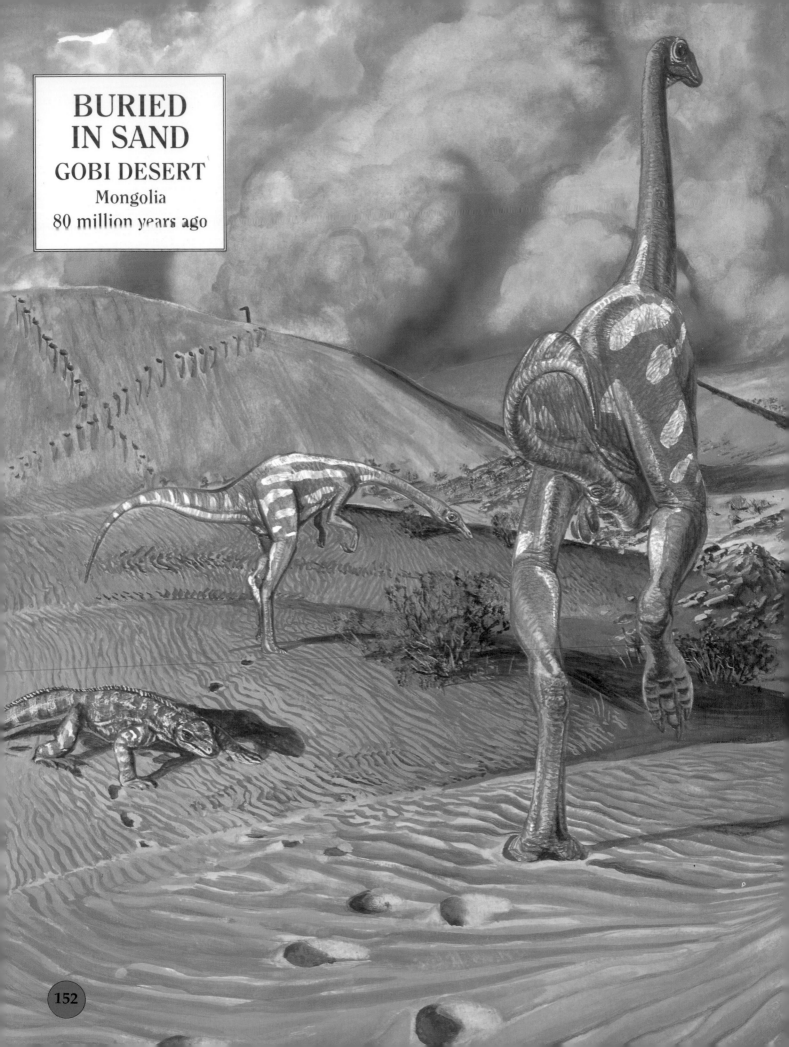

A nesting beaked dinosaur feeds a lizard to its newly hatched youngsters, unaware of the fast-approaching sandstorm. Ostrichlike ornithomimid dinosaurs and other desert-dwellers journey in search of scattered sources of food and water.

153

SHIFTING SANDS

Spectacular dinosaurs lived in Central Asia 80 million years ago. Their habitat was a dry, sometimes desertlike environment. The soft sands of the Gobi Desert preserved fossils so well that we know a great deal about Central Asian dinosaurs at that time. The first nests of dinosaurs were found here, with tiny babies and embryos, too.

North America and Asia were connected during much of the Cretaceous. Not surprisingly, the many fossil finds in the Gobi Desert include dinosaurs like those found in North America. But there are also many unusual creatures known from this region: giant lizards, long-armed carnivores, and giant sauropod dinosaurs. The sands of the Gobi preserved outstanding fossils of other creatures, too, from burrowing insects to mammals. Missing from this area are the large horned dinosaurs like *Triceratops*, so common in Late Cretaceous North America.

Plants adapted to dry conditions are also found as fossils here. The Gobi Desert is even drier now than when dinosaurs lived there.

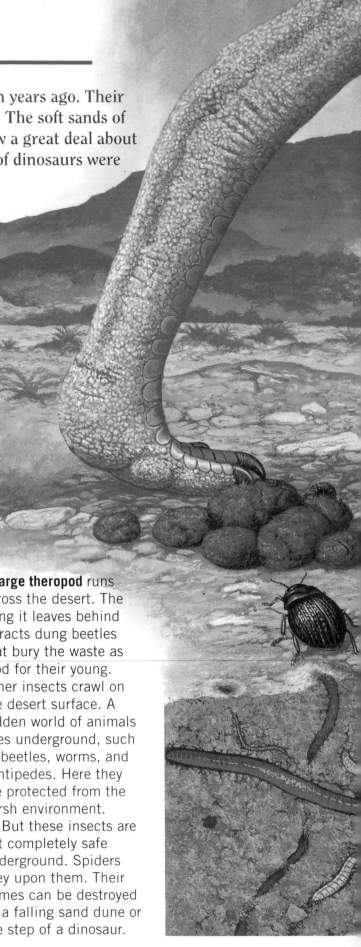

Gobi Desert—Today The Gobi is a crescent-shaped stretch of land nearly 1,000 miles wide in central Asia. Its climate varies from freezing to extremely hot. Divided between China and Mongolia, the desert is mostly barren, but dunes are rare.

A large theropod runs across the desert. The dung it leaves behind attracts dung beetles that bury the waste as food for their young. Other insects crawl on the desert surface. A hidden world of animals lives underground, such as beetles, worms, and centipedes. Here they are protected from the harsh environment.

But these insects are not completely safe underground. Spiders prey upon them. Their homes can be destroyed by a falling sand dune or the step of a dinosaur.

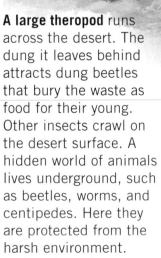

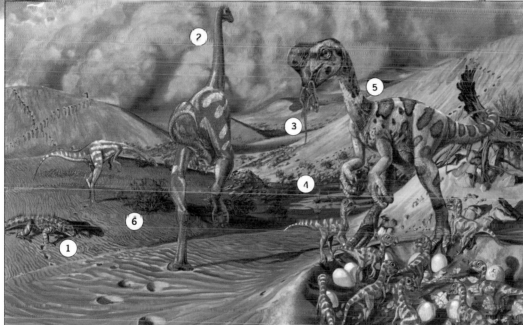

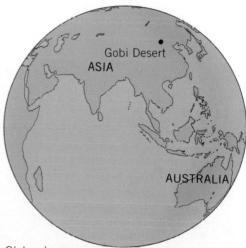

Mongolia was home to nearly one in five of all the meat-eating dinosaurs known.

ANIMALS
1. *Estesia* (ess-TEE-zee-ah)
2. *Gallimimus* (GAL-ih-MY-mus)
3. Lizard
4. *Mononykus* (MAW-no-NY-kus)
5. *Oviraptor* (O-vih RAP-tur)

PLANTS
6. *Ephedra* (eh-FED-rah)

ALSO AT THIS SITE:
Protoceratops (PRO-toe-SAIR-uh-tops)
Saurornithoides (SAWR-or-nith-OY-deez)
Tylocephale (TIE-luh-SEF-uh-lee)
Velociraptor (veh-LAW-sih-RAP-tur)
Dalembya (DAH-lem-BEE-yuh)
Kirengeshoma (ky-REN-guh-SHOW-mah)

Mongolia, Then and Now

Asia today looks much as it did 80 million years ago. But in the Late Cretaceous, sea levels were higher than they are now, and the Gobi was more humid, with shallow ponds and lakes during the wet season.

Globe shows
the position of the continents now

Gobi—Then

An *Oviraptor* feeds its nestlings with a small lizard it has caught. An ostrich-like *Gallimimus*, one of the fastest of all dinosaurs, runs off toward a stream while another *Gallimimus* looks on. A small bird, *Mononykus*, drinks from the stream. A large lizard, *Estesia*, slithers along the ground.

The sparse vegetation of Late Cretaceous Mongolia included the shrublike *Dalembya*; the bare-looking, weedy *Ephedra*; and the *Kirengeshoma* plant, with its shield-shaped leaves. These were food for dome-headed pachycephalosaurs, *Tylocephale*, and horned dinosaurs such as *Protoceratops*.

155

BIG BRAINS, LONG LEGS

The dinosaurs that lived in Mongolia 80 million years ago included some of the most intelligent and fastest-moving dinosaurs of all time. The resemblance to birds of some of these dinosaurs, particularly the lightly built meat-eaters, is striking. The birdlike Mongolian dinosaurs were not ancestors of birds. Birds had evolved from dinosaurs in the Late Jurassic Period or even earlier.

GALLIMIMUS
Meaning of name: "Chicken mimic"
Order: Saurischia
Size, Weight: 17 feet long, about 500 pounds
Location: Mongolia
Diet: Small animals and insects

Gallimimus had a long tail and a snout shaped like a goose's bill.

The skeletons of *Gallimimus* and ostriches have much in common. Both are long-legged, with hollow-boned and lightly built bodies. Some wrist and skull bones are also similar.

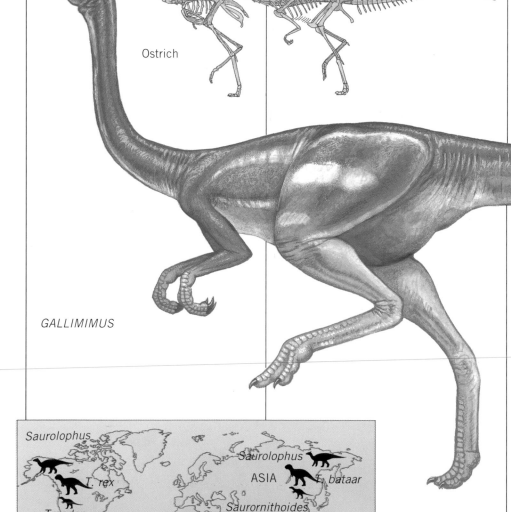

Ostrich

Gallimimus

GALLIMIMUS

Saurolophus

T. rex

Troodon

AMERICA

Saurolophus

ASIA   T. bataar

Saurornithoides

Many closely related animals lived in Asia and North America when these two landmasses were linked in the Late Cretaceous. Despite very different climates, the two continents share nearly identical dinosaur meat-eaters, from tyrannosaurs to raptors and ostrichlike speedsters. Duck-billed, domed, and small horned dinosaurs are also known from both continents. Large horned dinosaurs appear to have been absent from Asia. They may have needed a climate or type of food not available there.

The map shows *Tyrannosaurus rex* had a cousin in Asia called *Tyrannosaurus bataar*. The meat-eater *Troodon* of North America had an Asian "twin" called *Saurornithoides*. *Saurolophus*, a duckbill, lived on both continents.

PLANTS

Flowering plants became the dominant form of vegetation by the Late Cretaceous, at least in the Northern Hemisphere. In the Gobi, plant life was sparse in most places because there was little water.

But several kinds of flowering plants and trees are known from this region 80 million years ago. They include a climbing plant called *Kirengeshoma*, which had little oak-leaf-shaped leaves hanging down from its top. *Ephedra*, known as Mormon tea, is a shrub with climbing sticklike branches. *Ephedra* grows in dry climates today, such as those in Utah and in the Middle East.

Ephedra growing in scrubland in Israel. It also grows beside the Wailing Wall in Jerusalem.

SKULL
Oviraptor's skull was deep, with a high crest, but very light in weight. Its jaws were toothless, and it had a large beak.

OVIRAPTOR

TYLOCEPHALE

TYLOCEPHALE
Meaning of name: "Swollen head"
Order: Ornithischia
Size, Weight: 7 feet long, 120 pounds
Location: Mongolia
Diet: Plants

OVIRAPTOR
Meaning of name: "Egg thief"
Order: Saurischia
Size, Weight: 6 feet long or longer, 50 to 100 pounds
Location: Mongolia
Diet: Meat

Oviraptor was lightly built and had a wishbone. This bone is common in birds but not in dinosaurs. *Oviraptor* had large three-fingered hands with strong claws and three toes on each foot. It was toothless, but it may have been a good hunter. Remains of lizards near the stomach area of *Oviraptor* suggest it ate these reptiles. It may also have crushed eggs with its beak.

Dome-headed dinosaurs are known from both Mongolia and North America in the Late Cretaceous. *Tylocephale* is one of several smaller dome-headed dinosaurs from Mongolia. Only a part of a broken skull has been found. The skull was 4 inches thick and 5 inches high. The domed head is thought to have been used for butting rivals.

157

HEAT AND DROUGHT

Near the end of dinosaur time, as today, Mongolia was a place of great extremes. Nights were cool, but the midday heat was blazing. Water and plants were scarce. Wind-driven sandstorms could rage for weeks at a time. Sand dunes might suddenly collapse, suffocating unsuspecting animals.

Today in the Gobi Desert, animals travel far to find water and are adapted to going great distances without drinking. Some are nocturnal, avoiding the hot, dry days by becoming active only at night. Others, such as foxes, have large ears that act like radiators to help cool themselves in the heat.

How did dinosaurs cope with hot desert life? Perhaps many traveled and fed by night. Many, though not all, of the Gobi dinosaurs were small. Perhaps they could not find enough food to support a large body size. The stress of desert life favored small animals. Certainly, the quick, smart, and lightly built predators like *Velociraptor* and *Saurornithoides* were well equipped to kill small animals. It is possible that as pack hunters they also took on larger plant-eaters as well. Whatever the cause of their comparatively small size, the horned dinosaurs of the Gobi Desert grew no bigger than dogs, whereas in North America some were larger than trucks.

Two-humped Bactrian camels rest in the Gobi Desert today. Camels are the most famous of desert-living creatures. These animals, renowned for their ability to travel many days without water, draw nutrients from the fatty humps on their backs. Camels are also unusually adapted to reduce the amount of water lost from their bodies through breathing, sweating, and urination. And their thick, woolly fur blocks the entry of daytime heat.

Other animals today use a variety of strategies to cope with desert life. Many desert animals, such as the coyote, come out to hunt only at dawn, dusk, and night. Birds make their homes inside water-holding cactus.

158

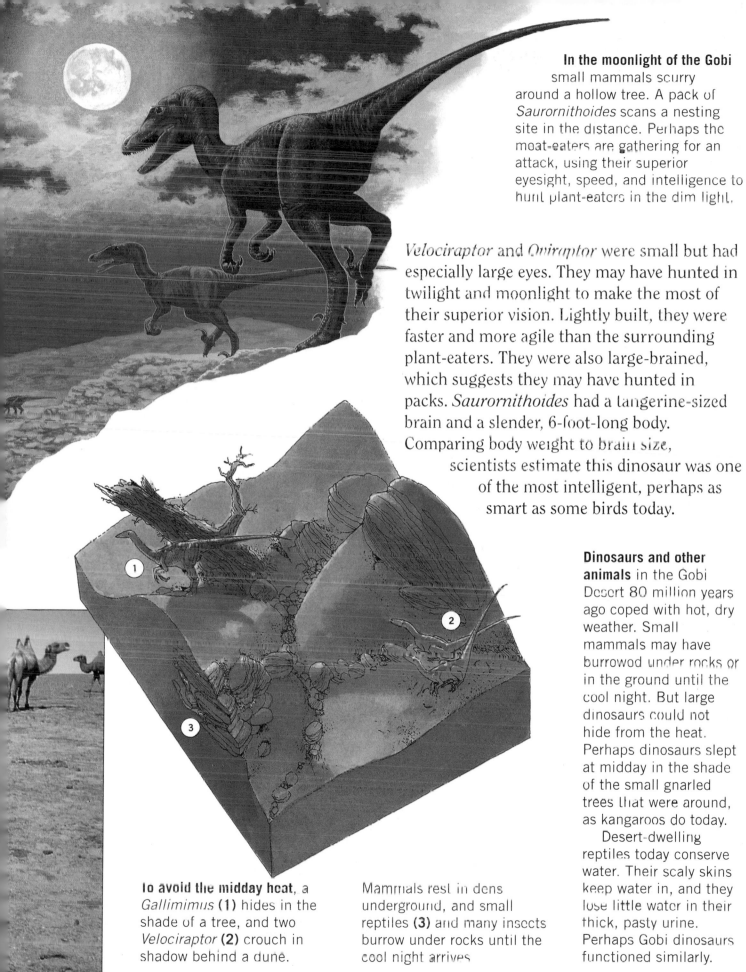

In the moonlight of the Gobi small mammals scurry around a hollow tree. A pack of *Saurornithoides* scans a nesting site in the distance. Perhaps the meat-eaters are gathering for an attack, using their superior eyesight, speed, and intelligence to hunt plant-eaters in the dim light.

Velociraptor and *Oviraptor* were small but had especially large eyes. They may have hunted in twilight and moonlight to make the most of their superior vision. Lightly built, they were faster and more agile than the surrounding plant-eaters. They were also large-brained, which suggests they may have hunted in packs. *Saurornithoides* had a tangerine-sized brain and a slender, 6-foot-long body. Comparing body weight to brain size, scientists estimate this dinosaur was one of the most intelligent, perhaps as smart as some birds today.

Dinosaurs and other animals in the Gobi Desert 80 million years ago coped with hot, dry weather. Small mammals may have burrowed under rocks or in the ground until the cool night. But large dinosaurs could not hide from the heat. Perhaps dinosaurs slept at midday in the shade of the small gnarled trees that were around, as kangaroos do today.

Desert-dwelling reptiles today conserve water. Their scaly skins keep water in, and they lose little water in their thick, pasty urine. Perhaps Gobi dinosaurs functioned similarly.

To avoid the midday heat, a *Gallimimus* (1) hides in the shade of a tree, and two *Velociraptor* (2) crouch in shadow behind a dune.

Mammals rest in dens underground, and small reptiles (3) and many insects burrow under rocks until the cool night arrives.

WHOSE NEST?

In 1923, American Museum of Natural History scientists found the first known dinosaur nests in the Gobi. The eggs were thought to belong to the plant-eater *Protoceratops*. The skeleton of a toothless meat-eater was found on top of one of the nests. It was named *Oviraptor*, "the egg thief."

In 1993, scientists from the same museum uncovered a nest in the Gobi with similarly shaped eggs. Some of these eggs contained embryos. The embryos proved to be bones of *Oviraptor*. *Oviraptor* was not an egg thief. It was an egg-laying parent, killed on top of its nest.

Chinese scientists dig for dinosaur bones in the Gobi Desert, near the site where American scientists first found the fossils of *Protoceratops*, *Oviraptor*, and dinosaur eggs in the early 1920s. The Chinese scientists uncovered many more dinosaur eggs as well as some materials left behind by the previous expedition.

OVIRAPTOR AS PARENT

Oviraptor may have sat directly on its eggs **(1)** to incubate them, as most birds do. Or it might have made a mound of plants over the eggs to keep them warm, as some reptiles and a few birds do today.
A dozen or more eggs, shaped like little loaves of French bread, were arranged in a spiral within the nest. As some of the chicks hatched, or even before, the *Oviraptor* may have had to leave the nest to feed. Perhaps it brought back food for its helpless young.

Here, the *Oviraptor* leaves the nest to try to frighten off a pack of very young *Velociraptor* **(2)**. As youngsters, these swift and smart hunters may have been egg thieves. As adults, *Velociraptor* were capable of hunting lizards and other prey.

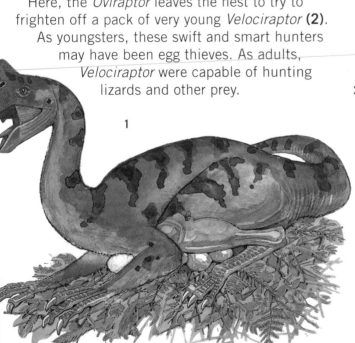

1

2

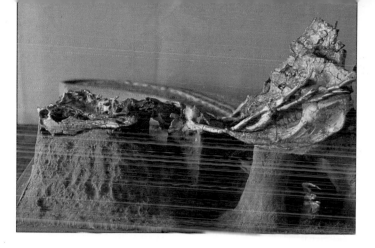

One dramatic find by the Andrews team was a meat-eating dinosaur the size of a large dog, with huge toe and hand claws. They called this lightly built long-legged hunter *Velociraptor,* "swift robber." It was one of the smallest raptor dinosaurs. The first raptors were as large as trucks. But Late Cretaceous raptors like *Velociraptor* and *Dromaeosaurus* (in North America) were small. *Velociraptor* was fast. It leaped into the air to slash its prey with its 4-inch-long second-finger and toe claws.

In the movie *Jurassic Park, Velociraptor* was portrayed as a pack hunter, with the speed of a cheetah and the intelligence of a chimpanzee. In reality, it was more likely as fast as a poodle. Although it was smarter than any mammal or dinosaur of its time, it fell far short of the brainpower of a chimpanzee. There is no evidence yet to suggest that *Velociraptor* traveled in packs.

Few fossil finds show the actual moment of death of prehistoric creatures. But the "fighting dinosaurs" reveals *Protoceratops* (right) and *Velociraptor* (left) grappling as a sand dune collapsed upon them. These amazing fossils were found by Polish paleontologists who explored the Gobi Desert from 1963 to 1971.

3

4

The *Oviraptor* is set upon by a pack of young and tiny *Velociraptor* (3). They leap at the *Oviraptor,* slashing it with their hand and toe claws and biting it with their sharp teeth.

But the young predators are too small to be a serious threat to the full-grown *Oviraptor.* It brushes some away with its tail and arms, and kills two of them by biting off their heads.

After chewing the baby *Velociraptor* to make it easier to digest, the *Oviraptor* will feed the meat to its young in the nest (4). The youngsters eagerly await their meal of raptor meat.

Within a few feet of the *Oviraptor* and its nest of embryos and eggs, the scientists discovered two crushed *Velociraptor* skulls. These skulls were scarcely an inch long and must have come from youngsters. The scenes shown on these pages offer one explanation of how the isolated and broken skulls of these *Velociraptor* babies might have come to be found so near the *Oviraptor* nest.

Along the lush banks of a river, a duck-billed dinosaur is startled by the approach of a big meat-eater. Insects, turtles, and mammals move among the tree branches and leaves. Birds and pterosaurs share the sky, while flowering plants compete with ferns to fill the damp ground around the trees.

DINOSAUR NURSERY

The rocks from the badlands of North America show us a time, 75 million years ago, when this was a lush, subtropical land. Small plant-eating dinosaurs nested beside the great colonies of duck-billed dinosaurs. Herds of horned dinosaurs roamed the countryside. Predatory dinosaurs, crocodiles, pterosaurs, birds, and little mammals lived amid many flowering and evergreen plants.

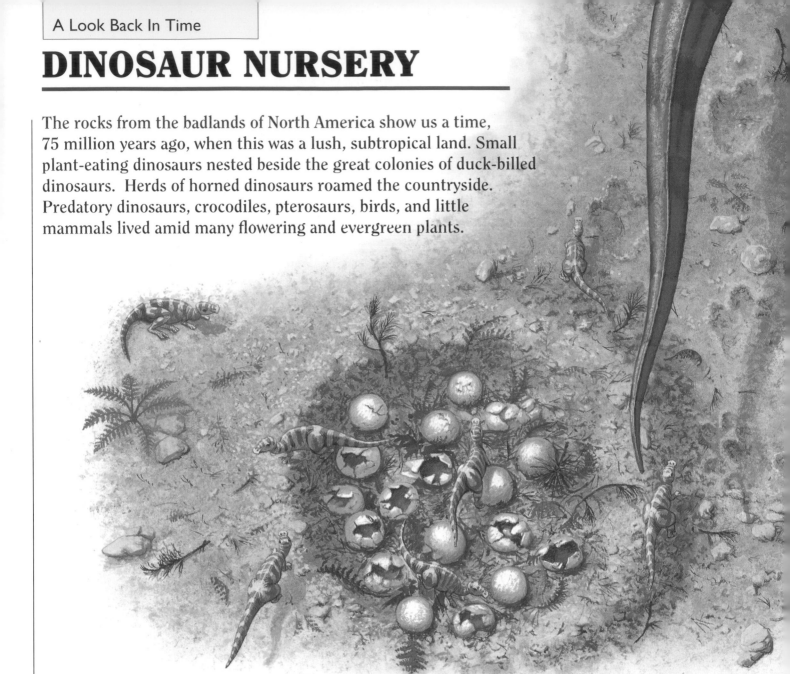

Badlands—Today
Devil's Coulee in Alberta, Canada, lies in the heart of badlands. These cliffs were created by rivers that vanished a few thousand years ago. Seventy-five million years ago this land was a lush river delta, full of nesting dinosaurs. Nests of duck-billed dinosaurs are found in nearby Montana, too.

Newly hatched duck-billed dinosaurs explore the area around their nest. The tiny dinosaurs still inside the eggs peck away with their egg teeth at the hard shell. Some eggs are cracking. A duckbill parent leaves the nest to find food. Parents may have regurgitated partially digested plants as food for the hungry young.

Like many birds, some dinosaurs might have been devoted parents that watched over their helpless young and brought them food in the nest. One scientist, Dr. John Horner, sparked excitement over this idea in the late 1970s. In Montana, he discovered the fossils of a new type of dinosaur, which he named *Maiasaura* ("good mother lizard"). Among other clues, he found the bones of hatchlings and juveniles lying together in and around their nests. He thinks the hatchlings stayed in the nest for weeks while their parents fed and protected them.

Other newly hatched dinosaurs were up-and-running immediately and needed little parental attention. Evidence for both of these styles of bringing up baby dinosaurs has been claimed from fossils found in the North American West.

FACT FILE

Badlands, Then and Now The badlands now have cold winters and hot, dry summers. In the Late Cretaceous, the Alberta badlands were wet lowlands. They are now prairie. The Montana badlands are in the foothills of the Rocky Mountains. In the Late Cretaceous, this area was a dry but fertile upland.

ANIMALS
1. *Albertosaurus* (al-BURR-toe-SAW-rus)
2. *Corythosaurus* (kor-ITH-o-SAW-rus)
3. Dragonflies and midges
4. *Centrosaurus* (SEN-tro-SAW-rus)
5. Leaf beetles
6. *Presbyornis* bird (PRESS-bee-OR-nis)
7. *Pteranodon* (tair-AN-o-dahn)
8. *Trionyx* (try-AW-nicks)
9. Unnamed mammal

PLANTS
10. Magnolia-like shrub
11. *Metasequoia* conifer (MEH-tah-suh-KOY-ah)
12. *Taxodium* conifer (tax-OH-dee-um)

ALSO AT THIS SITE:
Hypacrosaurus (hy-PACK-ro-SAW-rus)
Maiasaura (MY-uh-SAW-rah)
Orodromeus (OR-o-DRO-mee-us)

Globe shows the position of the continents now

Badlands—Then

An *Albertosaurus*, a large predator of Late Cretaceous Alberta and Montana, roams in search of prey, alive and dead. Among its victims may be duck-billed dinosaurs such as *Corythosaurus* or horned dinosaurs like *Centrosaurus*. These herbivores feast on the twigs of trees much like modern redwood and cypress conifers.

Little mammals scurry along the branches looking for midges, dragonflies, and beetles to eat.

Trionyx turtles that basked in the sun earlier in the day now cool off in the shade of the forest. Birds and enormous pterosaurs fly overhead.

In drier areas a few hundred miles away, duckbills called *Maiasaura* and *Hypacrosaurus* build nests and lay eggs. Other dinosaurs living in these areas include various kinds with horns, some with dome-shaped heads, others with thick, protective armored skin, and many kinds of small meat-eaters.

CANADA'S TREASURES

More kinds of dinosaurs are known from Alberta 75 million years ago than from any other time and place. Huge numbers of duck-billed and horned dinosaurs have been found there. These types dominated western North America from 75 million to 65 million years ago. While duckbills were successful around the world at this time, large horned dinosaurs are known only from North America.

The horned giants of North America sported a variety of frill and horn designs. It is uncertain whether these horns were ever used as defense against predators. But holes found in the heavy skulls indicate that the horns were used in battles among rival horned dinosaurs.

INSECTS

Cretonomyia is a fly that lives today and also existed 75 million years ago. A specimen was preserved when the living fly was trapped inside a glob of sticky pine sap in Alberta, Canada, between 83 million and 74 million years ago. The sap hardened into a piece of amber, with the dead insect preserved inside.

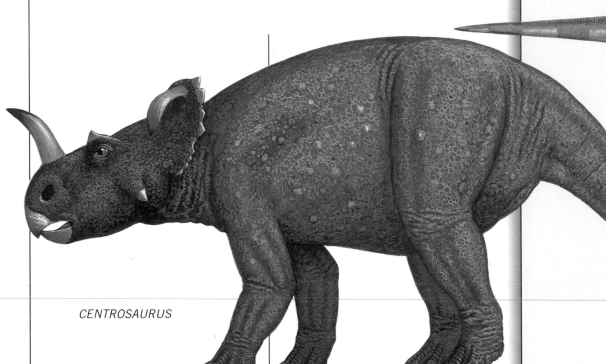

CENTROSAURUS

CENTROSAURUS
Meaning of name: "Sharp-pointed lizard"
Order: Ornithischia
Size, Weight: 17 feet long, 1 to 2 tons
Location: Alberta
Diet: Plants

Centrosaurus is one of the most decorated of all horned dinosaurs.

Its head frill had a thick edge, two hooks that pointed backward, and two horns that curved forward. *Centrosaurus*'s crest was notched with sharp edges. On some individuals the nose horn curved forward, while on others it stood straight up or curved backward. The differences in nose horn sizes and shapes may relate both to the age and the sex of the individual.

Flies of the *Cretonomyia* family are known today only from Australia. They cannot cross oceans and could not have crossed the Pacific from Canada 75 million years ago. They must have evolved more than 130 million years ago when the world's continents were still closely linked.

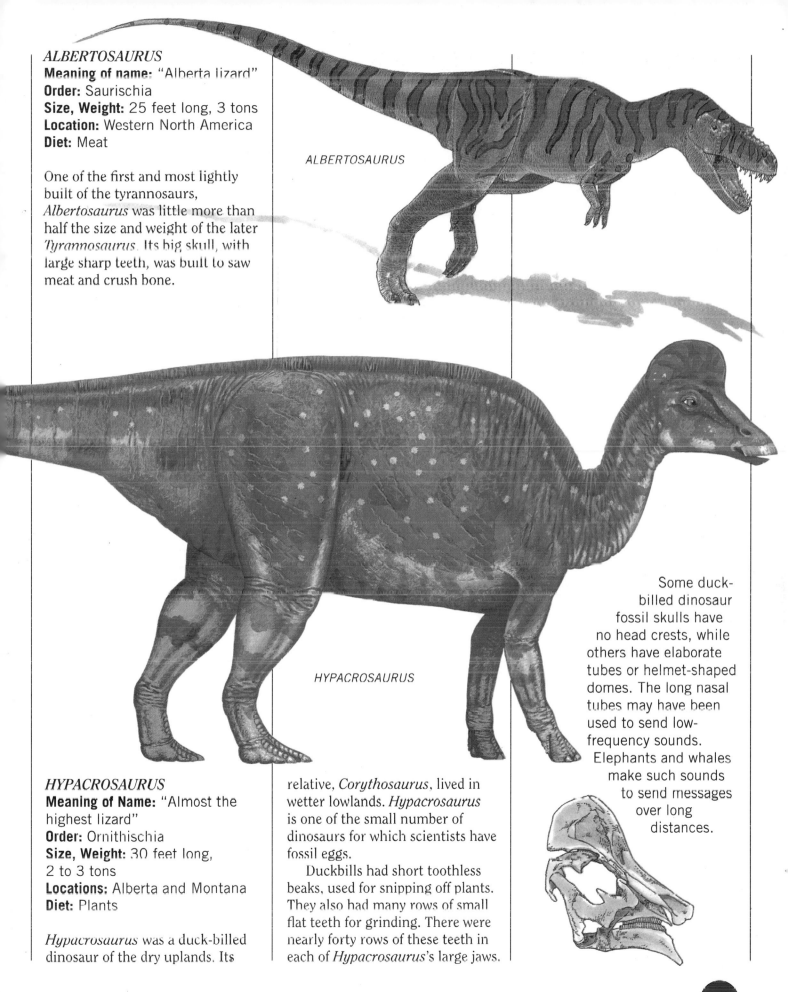

ALBERTOSAURUS

Meaning of name: "Alberta lizard"
Order: Saurischia
Size, Weight: 25 feet long, 3 tons
Location: Western North America
Diet: Meat

One of the first and most lightly built of the tyrannosaurs, *Albertosaurus* was little more than half the size and weight of the later *Tyrannosaurus*. Its big skull, with large sharp teeth, was built to saw meat and crush bone.

ALBERTOSAURUS

HYPACROSAURUS

HYPACROSAURUS

Meaning of Name: "Almost the highest lizard"
Order: Ornithischia
Size, Weight: 30 feet long, 2 to 3 tons
Locations: Alberta and Montana
Diet: Plants

Hypacrosaurus was a duck-billed dinosaur of the dry uplands. Its relative, *Corythosaurus*, lived in wetter lowlands. *Hypacrosaurus* is one of the small number of dinosaurs for which scientists have fossil eggs.

Duckbills had short toothless beaks, used for snipping off plants. They also had many rows of small flat teeth for grinding. There were nearly forty rows of these teeth in each of *Hypacrosaurus*'s large jaws.

Some duck-billed dinosaur fossil skulls have no head crests, while others have elaborate tubes or helmet-shaped domes. The long nasal tubes may have been used to send low-frequency sounds. Elephants and whales make such sounds to send messages over long distances.

THE NESTING SCENE

The nesting colonies of duck-billed dinosaurs found in Alberta and Montana have much in common with colonies of seabirds today. Huge numbers of animals build their nests in a crowded community. The large tightly packed group offers defense against predators that might eat the eggs or young chicks.

Maiasaura duckbills might have cared for their young as birds do. Their nests contained crushed eggshells, and a lump of half-digested plants was nearby. Some scientists think that *Maiasaura* hatchlings stayed in the nest, crushing their eggshells as they moved around, and that adults made baby food by spitting up chewed plants. Other scientists think the settling earth crushed the eggshells and preserved a lump of chewed nest-building material. The search is on for more clues.

   Maiasaura nests contain a dozen or more eggs. The size of the embryos at hatching is not known, though *Maiasaura* bones of individuals thought to be less than 12 inches long have been discovered.

Birds circle over the nest site, looking for stray hatchling *Orodromeus* to catch and eat.

This nesting colony, like that found at Egg Mountain in Choteau, Montana, belongs to long-legged little dinosaurs known as *Orodromeus* ("mountain runner"). Eggs were laid in a spiral in the nest, which was a mound of mud, packed by an adult. The eggs might have been covered with vegetation, and adults might have attended the nests. Each nest was separated from the next by the body length of an adult—about 6 feet. These baby plant-eaters could run immediately after hatching.

Two *Orodromeus* parents watch over their nests, which they have covered with plant material probably to incubate the eggs and perhaps to hide them from predators. Others busily gather materials to complete their own nests.

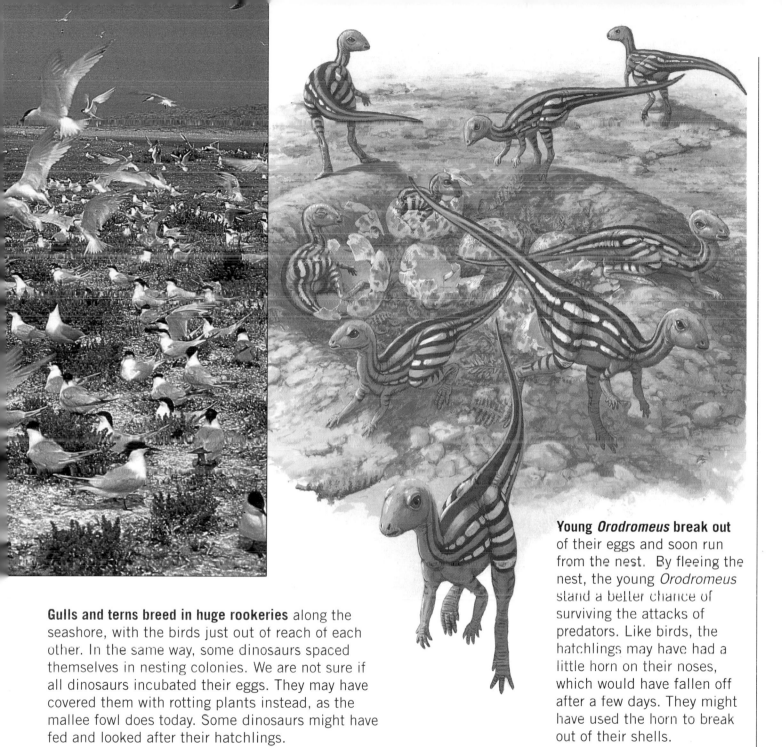

Gulls and terns breed in huge rookeries along the seashore, with the birds just out of reach of each other. In the same way, some dinosaurs spaced themselves in nesting colonies. We are not sure if all dinosaurs incubated their eggs. They may have covered them with rotting plants instead, as the mallee fowl does today. Some dinosaurs might have fed and looked after their hatchlings.

Young *Orodromeus* break out of their eggs and soon run from the nest. By fleeing the nest, the young *Orodromeus* stand a better chance of surviving the attacks of predators. Like birds, the hatchlings may have had a little horn on their noses, which would have fallen off after a few days. They might have used the horn to break out of their shells.

Small dinosaurs like *Orodromeus* had no defenses other than their speed. Their young may have needed to be strong runners from the moment they hatched in order to escape predators and survive to adulthood. The hatchlings of larger plant-eating dinosaurs could have relied more upon the size and strength of their parents to protect them during their early weeks of helplessness.

The duckbills might still have needed to grow quickly in order to join the annual migration. With the first change of season after the young hatched, the duckbills might have moved to new feeding grounds. In order to be big enough to migrate with the adults, the youngsters would have needed to grow fast. But the rate of growth for these dinosaurs is not yet known.

CENTROSAUR CATASTROPHE

Remains of thirty-seven different species of dinosaurs are preserved in the badland rocks of Dinosaur Provincial Park in Alberta, Canada. At least fifteen of these species are preserved in dozens of whole skeletons. A bed of hundreds of broken bones from many centrosaurs allows scientists to tell how a herd of these horned dinosaurs met their end 75 million years ago.

THE END OF A HERD

A herd of horned dinosaurs, young and old, attempts to cross a river in search of fresh feeding grounds. There are more than 300 individuals in the herd.

Like many dinosaurs, these animals can probably swim well. But, after recent rains, the current is too fast and the water too high for the dinosaurs to swim to the opposite bank. As they enter the water, they panic and thrash wildly, trampling one another and breaking many of their limbs **(1)**. These unfortunate animals drown. Their bodies are washed up on the riverbanks by the powerful waters.

A bone bed of centrosaur dinosaurs appears to be just a jumble of broken bones. To the trained eye of a paleontologist, however, stories of death and life are suggested by these fossils. The many sizes of limb bones indicate that the herd included animals of many ages. The sandstone and the pattern of how the bones were piled show that the animals' bones were jumbled by a fast-flowing stream. Then they were preserved by a blanket of river-bottom sand that later turned to stone. But how do scientists know that the animals broke one another's bones in a stampede? They don't.

Scientists think these dinosaurs died in an unusual situation because of the way the bones are broken. The fractures are spiral in shape. These "greenstick" breaks look like the uneven and incomplete break made when a green twig is bent or twisted. These fractures show that the bones were broken before they became fossils, probably within two years after death.

170

The bloated bodies of drowned dinosaurs lie on the riverbank **(2)**. *Albertosaurus* are attracted by the smell of the rotting flesh. They gnaw and strip the bones clean.

Over years, the river waters rise slowly and steadily. The water washes over the bones and moves them slightly **(3)**. The river carries sand and silt downstream, which settles over the bones. Over thousands of years it packs down. Minerals enter into the bones, making them harden into fossils. Millions of years later scientists uncover the bones for us to see **(4)**.

PLATEOSAURUS   PARASAUROLOPHUS   TYRANNOSAURUS   TROODON

Instead of a stampede, these centrosaurs might have died in a drought. As the herd searched for food and water, they became weaker and sicker. Near death, the animals collapsed one by one, trampling the weakest and the first to die before the last of them collapsed.

Other marks on the bones and cleaner breaks show that after these animals died they were eaten by predators. The marks match the teeth of large predators such as *Albertosaurus*.

BRAINY DINOSAURS

These dinosaurs' heads are drawn to the same size to show how scientists measure dinosaur intelligence. Since big animals need big brains just to handle the basic functions of their bodies, simple comparisons of brain size can make larger animals seem smarter, even when they are not. To get a rough idea of intelligence from brain size, scientists compare dinosaurs' brains as if the animals were all the same size. *Troodon* is the smallest of the four dinosaurs and has the smallest brain. But it is considered the smartest because it had the biggest brain for its size.

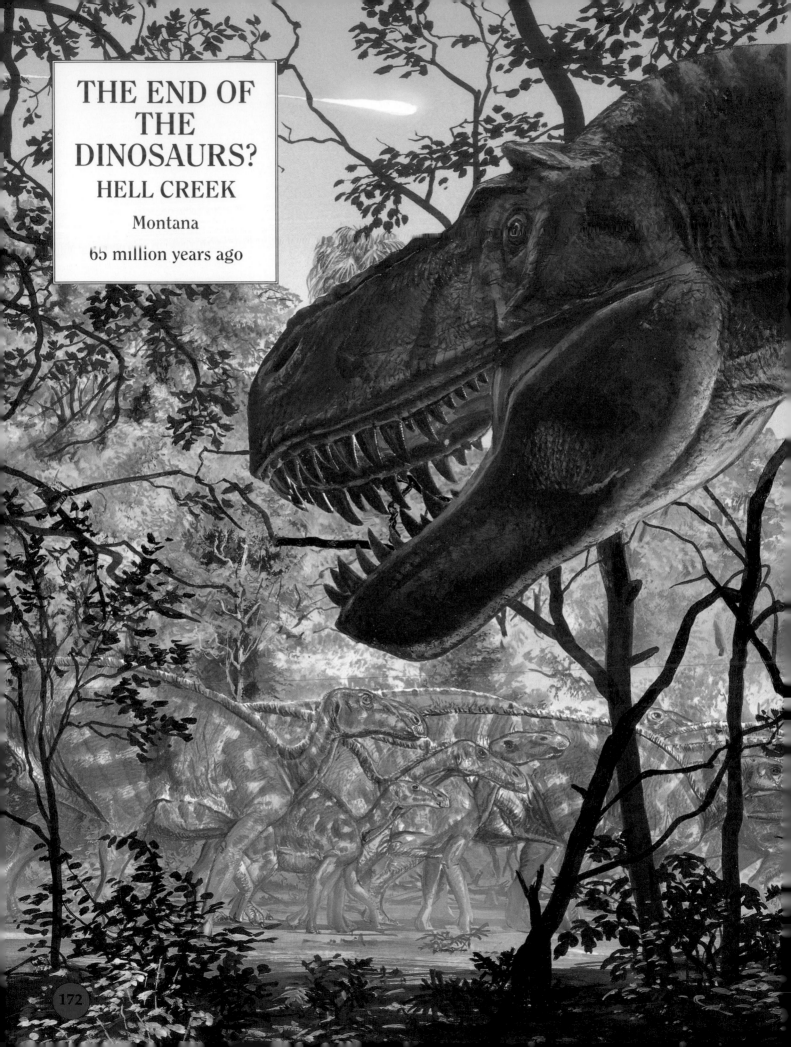

THE END OF THE DINOSAURS?
HELL CREEK

Montana

65 million years ago

Hidden among the trees of a warm, dry forest, a hungry *Tyrannosaurus rex* eyes a herd of duckbills, deciding which animal might become its next meal. A dragonfly flutters around the *T. rex* as a squat, heavily armored dinosaur looks on from a safe distance.

END OF THE LINE

The lush world of 65 million years ago contained the last communities of dinosaurs ever to walk the Earth. They included the best plant-chewers and some of the smartest, fastest, and most powerful meat-eating dinosaurs ever. Yet, within a million years dinosaurs were extinct.

What killed the dinosaurs? Scientists are not certain. One of the most popular recent theories is that a huge asteroid crashed into the Earth. The enormous collision would have sent a cloud of dust into the atmosphere, blocking the sunlight. Fires from the explosion would have added to the dust cloud and the heat. Shifting temperatures could have killed many animals and plants, including dinosaurs and giant reptiles of the sea and air.

Whether the end of the dinosaurs was caused by asteroid impacts, volcanic eruptions, or slow changes in climate and sea levels remains a mystery. There have been a handful of mass extinctions in the history of life. One of the most serious struck 65 million years ago. In the 163 million year history of dinosaurs, the world of the very last dinosaurs is the one we know best, but it is still largely a mystery.

Many of these fossils have been found in eastern Montana at a dig site known as Hell Creek. A range of herbivores and carnivores has been found, including fossils of the most famous of all dinosaurs, *Tyrannosaurus rex.*

Following the impact of a giant asteroid, the sun is colored red, since much of its warming light is blocked by dust in the air. The land can no longer support dinosaurs. Small mouse- and opossum-like mammals scurry over the corpse of a dead and decaying *Tyrannosaurus*. They clamber, too, on the dead branches of a nearby tree.

Hell Creek—Today In a remote stretch of badlands in eastern Montana, sandstone cliffs and valleys expose rocks from 65 million years ago—the end of the Cretaceous Period and the beginning of the following Tertiary Period. Much of the land is used for grazing cattle. Here paleontologists are using a mechanical shovel to raise a huge slab of rock containing fossils and load it onto a truck.

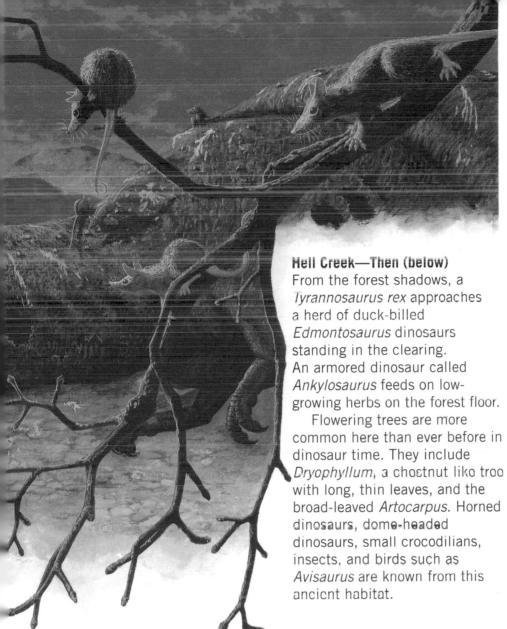

FACT FILE

The Montana of today is far different from the same land 65 million years ago. By the end of the age of dinosaurs, the continents had almost reached their current positions. But the world was still much warmer, and their were no polar ice caps.

Globe shows the position of the continents now

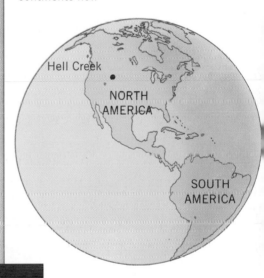

Hell Creek—Then (below)
From the forest shadows, a *Tyrannosaurus rex* approaches a herd of duck-billed *Edmontosaurus* dinosaurs standing in the clearing. An armored dinosaur called *Ankylosaurus* feeds on low-growing herbs on the forest floor.

Flowering trees are more common here than ever before in dinosaur time. They include *Dryophyllum*, a chestnut like tree with long, thin leaves, and the broad-leaved *Artocarpus*. Horned dinosaurs, dome-headed dinosaurs, small crocodilians, insects, and birds such as *Avisaurus* are known from this ancient habitat.

ANIMALS
1. *Ankylosaurus*
   (ang-KY-lo-SAW-rus)
2. Dragonfly
3. *Edmontosaurus*
   (ed-MAWN-toe-SAW-rus)
4. *Tyrannosaurus rex*
   (tie-RAN-uh-SAW-rus rex)

PLANTS
5. *Dryophyllum* trees
   (DRY-o-FILL-um)
6. Herbs

ALSO AT THIS SITE
Avisaurus (AY-vih-SAW-rus)
Crocodilians
Metasequoia conifers
   (MEH-tah-suh-KOY-ah)

TOOTHED TYRANT

Like the other tyrannosaurs, which appeared in the last 10 million years of the dinosaurs' existence, *Tyrannosaurus rex* had particularly large, strong jaws and teeth. But was *T. rex* really a killer most of the time? Or did it mostly scavenge for food? Paleontologists have differing opinions about *T. rex*'s feeding behavior.

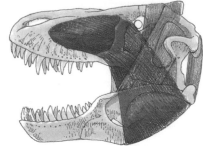

Skull of *T. rex* shows thick pointed teeth and a wide band of muscle that moved the hinged jaws.

Tyrannosaurus had a deep and heavy skull. A hinged lower jaw helped it open its mouth wide.

TYRANNOSAURUS REX

TYRANNOSAURUS REX
Meaning of name: "Tyrant lizard king"
Order: Saurischia
Size, Weight: 40 feet long, 7 tons or more
Location: Western North America
Diet: Meat

Tyrannosaurus's front limbs were so tiny that they could not touch each other. Yet they were strong, able to lift more than 450 pounds. However, its killing weapons—powerful muscular jaws—were enormous. More than 5 feet long, its skull held about fifty teeth the size of bananas. Each tooth was thick and pointed, good for breaking through bones. The jagged edges of these teeth could slice like a steak knife through thick muscle.

Scavenger or predator?
Tyrannosaurus rex was a huge meat-eater. Instead of hunting (below right), it might have fed off the carcasses of dead animals when they were available (below left). Huge herds of horned dinosaurs like *Triceratops* may have provided carrion.

PLANTS

Frlangdorfia was a flowering tree. Sixty-five million years ago, it grew 50 feet tall in the Hell Creek area. Its trunk was 12 inches or more in diameter, and its leaves had two or three lobes. Plant fossils from Hell Creek show that in this streambed community, by this time, more than nine in every ten plants were flowering plants and trees, not conifers or ferns.

INSECTS

The earliest bees and ants in the fossil record were found in amber from 65 million years ago. Slightly older plant fossils from Wyoming show damage from insects, including moths. Moth larvae had mined their way through the leaves of a tree.

AVISAURUS
Meaning of name: "Bird reptile"
Order: Enantiornithiformes
Size, Weight: 2- to 4-foot wingspan, about 2 pounds
Location: Montana
Diet: Meat

Avisaurus was a hawk-sized bird that probably fed on small animals, as many small birds do today. So far, it is known only from its foot and leg bones. *Avisaurus* belongs to an extinct family not closely related to modern birds.

AVISAURUS

ANKYLOSAURUS
Meaning of name: "Fused lizard"
Order: Ornithischia
Size, Weight: 20 feet, 3 to 4 tons
Location: Montana and Alberta
Diet: Plants

Ankylosaurus was one of the last and largest of the club-tailed armored dinosaurs. Built low to the ground, it had armor over much of its body, including its eyelids. Its tail club, which was made of several armor plates and was swung by the animal's stiff tail, may have been a good weapon. Barnum Brown of the American Museum of Natural History discovered *Ankylosaurus* nearly a century ago. (He also discovered *Tyrannosaurus*.)

Although *Ankylosaurus* has been famous for nearly 100 years, only three good specimens, none complete, have ever been found. It is named for the many fused bones in its skeleton.

ANKYLOSAURUS

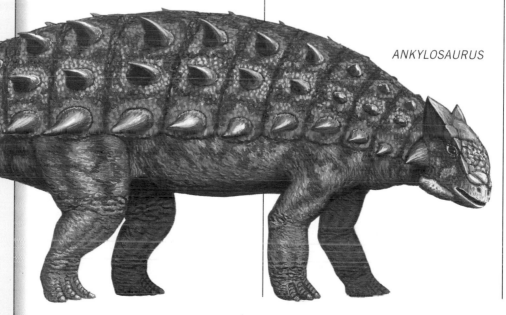

ACCIDENTAL DEATH?

For decades scientists have debated the question "What killed the dinosaurs?" Some of them have argued that dinosaurs died of digestion problems, or disease, or climate change. The cause remains unknown, but some interesting evidence in the last two decades supports another theory: a disaster from outer space.

The habitat of what is now Hell Creek Formation in Montana underwent a dramatic change 65 million years ago. Changes in leaf fossils show the effects of sudden cold and drier weather. In Montana and around the world, many plants and animals disappeared. An asteroid blasted a huge crater off the coast of Mexico at this time. The collision may have triggered fires and volcanic eruptions around the world. Huge clouds of dust thrown into the atmosphere first warmed the Earth, then cooled it to temperatures too low for dinosaurs and some other animals. For many creatures, the result was extinction.

1

2

3

4

An asteroid is pulled toward the Earth by the powerful force of gravity. Going through the atmosphere, friction turns the asteroid red hot. Much of it is burned away, but it is still more than 6 miles wide when it hits **(1)**.

The fiery blast makes a crater nearly 120 miles wide and sets off volcanoes around the world. As duck-billed dinosaurs browse, a volcano erupts **(2)**, destroying vegetation and killing many animals in the area.

Dust from fires, volcanic eruptions, and the asteroid impact cut off much of the light **(3)** needed by many plants and animals to survive. Smoke fills the air. Shock waves from the impact create floods from huge sea waves.

The land grows cooler and darker **(4)**. Rainfall is highly acid. Many kinds of plants die, leading to the deaths of plant-eating dinosaurs. Eventually, the meat-eating dinosaurs have no plant-eaters to consume. They also die.

So what actually killed off the last dinosaurs? Some scientists have suggested that the smoke and ash from the asteroid impact 65 million years ago first heated and then cooled the atmosphere. This killed off plant life, dinosaurs, and several other forms of large animals. Other scientists suggest that volcanic eruptions produced the same weather changes. Acid rain, cancer-causing radiation from the impact of objects from space, diseases, and gradual climate change are other proposed dinosaur-killers.

Mass extinctions
Dates are in millions of years ago.

TRIASSIC
250
225
JURASSIC
200
175
150
CRETACEOUS
125
100
65

Orange shaded area represents numbers of species of animals and plants becoming extinct. Peaks represent mass extinctions.

Trees are felled by a natural disaster. In human history there has never been an asteroid impact in an area where many people live. A possible collision of an asteroid with the Earth took place in Siberia in 1908. It caused fires and flattened trees for many miles around, as above.

Scientists imagine that the effect of an asteroid striking the Earth would be much like the devastation of a nuclear war. When an atomic bomb is set off, it creates a huge mushroom-shaped cloud that sends smoke and dust high into the air. The air is heated to a burning temperature for miles around. The only two atomic bombs set off in populated areas, in Japan during World War II, had terrible effects on all life in the area.

Some scientists have detected a pattern in the timing of the extinction events that strike the Earth. They see them occurring every 26 million years. The extinctions may be related to the cycle of the approach of some comets to the Earth. Impacts of some of these objects with the Earth at these times may cause the extinctions. Scientists who study fossils now think that changes in life-forms may not proceed at a steady pace. Brief periods of drastic change, including major extinctions, shape the history of life. So dinosaurs may have started their rise and met their end through accidental tragedies.

179

READING THE ROCKS

The rocks and fossils of the Hell Creek Formation offer some of the best clues about the world of the last dinosaurs and the start of the Age of Mammals. From fossils of animals and plants and from rare minerals in the rocks, scientists find clues to the life and death of the last dinosaurs. Many scientists do think that birds are living dinosaurs, direct descendants of meat-eating dinosaurs.

Scientists examine *Tyrannosaurus rex* fossil bones embedded in rock at Hell Creek Formation. At Hell Creek there are distinct layers of sandstone and coal. A layer of black coal marks the end of the Age of Dinosaurs. A few inches below that, scientists have discovered high concentrations of the rare element iridium. It is likely that the iridium came from a meteorite striking the Earth.

The most complete *T. rex* skeleton was found in the neighboring state of South Dakota in 1990. It was discovered by prospector Sue Hendrickson and has been nicknamed "Sue."

In the Hell Creek Formation, layers of rock laid down over millions of years contain fossils of the last dinosaurs and the animals and plants that lived with them. Above these layers are rocks formed in the hundreds of thousands of years after the dinosaurs disappeared. Near the boundary between the Age of Dinosaurs and the Age of Mammals, scientists discovered a layer of rock rich in iridium. Iridium is a rare element on Earth. It is more common in rocks, such as meteorites, which come from outer space. At several other places on the Earth, similar bands of iridium-rich clay have been detected from the same period. Other scientists point to changes in the shapes of leaf fossils at this time. These changes seem to reflect adaptation to a drastic change in climate as the Earth underwent a period of more variable weather.

The skull of a *Tyrannosaurus rex* exhibited at the American Museum of Natural History in New York. The skull is mostly original bone, not a cast. A new complete reconstruction of *T. rex* now stands in the museum.

The extinction of the dinosaurs left a gap in the web of life for large animals to fill. Mammals evolved into many new types of larger sizes and filled this gap. Now most of the common large creatures on land are mammals. Sixty-four million years after dinosaurs died out, humans evolved. Some day, in the distant future, humans and other mammals may become extinct as well. New creatures will rule the Earth. Dinosaurs will never live again, but their descendants, birds, live on.

A *Tyrannosaurus rex* rampages through the forest 65 million years ago. A tiny mammal watches, safely hidden on a tree branch. The mammal will survive the great extinction that is about to wipe out many species. Why? Perhaps mammals' small size or modest food needs helped them survive.

An animated model of the head and shoulders of a *Tyrannosaurus rex*.

FURTHER READING

FOR YOUNG READERS

Digging Up Tyrannosaurus rex by J. R. Horner and D. Lessem. Crown, 1994. A color pictorial portrait of excavating *T. rex*.

Dinotopia by James Gurney. Turner Publishing, 1992. An imaginative fantasy of an island of dinosaurs and humans created with astonishing artistry by the author-illustrator.

Dinotopia: The World Beneath by James Gurney. Turner Publishing, 1995. An elegant sequel to Gurney's fantasy.

Dougal Dixon's Dinosaurs by Dougal Dixon. Boyds Mills Press, 1993. An award-winning overview by a leading dinosaur author.

Jack Horner: Living With Dinosaurs by D. Lessem. Freeman Books, 1994. A children's biography of an accomplished dinosaur scientist.

The Great Dinosaur Atlas. Dorling Kindersley, 1991. Useful for its maps and attractive art work.

The Ultimate Dinosaur Book by D. Lambert. Dorling Kindersley, 1993. A lavish general portrait of dinosaurs.

The Visual Dictionary of Dinosaurs. Dorling Kindersley, 1993. A lively introduction with beautiful illustrations.

Troodon, The Smartest Dinosaur; *Gallimimus, The Fastest Dinosaur*; *Seismosaurus, The Longest Dinosaur*; and *Utahraptor, The Nastiest Dinosaur* —all by D. Lessem. Carolrhoda Books, 1996. A series profiling distinctive individual dinosaurs and how scientists study them, well-illustrated by Donna Braginetz.

FOR OLDER READERS

Digging Dinosaurs by J.R. Horner and James Gorman. Workman, 1989. One famous scientist's adventures in dinosaur hunting.

Dinosaurs – A Global View by Stephan and Sylvia Czerkas. Dragon's World, 1990. A huge and handsome book by a talented sculptor, which surveys dinosaur life.

Dinosaurs Rediscovered by D. Lessem. Random House, 1993. A survey of current dinosaur research across time.

Hunting Dinosaurs by Louis Psihoyos. Random House, New York, 1994. A beautiful pictorial survey of dinosaur studies.

Jurassic Park by Michael Crichton. Alfred A. Knopf, 1990. The clever fictional adventure upon which the movie was based. Contains violence.

Lost World by Michael Crichton. Alfred A. Knopf, 1995. The dramatic sequel to *Jurassic Park*.

Prehistoric Life: The Rise of the Vertebrates by David Norman. MacMillan, 1994. A good overview by a leading paleontologist, with many excellent color illustrations.

The Complete T. rex by J.R. Horner and D. Lessem. Simon & Schuster, 1993. A leading paleontologist recounts his and others' experiences excavating and speculating on *Tyrannosaurus rex*. With abundant illustrations.

The Illustrated Encyclopedia of Pterosaurs by Peter Welnhofer. Crescent Books, 1991. An outstanding and comprehensive guide by a world authority, with excellent art by John Sibbick.

The Rise and Fall of the Dinosaur by Joseph Wallace. Gallery Books, 1987. An enjoyable survey.

REFERENCE

The Dinosaur Society Dinosaur Encyclopedia by D. Lessem and D. Glut. Random House, 1993. A comprehensive dictionary of dinosaurs, and a useful reference.

The Dinosaur Data Book by D. Lambert and Diagram Visual Information, Avon, 1990. A useful, concise paperback reference.

The Dinosaurs of North America: An Odyssey in Time by Dale Russell. NorthWord Press, Inc., 1989.

The Illustrated Encyclopedia of Dinosaurs by David Norman. Crescent Books, 1985. Though dated, still the best encyclopedic reference on dinosaurs for a general audience. Beautifully illustrated.

The MacMillan Illustrated Encyclopedia of Dinosaurs and Prehistoric Animals by D. Dixon, B. Cox, R.J.G. Savage, and B. Gardiner. MacMillan, 1993. A useful general reference to animal life with good color illustrations.

Where to Find Dinosaurs Today by Daniel and Susan Cohen. Puffin, 1992. A useful guide to dinosaur museums, stores, and dig sites.

OTHER PUBLICATIONS

Dinosaurus Magazine. A color magazine for older children. 505 Fifth Avenue, New York, NY 10018.

Dino Times. A monthly newspaper for children of new dinosaur discoveries. Published by the Dinosaur Society, 20 Carleton Avenue, East Islip, NY 11730.

CD-ROMS

3-D Dinosaur Adventure. Knowledge Adventure, 1995. A fun activity and reference disk for younger children.

Microsoft Dinosaurs. Microsoft Corporation, 1992. An attractive reference with humorous commentary by "Dino" Don Lessem.

ACKNOWLEDGMENTS

Photographs
Page 4: Stan Grossfeld/Don Lessem. 12-13 (all photos): The Natural History Museum, London. 14: Dr. Paul Sereno, University of Chicago/Matrix Photo Agency. 18: Don Lessem. 22-23: Bruce Coleman Collection. 24: Dr. Paul Sereno. 28 and 35: Dr. Martin Sander, Institute of Paleontology, Bonn University. 32-33: Norbert Rosing/Oxford Scientific Films. 38: Don Lessem. 42-43: James H. Robinson/Oxford Scientific Films. 44 (left), 45 (right): Paul E. Olsen, Lamont-Doherty Earth Observatory of Columbia University. 44-45: Breck P. Kent/Oxford Scientific Films. 48: Dr. Mike Raath, Port Elizabeth Museum, South Africa. 52-55: George W. Frame. 55 (top left, top right): Dr. Anusuya Chinsamy-Turan, South African Museum, Cape Town. 55 (bottom): Dr. Mike Raath. 56: Mark A. Philbrick/Brigham Young University. 60: V.R. Hammer, Augustana College, Illinois. 64: Tom Leach/Oxford Scientific Films. 66 and 67: V. R. Hammer. 70: The Natural History Museum, London. 74: Breck P. Kent/Oxford Scientific Films. 76-77 and 77 (inset): The Natural History Museum, London. 81: Mark A. Philbrick/Brigham Young University. 83: Dr. Jeremy Burgess/Science Photo Library. 84-85: Anthony Bannister/Natural History Photo Agency. 87: Dr. David Gillette, Division of Antiquities, Salt Lake City. 90 and 93: Dr. Gunther Viohl, Jura Museum, Eichstätt. 94 95: Trevor McDonald/Natural History Photo Agency. 96: The Natural History Museum, London. 98 and 102: Dr. Paul Sereno. 104: Norbert Wu/Natural History Photo Agency. 107: Oxford Scientific Films/C.C. Lockwood, Earth Scenes. 109 (both photos): Dr. Paul Sereno. 113: Francois Gohier Pictures. 116: George W. Frame. 118: Francois Gohier Pictures. 122: The Natural History Museum, London. 124: Oxford Scientific Films/ London Scientific Films. 126: Natural History Photo Agency/A.N.T. 128 and 129 (all photos): The Natural History Museum, London.

132: Earthwatch, Massachusetts. 136: Lory Herbison Frame. 138: Bill Hopkins/Dr. P. Vickers-Rich, Monash Science Centre, Monash University. 139: Dr. P. Vickers-Rich. 140: The Natural History Museum, London. 144: Ignacio Salas-Humara/Don Lessem. 149: George W. Frame. 150: Carlos Goldin/Science Photo Library. 154: Thomas Jerzykiewicz/Don Lessem. 156: Dr. J.A.L. Cooke/Oxford Scientific Films. 158: George Holton/Photo Researchers/Oxford Scientific Films. 160: Don Lessem. 161(top): Don Lessem. 161 (bottom): The Ex-Terra Foundation, Edmonton. 164: Don Lessem. 168: Roger Tidman/ Natural History Photo Agency. 171 and 174: Don Lessem. 178-179: Novosti Press Agency/Science Photo Library. 180 (top): Bruce Selyam/ Museum of the Rockies, Montana. 180 (bottom): American Museum of Natural History. 181: The Natural History Museum, London.

Illustrations
All major double-page scenes by Steve Kirk.
All other major illustrations by James Field.
Ecology diagrams and small featured creatures by Jim Robins.
Step-by-step sequences by John James.
Maps by Ron Hayward.
Fish on pages 102-103 by John Rice.

Every effort has been made to contact copyright holders of any material reproduced in this book. Any omissions or errors will be rectified in subsequent printings if notice is given to the Publisher.

Bender Richardson White would also like to thank the following for help in producing this book: John Stidworthy; Madeleine Samuel; Alan Richardson; Martin Pulsford of the Photo Library, The Natural History Museum, London; Rose White; Dr. Robert Spicer, Open University, England.

GLOSSARY

aetosaurs (ay-EE-toe-sawrs) plant-eating reptiles up to 16 feet long that resembled crocodiles with stubby snouts. They are known only from the Late Triassic Period.

ammonites (AM-uh-nights) an ancient group of shelled animals, related to modern squid, cuttlefish, and octopuses. They died out at the same time as the dinosaurs.

amphibians (am-FIB-ee-uns) vertebrate animals (those with a backbone) that lay their eggs in water but usually spend their adult life on land. Modern amphibians include newts and frogs.

anatomy (ah-NAT-o-mee) the study of the structure of living things—for example, how a dinosaur's bones fitted together, and the size and shape of the various parts of its body.

araucarians (AIR-ah-CARE-ee-uns) a group of conifer trees common in dinosaur time and still found. The monkey puzzle tree of the Southern Hemisphere with its tall trunk and fanned branches is a modern araucarian.

atmosphere (AT-muss-feer) the layer of gases that surrounds the Earth; also known as the air.

beak a horny toothless mouth structure that is found on birds and on some dinosaurs. More lightweight than teeth, it also serves to bite and tear food.

bird-hipped having hipbones that resemble those of a bird. This term applies to a major group of dinosaurs—the bird-hipped dinosaurs, which are also called ornithischians, or members of the order Ornithischia. (See page 53.) All of the bird-hipped dinosaurs were plant-eaters.

browse to feed on shoots, leaves, and bark of shrubs and trees.

camouflage (KAM-uh-FLAWZH) a natural color scheme or pattern that allows an animal to hide by blending in with its surroundings to avoid detection.

carnivore (KAR-nih-vor) a meat-eating animal.

climate the average weather conditions in a particular part of the world. ("Weather" is the day-to-day variation in climate.)

cold-blooded a term used to describe an animal that cannot sustain a constant body temperature and so has a body temperature influenced by external conditions.

conifers (KON-ih-furs) trees that produce seeds in cones, for example, pines, firs, and larches. Their needlelike leaves usually stay on the trees year round.

continent (KON-tih-nent) a huge area of land, such as North America, Europe, and Australia.

crest a structure on top of the head, usually designed as a display feature to threaten rivals and attract mates.

Cretaceous (kree-TAY-shus) the period of geological history between 145 million and 65 million years ago, which ended with the extinction of dinosaurs and many other life-forms.

crocodilians (CROCK-o-DILL-ee-uns) a large group of reptiles that includes modern crocodiles and many extinct forms. In the Cretaceous Period some crocodilians were larger than any meat-eating dinosaurs.

This cutaway shows the major body parts, or organs, of a *Plateosaurus*, a typical dinosaur of the Late Triassic Period.

cycad (SY-kad) a type of non-flowering plant common in dinosaur time and still living in warm climates. Cycads are related to conifers and consist of a stout trunk with pineapple-like bark and radiating, palmlike leaves.

cycadeoids (sy-KAD-ee-oyds) extinct non-flowering plants with swollen globe-shaped trunks, spirals of fernlike leaves, and flowerlike cones on their trunks. They resembled cycads.

cynodonts (SY-no-dahnts) mammal-like reptiles with doglike, stabbing canine teeth. They lived from before the Triassic to well into the Jurassic Period. They were direct ancestors of mammals.

deposit in geology, rock material such as sand and pebbles laid down in an area after having been carried from elsewhere by rivers, wind, glaciers, or the sea.

dicynodonts (die-SY-no-dahnts) mammal-like, plant-eating reptiles. Their scientific name means "two dog-teeth," and comes from the two tusklike teeth (similar to those of dogs) in their upper jaws.

digest (die-JEST) to break down food in the stomach and intestines into a form that can be absorbed and used by the body.

dinosaurs (DIE-no-SAWRS) a highly successful and varied group of land reptiles with fully upright postures and S-curved necks that lived from the Late Triassic through the Jurassic and Cretaceous Periods (228 million to 65 million years ago). Crocodilians are the closest living relatives of dinosaurs. Birds are dinosaurs' descendants.

environment (en-VY-ron-ment) the living conditions of animals, including landscape, climate, plants, and animals.

evolve (ee-VAWLV) to change, over many generations, to produce a new species, body feature, or way of life.

ferns nonflowering plants with finely divided leaves known as fronds. Ferns reproduce by means of spores that develop under these leaves.

flash flood a sudden rush of water down a river valley following rainfall in higher areas nearby.

fossilized turned into fossils.

fossils (FAW-sils) remains or traces of once-living plants or animals that are preserved, usually in rock.

185

fronds (frawnds) the large, often finely divided leaves of fern and palm plants.

geography (jee-AWG-ruh-fee) the study of the land, sea, and air on Earth.

geology (jee-AWL-uh-jee) the study of rocks, minerals, and fossils.

ginkgo tree (GINK-go) cone-bearing tree with fan-shaped leaves that are shed in the fall. There is only one living species, the maidenhair tree.

Gondwana (gawnd-WAH-nah) the more southern of the two supercontinents formed by the breakup of Pangaea in the Age of Dinosaurs, including what are now Australia, South America, Africa, Antarctica, and India.

graze to eat low-growing plants. Modern grazers, which eat grass, include sheep, goats, many antelope, and cattle.

greenhouse effect a heating up of the Earth's atmosphere because a change in the makeup of the atmosphere stops the warmth from the ground from escaping into space.

growth rings rings seen in the cut ends of the bones of some animals and resembling the growth rings seen in the cut end of a tree. In both animals and trees, they are formed during periods of nongrowth.

habitat (HAB-ih-tat) the local area in which an animal or plant lives, for example, a desert, forest, or lake.

hatchling an animal that is newly hatched from its egg.

herbivore (ER-bih-vor) a plant-eating animal.

horn a pointed structure that may be made of bone or hair.

horsetail a tall plant found along watercourses. Related to ferns, it has sprays of green branches with tiny leaves along an upright, jointed stem.

ichthyosaurs (ICK-thee-o-sawrs) air-breathing marine reptiles that ate fish. They lived throughout the Cretaceous Period.

impression a mark or print in the surface of the ground or a rock made by something pressing against or in it.

intestines (in-TESS-tins) the parts of the food canal beyond the stomach from which nutrients are absorbed for use by the body and by which wastes are transported out of the body.

invertebrates (in-VER-teh-brayts) animals without backbones. Marine invertebrates such as jellyfish are well preserved among other fossils of the Late Jurassic.

Jurassic (jur-RAA-sick) the period of geological time between 208 million and 145 million years ago.

labyrinthodonts (LAB-uh-RIN-tho-dahnts) fat-bodied amphibians of many forms and sizes, most of which had a pattern like a maze, or labyrinth, inside their teeth.

Laurasia (law-RAY-zhah) the more northern of the two supercontinents formed by the breakup of Pangea in the Age of Dinosaurs, consisting of what are now North America, Europe, and most of Asia.

limestone a rock made up mainly of the mineral calcite from the shells of sea animals that died long ago and were buried on the sea bed.

lizard-hipped having hipbones that resemble those of a lizard. This term applies to a major group of dinosaurs—the lizard-hipped dinosaurs, which are called saurischians, or members of the order Saurischia. (See page 53.) This group included both plant-eaters and meat-eaters.

lungfish fish that have lungs as well as gills and so can breathe air. They can survive droughts or live in stagnant waters.

mammal-like reptile a member of a group of reptiles that were common in the Permian Period, before dinosaurs evolved, some of which lived on into the beginning of the Age of Dinosaurs. They eventually evolved into mammals.

mammals (MAM-uls) an order of animals with hair, whose members nurse their babies. Mammals were present throughout the Cretaceous Period, though they never grew larger than house cats.

meteorite (MEE-tee-o-right) a lump of rock from space that falls to Earth.

migrate (MY-great) to move from place to place as conditions change or for mating or reproduction.

minerals (MIN-er-uls) substances formed naturally in the ground that make up rocks. They include compounds formed of elements such as iron, aluminum, carbon, silicon, oxygen, and hydrogen.

Ornithischia (OR-nih-THIH-skee-ah) the order of bird-hipped dinosaurs, which were all plant-eaters. (Compare with Saurischia, and see page 53.) This order includes the two-footed plant-eaters, the plated dinosaurs, the armored dinosaurs, and the horned dinosaurs.

paleontologist (PAY-lee-on-TAW-luh-jist) a scientist who studies fossils of plant and animal life of the past.

Pangaea (pan-JEE-ah) the name given to the supercontinent that once existed in which all the continental masses of the Earth were joined.

Permian (PURR-mee-un) the period of geological time between 290 million and 245 million years ago. The time immediately before dinosaurs appeared when reptiles were taking over from amphibians.

plesiosaurs (PLEE-zee-uh-SAWRS) swimming reptiles, distantly related to dinosaurs, from the Age of Dinosaurs. These animals had squat bodies and limbs shaped like paddles.

predators (PREH dah-turs) meat-eating animals that hunt and kill.

prey an animal that is hunted and eaten by a predator.

pterodactyls (TAIR-o-DACK-tills) pterosaurs with long necks and short tails that lived in the Jurassic and Cretaceous Periods.

pterosaurs (TAIR-o-SAWRS) flying reptiles, the first vertebrates to fly.

rhamphorhynchids (RAM fo-RING-kids) small Jurassic pterosaurs with light skulls and long tails with diamond-shaped flaps.

rauisuchians (RAO-ih-SOO-key-uns) four-legged meat-eating reptiles of the Triassic Period, that grew to 20 feet in length.

reptiles vertebrate animals that reproduce by laying hard-shelled or leathery eggs on land. Snakes, lizards, turtles, and crocodiles are some modern types of reptiles.

rhynchosaurs (RINK o-sawrs) pig-sized plant-eaters, with bodies low to the ground, common in the Late Triassic. They snipped plants with their hooked beaks.

Saurischia (saw-RIH-skee-ah) the order of lizard hipped dinosaurs. (Compare with Ornithischia, and see page 53.) This order includes all of the meat-eaters and the largest of the plant-eaters.

sauropod (SAW-ro-pod) long-necked, lizard-hipped plant-eating dinosaurs that walked on all fours, such as *Apatosaurus*.

scavenger (SKAA-ven-jur) a meat-eating animal that does not make its own kills but eats the bodies of animals already dead.

sediment (SEH-dih-ment) tiny pieces of soil, earth, or stone that are picked up, carried along, and deposited in layers by wind, rivers, ice, or rain and are slowly compressed into rock.

seed ferns extinct woody swamp forest plants with large seed-bearing fronds, often with exposed roots and treelike trunks.

species (SPEE-sheez) a group of living things of the same kind that can reproduce with one another.

tendons (TEN-duns) tough pieces of animal tissue that attach muscles to bones.

thecodonts (THEE-ko-dahnts) mostly meat eaters, these were the earliest of the "ruling reptiles," the archosaur group. This group included ancestors of dinosaurs, as well as aetosaurs, phytosaurs, and rauisuchians. They were common in the Triassic, but died out before the Jurassic Period.

theropod (THEH-ra-pod) a meat-eating dinosaur and a member of the Saurischia, such as *Tyrannosaurus rex*.

tree ferns ferns that grow to 80 feet or more in height. There are only a few living species, but they were plentiful at the beginning of the Age of Dinosaurs.

Triassic (try-YAA-sick) the period of geological time between 245 million and 208 million years ago when dinosaurs, flying reptiles, and large marine reptiles first appeared.

tritylodontids (try-TIE-lo-DAHN-tids) mammal-like reptiles that grew to the size of beavers in the Early Jurassic Period.

vegetation (veh-jeh-TAY-shun) plant life.

vertebrates (VER-teh-brayts) animals with backbones, including fish, mammals, birds, reptiles, and amphibians.

warm-blooded a term used to describe an animal that regulates its internal temperature, often at a high and steady level. Birds and mammals are warm-blooded animals alive today. (Compare with cold-blooded.)

INDEX

INDEX CONTINUED

INDEX <small>END</small>